Books of Merit

WHAT HAPPENED LATER

Ray

ROBERTSON

WHAT HAPPENED LATER

Thomas Allen Publishers
Toronto

Library and Archives Canada Cataloguing in Publication

Robertson, Ray, 1966 –
    What happened later / Ray Robertson.

ISBN 978-0-88762-279-3

1. Kerouac, Jack, 1922-1969 – Fiction.
2. Robertson, Ray, 1966 – – Childhood and youth – Fiction.   I. Title.

PS8585.O3219W43 2007   C813'.54   C2007-902563-3

Editor: Janice Zawerbny
Jacket and text design: Gordon Robertson
Jacket image: Veer

Published by Thomas Allen Publishers,
a division of Thomas Allen & Son Limited,
145 Front Street East, Suite 209,
Toronto, Ontario M5A 1E3 Canada

www.thomas-allen.com

  **Canada Council
for the Arts**

The publisher gratefully acknowledges the support of The Ontario Arts Council for its publishing program.

We acknowledge the support of the Canada Council for the Arts, which last year invested $20.0 million in writing and publishing throughout Canada.

We acknowledge the Government of Ontario through the Ontario Media Development Corporation's Ontario Book Initiative.

We acknowledge the financial support of the Government of Canada through the Book Publishing Industry Development Program (BPIDP) for our publishing activities.

The author acknowledges the support of the Canada Council for the Arts and the Ontario Arts Council.

11 10 09 08 07   1 2 3 4 5

Printed and bound in Canada

B. M. H.
1993-2006

J. C. H.
1937-2001

M. A. K.

This part is my part of the movie, let's hear yours.

— Jack Kerouac, *Tristessa*

WHAT HAPPENED LATER

Well, there's Jack Kerouac, back on the road again.

Even Jack had to laugh at that.

Flat on his back and soggy drunk, lying across the Northport streetcar tracks, he'd told his buddy Stanley Twardowicz that he wasn't getting up until either the streetcar or an automobile arrived and he was finally free of the wheel of the quivering meat conception and safe in heaven dead.

Actually, *Fuck off, I'm not getting up,* is what he said, but Stanley knew what he meant.

Right back to the bright, clear days of New York in the fifties, backslapping double shots of Jack Daniels at the Cedar Tavern with Pollock and de Kooning and Kline and all the rest, Jack had always enjoyed the company of painters. Painters tend not to talk about things like the pros and cons of third-person limited versus third-person omniscient narration or how much money what's-his-name's agent got for him for his last paperback reprint deal or who the *New York Times* has anointed as this week's 100 percent guaranteed wunderkind to watch out for. Jack liked to hang around Twardowicz's Northport studio in the afternoon while Stanley was working, liked to quietly putter away and sip from a tall can of Colt 45 or sometimes spend entire hours watching Twardowicz lay down some fresh new colour and light and line.

Being at the studio was also a way of getting away from his mother for a while, as well as a place he could retreat to to avoid the Long Island teenagers who still showed up at his front door looking for the guy who wrote *On the Road*. Mémère would try her best to shoo them away, but Jack would yell at his mother in French and she'd yell back at him in even louder French and one of the kids would have brought along a six-pack and it wouldn't be long before Jack would lift his whiskey bottle and put on his clown nose and be the brilliant buffoon everybody wanted him to be. He'd wake up two days later with a crippling hangover only to discover that one of his notebooks, a couple first editions of his own novels, and even some of his pencils were missing — pencils, after all, once owned and used by Jack Kerouac, King of the Beats, *Time* magazine tells us so.

And now Jack wouldn't get up.

For nearly ten minutes Stanley had tried everything: reasoning, pleading, even threatening. One honking car had already had to swerve around Jack in the dark, and the streetcar was eventually going to come. It hadn't come yet, but it was coming.

Finally:

Well, there's Jack Kerouac, back on the road again.

Even Jack had to laugh at that.

Jack laughed, picked himself up off the street, and he and Stanley headed back toward Gunther's, the fisherman's bar where they liked to drink. He put his arm around Stanley's shoulder as they crossed the road.

Ah, Stash, you knew I wasn't going to do it, you know I'm a good Catholic, you know I have to take the slow way out.

What do you mean, 'Take the slow way out'?

Jack raised a single forefinger in the salty Long Island night air.

Suicide is a sin, Stash, you know that. C'mon, let's get a table, let me buy you a boilermaker.

Before Jack Kerouac could change my life, Jim Morrison had to save it. Every Almighty needs an ambassador down below to do his dirty work. Mine wore tight brown leather pants and shouted out his rock and roll couplets like it somehow actually mattered.

You can read William James' *The Varieties of Religious Experience* or you can take my word for it, but walking on water wasn't built in a day, every epiphany has to pay its own way. Jamie Dalzell and I were being bored together in his bedroom one afternoon after school when he slipped the Doors' *Greatest Hits* onto his stereo turntable as casually as anybody who's ever transformed somebody else's life without trying. Forget about music videos, I'd only just discovered FM radio the year before. I thought Elton John was a poet. I thought Kiss were punk rock. We all had ten-speed bicycles, and the city buses snaked our neighbourhoods until six p.m. five nights a week, nine p.m. on Fridays and Saturdays, and the suburbs that connected us seemed like they went on forever.

The Doors were Morrison—you knew, because it was his chiselled cheekbones and dripping brown curls that crowded out the faces of the other three on the album cover—but the music was what made me sit down on the edge of Jamie's bed and be quiet and listen. You didn't have to sit down and be quiet in order to listen to REO Speedwagon. When I headed home for supper in the early evening February grey, my red Adidas bag full of school stuff hanging from one hand, the borrowed record album cradled tight in the other, the nightmare soundtrack organ sound of "Light My Fire" hummed me the half-mile walk back to my house.

My sneakers crunched in the snow in the frozen dark. No one over the age of fifteen worth talking to ever wore boots or hats in the winter, no matter how nasty frosty it got. The less you wore, the cooler you were. The really, really cool guys in grade thirteen came to school in jean jackets that they let flap open in the freezing breeze in the parking lot while they smoked. That, and getting a girlfriend and scoring touchdowns and potting hat tricks in hockey, was about as good as it was ever going to get.

I had no idea. I pulled the Doors album closer. I really had no idea.

In Lowell, Massachusetts, in the rectory of the St. Louis de France Church, in Centralville, Lowell's French-Canadian ghetto, in 1922, on March 12, at five-thirty in the afternoon, a Sunday.

Then New York, in school and out of school; then marriage and divorce in Ozone Park, Michigan; then merchant marine ships and sailing seas; then the war and then the psycho ward and then the war no more; then New York; then more ships and more seas; then meeting Cassady and then, therefore, itchy highway thumbing or, if rideless, Greyhound back seat slouching, the roads of America the veins of America, up and down its tired tar arteries listening for its fluttering, not-yet-flatlining heart; then New York; then San Francisco; then Mexico City; then New York; then San Francisco; then New York; then North Carolina; then Mexico City; then Berkeley, California; then Desolation Peak, Washington State; then San Francisco; then New York; then Tangiers; then Berkeley; then Orlando, Florida; then Northport, Long Island; then Big Sur, California; then Mexico City; then Orlando, Florida; then New York; then Northport; then

St. Petersburg, Florida; then Paris and Italy; then Hyannis, Cape Cod; and then, finally, Lowell again.

After that, one more year more or less, with just enough time left over for a traveller's-cheque blur through Europe (Lisbon, Madrid, Geneva, Munich, Stuttgart), a three-day pilgrimage to Rivière-du-Loup, Quebec, to seek out his paternal grandfather's potato farm, and then St. Petersburg one last time.

Florida was for his mother, for her health after her stroke. But after the last time Mémère said she didn't want to go back east, didn't want to go back to Lowell again—they'd tried it the year before, for Jack, but Mémère claimed she was always so cold, she could never get warm, and especially now after her stroke she needed to keep warm—Jack said okay, they'd wait out the winter in St. Petersburg and go back in the spring, said to his wife, *Who says you can't go home again?*

A few weeks later, after not being able to sleep—still infuriated at the next-door neighbour for cutting down the towering Georgia pine in their front yard through whose branches Jack had liked to listen to the wind talking to him at night—and after lying outside in the backyard on his cot watching the icy stars prickle the sticky southern night; in the morning, early in the morning, after eating a can of tuna fish straight from the can over the kitchen sink and then plopping down in front of *The Galloping Gourmet* on television with the sound turned off and the living room curtains shut tight to the stupid Florida always sun; an open notebook on his lap and sketching out plans for a new novel, this one about his father's old printing shop in Lowell when he was boy:

His wife heard a sound coming from the bathroom.

On his knees (praying, maybe), vomiting blood into the toilet bowel (definitely not praying): *I'm hemorrhaging,* he said. *I'm hemorrhaging, Stella.*

Three days later he got what he'd wanted, was back in Lowell for good, an open casket in the Archambault Funeral Home on Pawtucket Street followed by the funeral the next morning at St. Jean Baptiste Roman Catholic Church, Jack all dressed up in his checkered sports jacket and red bow tie and a tiny bald spot and nowhere to go but where everybody goes.

Who says you can't go home again?

Before the mall showed up to make Chatham modern, the same as everywhere else, there were different stores you had to go to for all of the different things you wanted or needed. Lewis' Variety on St. Clair Avenue was where you went when you wanted a magazine that they didn't stock at the checkout line at the grocery store. My dad bought his *Hockey News* there. Lewis' carried both the *Detroit Free Press* and the *Detroit News* and even the day before's *New York Times*, but I never knew anybody who bought any of those. I liked Lewis' for the two entire rows of shiny sports magazines they kept.

The day I had my wisdom teeth removed we stopped off at Lewis' on the way home from the hospital so I could pick out a hockey magazine to help pass the time while the anaesthetic wore off. I wasn't in any pain, but my mouth was still frozen from the operation and I had to hold a handful of tissues to my bottom lip because I couldn't feel it whenever the blood would occasionally bubble over and dribble down my chin. My dad saw somebody he knew buying lottery tickets at the cash register. It seemed like my dad always knew somebody no matter where we went, either from Ontario Steel, where he worked, or from when he used to play hockey or from the east end, where he grew up.

Grab a couple magazines but don't be all day, he said. I usually got to pick out only one magazine when we went to Lewis'. He must have felt sorry for me for having to go into the hospital, it must have been all the bloody Kleenex.

I never made it as far as the magazine section. Here and there throughout the store were black metal revolving paperback racks displaying the usual variety-store-as-bookstore wares: unauthorized celebrity biographies, romance novels and spy novels, weight loss books, books on flying saucers and Big Foot and killer sharks. And *No One Here Gets Out Alive*, the biography of Jim Morrison.

The Doors' *Greatest Hits* hadn't left my turntable since I'd carted it home from Jamie Dalzell's house a couple of weeks back, but all I knew about Morrison was what Jamie had told me when he'd lent me the record: that he was dead, that he'd died young, that he was buried somewhere in Paris. I took the paperback with Morrison's brooding face and naked chest on the cover down from the rack and brought it to the cash register where my dad was still talking to his friend.

You about ready to go? he said.

I nodded, placed the biography on the counter. It was hard to make myself understood with a frozen mouth. My dad looked down at the book.

I thought you were getting a magazine.

I was ready for this. As clearly as I could, *It's not much more than two magazines*, I said. I sounded like a nasally cross between a Mafia don and Mr. Howell from *Gilligan's Island*.

How much is it? he said.

Only four ninety-five.

How much?

Only four ninety-five.

Jesus Christ. Wouldn't you rather have a hockey magazine, a couple magazines?

I want this, I said.

He looked at the skinny, bare-chested man with curly shoulder-length hair on the cover of the paperback again. Maybe he thought that the painkillers they'd given me had finally kicked in. He put his hand in his front right pocket and took out a thin fold of bills, peeled off a ten.

All right, hand it to the lady, let her ring it in. Your mother's going to wonder where the hell we got off to.

When we got home I went to my room and lay down on my bed and stuck both pillows underneath my head and opened up the book. My mother had made me exchange my fistful of crusty tissues for a warm washcloth, and I held the rag to my mouth with one hand while turning the pages of the paperback with the other.

The nurse had said that the painkillers might make me drowsy, and two or three times while I was reading I woke up to find out that I'd fallen asleep, my mouth full of salty blood like a sticky ditch, the book lying beside me on the bedspread. And every once in a while I'd have to get up and go to the bathroom to take a pee or wring out the blood from the cold washcloth and make it clean and hot again. But by the time I could feel my mouth again, could run my tongue over the holes where there used to be teeth, I'd finished reading the book, all 379 pages.

Jim growing up, I read—Jim around my age—had been part parking-lot stoner, part straight-A egghead, part chess-club outcast, all three all wrapped up with a James Dean who-gives-a-fuck shrug and a young Elvis' lip-curling sneer. Jim Morrison didn't play quarterback, but he still got any girl he wanted. Jim Morrison made being an outsider seem like the only honourable way of fitting in.

Jim, I went on to learn, did everything, went everywhere, touched everyone, and drank and drugged himself to an early grave. Finally, a role model I could look up to.

Also—surprise—I learned that Jim Morrison read books. Lots and lots of books. *No One Here Gets Out Alive* catalogued all of the ones that had made the biggest impact, the ones that went into making Jim Jim: a German philosopher named Nietzsche, a French poet called Rimbaud, and a bunch of American writers who called themselves Beatniks. The Beatnik that Jim liked the best was named Jack Kerouac. Jim read Kerouac's novel *On the Road* when he was fifteen, the year after it was published, and the day after he finished it he opened it up again and started over from the beginning.

As soon as I got a chance to read *On the Road*, Jack Kerouac was going to be my favourite author.

He always came back. No matter where he was living, he always came back. A week, a couple of days, sometimes just overnight. But he always came back.

Old friends, childhood friends, leaning-in-downtown-doorways-and-spitting friends — G.J., Scotty, the Sampas clan — and the excited phone call from the downtown Lowell bus depot:

I'm back.

When nobody was anybody yet, when everybody was still who they'd be, it was all right, it was great, *C'mon, Jack's back, let's go.*

A shared six-pack of Ballantine Ale for supper at somebody's kitchen table, maybe some eggs and toast and bacon if somebody's mother or young wife was making it, and, by and by, in time's rear-view mirror, one more snapshot hello at yesterday's long slow goodbye: St. Louis de France School and St. Joseph's Parochial School and Lowell High (especially the Lowell High football field) and the Stations of the Cross and all the busy baseball diamonds and all the smoking, stinking mills and the house on Beaulieu Street where

Gerard, Jack's eight-year-old brother, died of rheumatic fever, and Kearney Square and the City Hall clock and the wrinkly tar sidewalk of Moody Street and the Textile Lunch and the Sportsmen's Athletic Club and Liggett's Drugstore and Paige's Drugstore and the Number One soda fountain and the trolley stops and the B.F. Keith theatre and the Catholic churches and the single Chinese restaurant and the Pawtucket Falls and the Moody Street Bridge and the ceaseless, immutable Merrimack River.

Later, years later, when Jacky was Jack Kerouac, when Zag became King of the Beatniks, he still came back.

Only now the phone call always came in the middle of the night and he was always drunk, whiskey drunk. And it always seemed like it was snowing.

People had things to do now, jobs to go to, children who were sleeping, other people besides themselves to think about.

For Christsake, Zag, I've got to get up and sell insurance in the morning.

One time, G.J. had to order him to leave his house. Jack had been loud, had been monologuing, not talking sense and practically shouting, scaring G.J.'s wife and his two small children. Then he tried to get up and dance on top of the living room piano.

You gotta go, Zag, you gotta go right now.

In his sneakers and a white T-shirt and a dirty grey raincoat he'd always end up at the Sportsmen's Athletic Club because it used to be the Hi-Ball where everybody used to hang out when everybody was young, before the war. He'd give noisy lectures that no one asked to hear on Shakespeare and Wolfe and Celine and Spengler and, even louder still, belt out a few verses of Sinatra or Nat King Cole and tell anybody who would listen about how much money he could make writing stuff for the slicks if he wanted to, if he was that kind of a writer. He'd drink whiskey and sodas until he pissed his pants and passed out in his chair.

And all of his brand new friends who'd never read his books but who knew who he was would laugh along and slap him on the back and get him to sign cocktail napkins that they'd put away in their scrapbooks because who knows? Maybe they'll be worth something someday.

When he got back home, home to wherever he and Mémère were living at the time, he'd write sober letters of apology to every old friend he'd offended.

What's happened to me? they'd say.

Let's go around, I said.

An August afternoon Sunday when I was six, an idling '69 Buick Skylark with power windows but no air conditioning, a train that wouldn't end like Christmas will never come and summer vacation will go on forever.

We can't go around, my dad said.

Why not?

I was hot and bored and thirsty and there was cold pop at home on the bottom shelf of the bar fridge in the basement. Every other Friday I'd get to ride in the front seat and go with my dad to the beer store where he'd hoist over his box of twenty-four empties to the man behind the counter who'd hand him back his deposit and we'd wait for a brand new case of Labatt Blue to come rolling down the conveyor belt. Then we'd drive to the Pop Shoppe to return my own red plastic case of empty bottles and I got to pick out the pop that I wanted: root beer and orange and cream soda, but also black cherry, lemon-lime, and Sparkle Up, just as good as 7Up, just cheaper, my dad said so, so it had to be true. I never had to ask my mom or dad if I could have a pop from the fridge when I wanted one. Other kids, when they came over to play, couldn't believe it. Other kids always liked to come over to my house to play. I had a slip-on beverage cooler that said BLUE SMILES ALONG WITH YOU, just like my dad.

Because they'll put you in a box and put you in the ground and they won't let you out.

I thought about what he said. It didn't make sense. I said the only sensible thing I could think of.

But you'd let me out, I said.

My father leaned against the steering wheel and craned his head left, looked as far down the railroad track as he could. Sweat rivered down the back of his neck. He looked in the rear-view mirror to make sure there was no one behind us; put the car in reverse and gave the steering wheel a sharp tug to the right. We weren't going to wait around anymore. Finally, we were moving. Looking in the mirror again, this time at me in the back seat:

I don't want to see you fooling around when there's a train coming, he said.

I won't.

You either stand back and wait for it to go by, or you walk around to where it isn't, you hear me?

I know.

Hey?

I will, I'll wait for it or walk around.

My mother sucked a last suck from her Player's Light and pulled the ashtray out of the dash, crushed out her cigarette on the metal lip. It was full of mashed cigarette butts crowned with red lipstick kisses.

Because when they put you in that box in the ground, boy, that's it, nobody can help you, not even me.

But, I wanted to say, *But . . .*

But I didn't say anything. And my dad, I waited, but he didn't say anything else either.

If you're serious about going, you know I'm game. When are
you thinking of leaving?

Game? Jack said. *Game, Joe? You want a game, I'll give you*
a game, here's a game for you: tell me what Kerouac means.

Jack, I don't even know what Chaput means.

Very smart, Joe, very smart. The wise man is wise because
he knows he is not wise.

Socrates?

No, W.C. Fields.

They were at Nicky's, Nick Sampas' bar, Jack's brother-
in-law's place. Since the move back to Lowell a couple of
months before, Stella, Jack's wife, tried to get him to drink at
home as much as possible. But if he was going to go out, it
was best if he ended up at Nicky's where at least her brother
could keep an eye on him. Stella had enough on her plate
helping to nurse Mémère back to health after her stroke, she
didn't need the phone calls from the police station at three
a.m., Jack in the drunk tank again, a public nuisance, pissing
in the street, worse. She especially didn't need the phone
calls from the hospital, this time cracked ribs, the time before

that a busted nose, the time before that a concussion from a pool cue to the back of Jack's head. To help keep him at home, sometimes Stella would hide his shoes. The next day somebody would say to somebody else, *You're not going to believe this, but I saw Jack Kerouac walking down Moody Street in his stocking feet.*

Okay, Jack said, *since you don't know, now I have to tell you, now you have to ask me what Kerouac means.*

All right. Hey, Jack, what does Kerouac mean?

I'm glad you asked me that, Joe, I'm very glad you asked me that, let me tell you.

Jack drained the Johnnie Walker left in his glass. He recognized Bunny Berigan's "I Can't Get Started" playing on the jukebox just in time to expertly mime the song's trumpet part, *buh buh buh baba buh.* Joe looked at the two neat rows of liquor bottles behind the bar, slowly nodded his head in time to the music. Solo over, Jack turned back to Joe.

Kerouac is the oldest Irish name on earth, I bet you didn't know that, did you, Joe? I bet you also didn't know that Isolde was a Kerouac—that's right, that's what I said, Isolde—a Kerouac kidnapped by Tristan, an abominable Cornishman as all Cornishmen are. I bet you also didn't know that after immigrating to Brittany we became the Lebris de Kerouacs, one of whom—pay attention now, Joe, you will be tested on this material at the end of term—one of whom, the Baron François Louis Alexandre Lebris de Kerouac, went to Quebec to help Montcalm fight Wolfe for the valley of the St. Lawrence, after which, after the French lost that unfortunate war as you well know, Joe, he was granted one hundred miles of land along Rivière-du-Loup for exceptional gallantry and service to the king of France, where he met and married an Iroquois princess with whom he sired six sons who sired six sons of their own — say that six times fast, Joe — and these families, these families became known as les tucsons.

The tough ones.

The tough ones.

Jack caught Nick's eye, made a peace sign that meant two more drinks. The jukebox was silent, the bar quiet now, now that Jack had stopped talking. He closed his eyes and slapped out an unaccompanied drum solo on the lip of the wooden bar. The other drinkers ignored it, ignored him. What were you going to do? That clown was Nicky's brother-in-law.

Joe had been the only university graduate in Nicky's the night he recognized the man sitting at the bar as the author of *On the Road*. A recent widower with a missing son, Joe was happy not to be at home any more than he had to be, and his taste for Scotch and good books, and not just Jack's, made the two men almost immediate friends. Mémère even liked him, Stella too. Unlike most of the walking talking trash Jack would haul home with him from the bars at three in the morning so he wouldn't have to go to sleep and therefore wake up to himself again, Joe was French on both parents' sides, was polite to his elders, and was an honest admirer of all of Jack's work. Everybody liked Joe. If you couldn't get along with Joe, you couldn't get along with anybody.

Hey, Joe, do you know what Dr. Johnson said?

Dr. Johnson said a lot of things, Jack.

Hey, Joe, do you know what Dr. Johnson said?

No, Jack, what did Dr. Johnson say?

Dr. Johnson said, and I quote, "Patriotism is the last refuge of the scoundrel."

He said that, did he?

The drinks appeared on the bar in front of them. Jack immediately picked up his and peeled away the moist paper napkin hanging from the bottom of his glass; raised his Scotch to his lips.

He sure as hell did, Joe.

I didn't know I was Canadian until September 28, 1972.

I was only six years old, but I knew it was about more than hockey when they wheeled several television sets into the school gymnasium and let us watch the eighth and deciding game of the Canada–Russia Summit Series, the one where Paul Henderson scored the winning goal with less than a minute to play and everything turned out all right after all, we'd won, we'd won. Even then I didn't really get it—I screamed and cheered along with everybody else, but not having to be in class and getting to sit beside and talk to Jeff Jones and Phil Jackson were still the best parts of it—and it wasn't until that night, after my dad got home from work, that I knew.

Fathers on TV shaved and showered and got dressed up before they went to their jobs, but my dad got cleaned up at the end of the day, after he got home from the factory. Sometimes that was after I was asleep, when he worked what he and my mom called *midnights*, the four in the afternoon until twelve at night shift. Other times it was in the morning when I was getting ready for school, when he was working what they called just plain *nights*. If it was up to him and my mom and me he would have always worked *days*, leaving in the morning and coming home before it got dark. But although my grandfather and three of my dad's brothers had worked at Ontario Steel, everybody had to take turns working all of the different shifts until you'd built up enough seniority to apply to get *steady days*. Whenever I asked my dad how long it'd be until he got seniority and he could eat supper with us every night instead of every third week, he always said the same thing: *Not for a long time.*

The day that Henderson scored his goal—the game was in Russia, it must have been evening over there—my dad was working days. Men lugged the television sets from their family rooms into the factory. Transistor radios talked to each other from all over the plant, Foster Hewitt calling out the action, trying to make himself heard over the smash and crash of the bumper presses and rivet guns. My grandfather got drunk at home in front of the TV and showed up at the factory on his bicycle to tell my dad that Canada had won. The supervisors drank from the same cases of beer as the guys who'd brought them in, the men who worked the floor.

If he was working days, my dad would usually take a bath before we ate supper. Sometimes I'd sit on the toilet seat and talk to him while he'd scrub the dirt out of his ears and brush the grease from underneath his fingernails. I told him we'd got to watch the game at school and that the men teachers shook hands after it was all over and the women teachers hugged each other in front of everybody in the gym. Then, I said, we'd all sung "O Canada."

Do you know all the words all by yourself? my dad said.

We sing it every morning.

So you know how all of it goes?

Uh-huh.

Why don't you sing it for me, then.

How come?

If you don't want to, you don't have to.

I want to, I said.

I stood up from the toilet seat and kept my hands straight at my sides while I sang, just like Mrs. Jackson made sure we did every day at 9:05 a.m., no fidgeting around or slouching. My dad only got as far as grade eight in school, left early to work washing cars at a cab stand and running errands at Morris Auto Supply. My mother went a little further, almost made it to Christmas of grade nine before dropping out to take a job my Aunt Yvonne got her working where she worked, in the hospital cafeteria at Chatham General. Whenever I didn't feel like getting out of bed for school or came home with a weak report card, my mother would always say, *You get an education, you don't want to have to end up working in a dirty factory like your father.*

I sang "O Canada" while my dad lay back in the tub with his eyes closed. He liked his baths hot when he got home from the factory; steam lifted off the water like in the movie

I saw the Saturday afternoon before on Sir Graves Ghastly's horror show, *The Creature from the Black Lagoon*. When I was finished singing the anthem, his eyes stayed shut. I thought maybe he'd fallen asleep. He finally opened them.

Good boy, he said.

I stayed standing there, ready to sing again if he asked me to. I had goosebumps on my arms and on the back of my neck. *We won, didn't we, Dad?*

Yes, sir, he said. He sat up in the tub. The bathwater turned choppy; threatened to, but didn't, splash over the sides.

Now hand me that towel, he said. *Your mother's going to have supper on the table any minute now.*

Joe drove, Jack drank from a bottle of Rémy Martin.

The cognac was in honour of Jack's return to Canada, to his Québécois roots. His father's father had been a farmer in a small village on the outskirts of Rivière-du-Loup, and that's where they were headed, yesterday such an appealing destination when today and tomorrow just blank days and emptier nights. Joe was behind the wheel because Jack didn't have a driver's licence, never had. The author of *On the Road* didn't drive.

Just outside of Lowell they picked up a hitchhiker. The kid ran after the car and threw his knapsack in the back, climbed inside.

Thanks, man.

No problem, Joe said.

It had been Joe's idea to stop. Since getting picked up near Kearney Square for having an open bottle of beer and then catching strep throat later that night in his cell, Jack was extra wary of cops. Not that he blamed the police. It was all the damn civil rights and anti-war protesters and all their mad marching that had made the cops so jaily jittery these days. Ginsberg with his messianic beard and all his Castro-loving band of Communist buddies.

Where are you headed? Joe said.

The kid used all ten fingers to lift his long greasy hair off his forehead and out of his eyes. *I've got some friends up near Haverhill.*

Well, we're going a little further north than that, but you're welcome to ride with us as long as you want.

Cool, man, that's cool. The kid eased back in the seat, locked his hands behind his head, looked out the window at the speeding Massachusetts countryside. *I'm in no hurry to get nowhere, man, I'm just riding, I'm just digging life on the road.*

Joe clicked on the turn signal and steered into the passing lane, looked over at Jack grinning into his bottle. Jack took a swallow. Joe looked in the rear-view mirror at the kid.

Hey, Joe said, *you ever read that book by Jack Kerouac, what's it called,* On the Road?

The kid shimmied forward to the edge of the seat. *Oh, man, are you kidding me? I read that when I was a kid, when I was, like, sixteen or seventeen, it blew my mind, it totally blew my mind. That guy did it all, man, went everywhere and saw everything. I think I heard he was born around here, actually.*

So you think he's a pretty good writer? Joe took the bottle from Jack, took a quick pull.

Oh, yeah.

Joe winked at Jack, handed back the cognac.

I'm not sure if he's still alive, though, the kid said. *A friend of mine, he said he read somewhere that he'd gone crazy and joined the John Birch Society or something. Man, imagine that. Wow, what a trip.*

Jack could have laughed. Could have. Probably should have. The Jack of fifteen years before, the raggedy ass, hand-to-mouth, sponging-off-his-mother-who-slaved-in-a-shoe-factory-for-years-so-that-he-could-drink-and-drug-and-dream-and-ramble-and-write-and-write-and-write Jack would have. That same guy—the one who liked the Buddhist idea of Nothingness so much because, among other things, it was spiritual salve to worldly sores such as his friend John Clellon Holmes bagging a $20,000 advance for a finely manicured mediocrity like his novel *Go* while Jack's own accumulated half-dozen novels and two books of poetry and two thick Buddhist wake-up treatises were over and over again rejected and rejected or outright ignored— that Jack, too, would have laughed at the cosmic cut-up of how everything always turns out exactly like you have no idea how it'll turn out. Wouldn't have been able *not* to laugh.

But a sense of humour is 20/20. And to keep sane, you shouldn't be able to see too well, just good enough to get around and not get lost. Or at least not get too lost.

You're right, he's dead, Jack said, speaking for the first time.

Oh, yeah? the kid said.

Yeah, Jack said. *I killed him myself last Thursday night. He forgot to say his rosary so I stabbed him in the heart with my Smith-Corona.*

The celebrities of the hallways were hockey players. Officially they were known as the travel team, although everybody called them what they were, the All-Stars. It wasn't any coincidence that none of them had straight stringy hair like me or wore North Star running shoes to school like the ones my mother bought for me every August at Zellers. Their hair was blow-dried and feathered, perfectly parted in the middle, and nothing but Nike or Converse—high-tops usually, most often leather—would do for their feet for when they weren't wearing skates.

Most of us played what was called house league—one game a week, one practice every other week, a banquet at the end of the year and it's not whether you win or lose, boys, it's all about having fun—but the All-Star team was reserved for Chatham's best. The All-Stars played half of their games in Chatham, the other half on the road at the rinks of all the other neighbouring towns with their own All-Star teams: Dresden, Wallaceburg, Blenheim, Sarnia. When they did play at home, they played at Memorial Arena, where the Chatham Maroons, the Junior B club, played, seating capacity

1,700, with a press box and a tuck shop and a time clock sponsored by Coca-Cola that hung high over centre ice. Memorial Arena was built in the 1940s and named in honour of the fallen veterans of the Second World War. Northside Arena, where the house league teams played, was built in the early 1970s and was called what it was because it was built on the city's north side.

Every school had their share of All-Stars, and Indian Creek Road Public School wasn't any different. We had Miles O'Neil and Jerry Bechard and the two Jeffs, Jeff Jones and Jeff Dunford. We had Jamie too, but only for one year, for grade eight, after his dad, the Reverend Dalzell, changed churches and the entire family moved across town and Jamie and his brother Gordon came to Indian Creek. Even if you didn't know anything about hockey, you knew who the All-Stars were.

If you were an All-Star you got to wear a maroon winter jacket with white leather sleeves with CHATHAM written across the back and your first name stitched across the right breast. The results of the All-Star games got written up in the sports section of Monday's *Chatham Daily News* — "Jones Pots Pair as Pee Wees Clobber Sarnia," the headline would read — just like an actual NHL game. The All-Stars ate lunch together and stood around together at recess and walked the hallways to class together. Their parents took turns driving them four or five to a car to out-of-town games on the weekends and they ended up being best friends too, Jeff Jones' dad and Jeff Dunford's dad and Mr. O'Neil always going golfing together, sometimes bringing along Jeff and Jeff and Miles to make up their own nine-hole threesome. Most of the mothers would sit next to each other in the frozen stands of the arena under shared maroon blankets laid across shivering knees and ring their cowbells and cheer on their sons with chants of *Let's-Go-Chatham, Let's-Go! Let's-Go-Chatham, Let's-Go!*

Jamie wasn't all All-Star, though, not all the time, not like Jeff and Jeff and Miles were. We'd do Monty Python skits at recess, do them over and over so often that we'd sound more like the records than the records did. We had an exercise book (*Cahier d'exercice*) that was intended for French verbs that we appropriated and entitled the *Standard Ja Ra Dictionary*, a numbered catalogue of Jamie and Ray's favourite Monty Python and Steve Martin lines, the nicknames we made up for the teachers and the other students, and words and expressions that seemed to us just hilarious.

Near the end of grade eight, someone from the board of education came in to talk to our homeroom classes about what high schools we were going to attend. John McGregor, Chatham-Kent Secondary School, Tecumseh, St. Ursuline, Chatham Collegiate Institute — the choice was ours, the man maintained, just be careful when making your decision, talk it over with your parents, consider all of your options. Jamie didn't bother to take his form home with him like the man suggested, filled it out as soon as it was handed to him with his name and address and phone number and, under "Desired Secondary School (First Option)," *Chatham Collegiate Institute*. I wrote down what Jamie did.

Jamie was the only All-Star who signed up for Chatham Collegiate Institute. CCI was for the smart kids, the ones who were planning on going on to university, whose parents had been there themselves a generation before. Jamie's dad had studied divinity at Yale, and Jamie was expected to do the same at either U of T or Queen's or, at the very least, Western. I wasn't supposed to end up at CCI.

After school, walking to the bike rack, Jeff Dunford asked me where I was going to go. We lived in the same subdivision. Although I was only a house league player, he talked to me sometimes because I'd beaten him in the 100-metre dash during field day two years in a row.

CCI, I said. An hour before, I'd never even heard of it. Now I was calling it my school.

CCI is for fags, Jeff said. Jeff was short but wiry, as quick on his skates as he was on his feet, a pesky second-line centre especially good at killing penalties and agitating the other team's best players. He had sculpted blond hair like Leif Garrett and was the first guy I knew who had a girlfriend, Karen Fenton.

Jamie's going to CCI, I said.

Jeff bent over to undo his bike lock, blew at a strand of hair stuck in the corner of his mouth. He shrugged. *It's still for fags*, he said.

I pretended like I didn't hear him, climbed on my bike and started pedalling. I didn't care what he thought.

Columbia University wanted him, but only after a year of prepping at Horace Mann, a year of getting the Lowell washed and rinsed out of him—as quick and slick a halfback as he was, not quite yet up to Ivy League academic standards in chemistry and math and even French (*Parlez-vous français?* French, not nearly the same as Mémère's home-jawed *joual*). But Columbia wanted him. Lou Little's recruiters were dangling not only a full athletic scholarship but hints that their almighty alumni could finally get the ink off his father's fingers and rescue him from the rut of the printing shop. Jack's old man, though, didn't trust either Little or his offer, thought he was just a show-offy little wop, wanted Jack to take Boston College's offer instead. The shop Leo worked at, Sullivan Printers, handled the entire BC printing account and was busy doing its own hinting, namely that Leo would most likely get a promotion if his son committed to the local school, a probable pink slip if he didn't.

But Jack wanted to go to Columbia. Anybody who spent a lifetime of Saturday afternoons at the movies knew that New York was where you wanted to be. Mémère wanted him to end up there too. Columbia, she told everyone, her husband included, was the best place for her Ti Jean to go to learn how to be a successful insurance salesman. She bought him a new sports jacket, shirt, and tie with her savings from the shoe factory so that Jacky wouldn't have a problem fitting in with the better class of people he was going to meet up there.

Mémère arranged to have Jack stay with her stepmother in Brooklyn during his two terms at Horace Mann. The round-trip subway ride to school and back was two and a half hours long, and after a full day of classes followed by a couple more hours of football practice, there wasn't much time to do much else when he got home besides eat and sleep and get up for school again. He did most of his homework on the subway and skipped classes often enough that Times Square became his favourite subject.

The Apollo and the Paramount movie theatres; the hookers and the pushers and the panhandlers; Bickford's Cafeteria and the New York Public Library and the guys on the sidewalk selling watches underneath their overcoats; the Negroes and the Italians and the Asians and the tens of thousands of entirely other others who had nothing better to do at one o'clock on a Tuesday afternoon than walk around being themselves in order to be the supporting cast to the brilliant new movie of Jean-Louis Kerouac's brand new life starring the one and the only Jean-Louis Kerouac of Lowell, Massachusetts, US of A.

His first month there, Scotty and G.J. went up to visit him. Zag showed them all the sights, gave them the tour of the Horace Mann and Columbia campuses, made sure they had a chance to say they'd stood outside Madison Square Garden and ridden the elevator up the Empire State Building, and marched them down busy Broadway on a warm Saturday night, red neon tans and sore necks for everybody to bring home with them from staring up at the skyscrapers taking over the sky.

They finished off the evening at a restaurant with white tablecloths and a maître d' and a two-page wine list. They went all out, did it up right, ordered a seven-course meal and took their damn sweet time eating it. When the waiter saw Jack attempting to use his butter knife to sever the string holding together his Cornish hen, he came over and tapped him on the shoulder.

Excuse me, sir, he said, *but perhaps you'd have more success with your other knife.*

Jack just kept sawing away. *That's all right, Mac,* he said. *I've got a pretty strong arm.*

School, like being young, was to be endured.

High school, it turned out, wasn't much different from grade school. Sports were good, and so was the chance to meet girls, or at least stare at them in the hallways or at lunchtime from the safe side, the boys' side, of the cafeteria, but more and harder homework and more kids in class with their hands stuck up in the air more than made up the difference. One thing you had to look forward to in high school, though, was that starting in grade eleven everybody got a spare class built into their schedule, fifty free minutes to do whatever you wanted. And Jamie said that when you were in grade thirteen you didn't need to get a note from your parents if you were late for school or even if you missed an entire day, you got to write your own. So there was that to look forward to.

But that was all PJ—pre-Jim—before I knew there were things I needed to know if I wanted to be a rock and roll poet too who conquered the world only to give it all back at age twenty-seven under mysterious circumstances in a bathtub full of lukewarm water at dawn in Paris. Things I needed to know that could only be learned by shutting up and being quiet and letting men and women I didn't know talk to me through the husks of themselves they'd left behind for us, their books. Jim at seventeen, his biography told me, wasn't on a sports team, didn't talk to his girlfriend all night on the telephone, wasn't even in a rock band. Jim at seventeen liked to hang around the library. The *library*. Getting to know the dead people who told him how to live. Clearly I needed better friends. I didn't write out a list, but if I had, there could only have been one book at the top, Jim's all-time favourite, *On the Road*.

There were two bookstores in Chatham: Coles downtown and another Coles in the Woolco mall off Highway 40 that you could get to if you got a transfer from the bus driver at the depot and then got dropped off in the last subdivision in town and then got picked up by another bus that let you off in front of the mall. I tried the bookstore downtown first, went after school, looked under *K* under Fiction, but *On the Road* wasn't there.

I was the only person in the store besides the woman who worked there, but she hadn't looked at me since I came through the door, was busy setting up a display of desk calendars and daybooks on a white-cloth-covered table near the cash register. I thought about asking her to help me find the book, but she looked like she was angry about something. Besides, I figured there wasn't any point. I didn't know how to pronounce Jack What's-His-Name's name anyway.

Becoming an overnight success only took seven years.

Seven insolvent (self-elected, but no less so for being so) years after the publication of his first novel, *The Town and the City*, the same seven long years during which his next, *On the Road*, was rejected by every oh-so-insightful and obviously super-astute literary sensibility that read it (Harcourt Brace, Ace Books, Criterion, Bobbs-Merrill, Scribner's, Ballantine, Little Brown, Dutton, Knopf, Dodd Mead) until one day some bright boy in marketing at Viking thought, Hey, I think we can actually sell this thing, I could get this guy's picture in *Vogue*, he's handsome enough I think I could get him on TV, if we all work together I'm sure we could make this thing happen. This new music all the kids are talking about, this rock and roll crap; and Marlon Brando and James Dean and all these articles about juvenile delinquency you see in every newspaper and magazine you pick up these days. I'm telling you, this thing could take off, with the right kind of push, the right kind of angle, this thing could become a phenomenon, could turn out to be the goddamn bible of an entire generation.

On the Road was on the *New York Times* bestseller list for
five weeks in 1957, was reprinted three times during the very
first month it appeared.

Never underestimate people who have paper clips for
souls. What's wrong is what's right and they don't have to lie
to themselves to make other people believe it. People like the
people who believe that *Life* magazine is life. People like
the man in the Brooks Brothers suit inside everyone. People
like Jack. That's right—Jack. It wasn't as if he said what he
should have said right from the start, that Beat Generation
Meat Generation Feet Generation Bleat Generation, thanks
for the cover story and all the nice money, folks, but try to
understand, it was just me and a bunch of guys I knew trying
not to be bored.

So:

In bars, men would pick fights with him, what a thrill to
say you'd cleaned the clock of the King of the Beats. One
time, Jack and Gregory Corso got jumped coming out of the
Kettle of Fish and some guy got Jack down on the ground
and kept slamming his head against the pavement, *smack
smack smack*. Jack didn't set foot in New York again for
nearly a year.

His agent had no problem placing any of his unpublished
manuscripts anymore, but some of the editors at some of the
larger publishers wondered if, perhaps, a gentle grammati-
cal flossing might make some of Jack's more . . . challeng-
ing sentences a little more . . . let us say, accessible. They
were, after all, operating a business. They were, after all,

making a significant financial investment in the continued success of Jack's burgeoning literary career.

And before too long, before his next book, *The Dharma Bums*, even landed on the bookstore shelves: Oh yeah, about that career thing— Remember how last week you were a spontaneous prose poet, a singular bard of bop, a lyrical visionary declaiming a previously unknown hipster-rich American underbelly? Yeah, well, now you're a sloppy, undisciplined, self-indulgent media creation prone to sentimentality, immorality, and obvious sensationalism. Next, please.

And then there was the booze. Yes, there was that.

But what comes first, the chicken or the alcoholic? Jack always drank, now he really, really drank. Before, it was because of blah blah blah; now, it was because of et cetera et cetera. Give a junkie junk and he'll give you a reason. Chemistry will find a way.

An old girlfriend ran into Jack, droopy drunk and echoed out by a group of loud strangers at the Cellar Door in the Village, and asked him what it was like to be famous.

Like old newspapers blowing down Bleecker Street, he said.

The first rich person's house I ever visited—rich for Chatham, anyway—was Larry Franklin's. His father was an ear, eye, nose, and throat specialist, and everyone from our grade ten class got invited to the Franklins' big house out in the country for Larry's birthday party. We were told to bring our bathing suits. Somebody said Larry had an indoor swimming pool. Somebody else said he had a sauna.

Larry was a doughy red-headed kid I'd gone to the same public school with and he was all right, he'd liked dinosaurs like I did in grade four and told pretty good dirty jokes. And unlike the other kids whose parents weren't auto workers or cafeteria workers like mine were, he wasn't very good at school. I liked that about him.

Larry hung around with everybody, but especially with Mike Rankin and Craig Wellington and Mark Shillington, a lawyer's son and a dentist's son and the son of an architect. To their credit, they didn't talk about being better off than everybody else, but they didn't have to, all you had to do was look at them. They were the ones who came back from Christmas vacation with buttery Bermuda tans. They were the ones whose mothers packed King Dons and Twinkies and Hostess Fruit Pies in their lunches instead of maple leaf–shaped maple cookies and glow-in-the-dark, finger-length pink wafer cookies that our mothers hand-wrapped in thick wax paper. Later on, during high school, they were the ones who showed up first in all of the new fashions: white painter's pants; leather deck shoes; brightly coloured shirts with a little black alligator stitched over the left breast.

One day during grade ten the collars on their shirts were suddenly all turned up. At first I thought it was a mistake, that somebody didn't know that his collar wasn't right, but then I noticed that all of them were wearing them that way. I asked Jamie what was going on. Jamie was smart, not because his parents were wealthy, but because his dad, who had floor-to-ceiling bookshelves in his office at the church, made him study hard.

What's that supposed to mean? I said.

It means they're rich.

I don't get it.

You're not supposed to, you're not rich.

I almost didn't go to the party. There was a girl who I thought liked me who, it turned out, didn't like me, which I only discovered after I asked somebody to find out if she liked me, as sure a sign as any that I liked her. It was touch and go for a while, but the wound, after all, wasn't fatal, I was going to pull through. It was still pretty raw, though, and there was no way I was going to chance running into her at Larry's party.

I was helping my dad cut the grass, occasionally being allowed to man the mower for a few apprentice swipes of the lawn, but mainly being responsible for assisting in emptying out the clippings from the side-catcher. The old man cut the engine. Always turn off the engine when you're emptying the clippings from the side-catcher.

You should probably be getting cleaned up for your party by now, he said. We were both bare-chested and dripping hot, our T-shirts hanging over the rail of the deck he'd built that summer with Mr. Deboir, our neighbour. Each of us was wearing what we always wore all summer, Adidas gym shorts, mine blue ones with white stripes up each side, his red ones with white stripes.

I'm not going.

He unhooked the cloth side-catcher from the mower. I opened up the garbage bag, got it ready.

Why not? he said.

I don't know. I don't feel like it.

You sick?

No. I just don't feel like going.

He lifted up the side-catcher and placed it inside the garbage bag, shook it, and kept shaking it until it was empty. The bag grew heavy in my hands. It always surprised me how heavy a bag full of blades of grass could end up being.

Dr. Franklin's got an indoor pool out there. He's got a sauna too, I hear.

I know. Of course I knew. I was the one who'd told him.

Go get showered up, then, he said. *I'll be done by the time you get ready, I'll drop you off.*

I shrugged my shoulders.

My dad pulled a green garbage bag tie out of his back pocket. It was important not to fill the bags too full or else they'd get too heavy and when you put them out on the curb the garbageman might not take them.

You do what you want, he said, *but if you're not going to the party like you said you were, you're gonna stay around here and help me with the trimming and the hedges.*

He spun the bag around by its bunched plastic top, twisted the tie tight.

I guess I'll take a shower, I said.

I'm ready to go when you are.

Everybody was there, everybody, it seemed, except Jennifer Hastings. Somebody ended up telling me that her parents were Jehovah's Witnesses and that she wasn't allowed to go to parties or dances or to do it until she was married to another Jehovah's Witness. I started to feel better about her not liking me. Who wanted a girlfriend who couldn't do it until she got married?

Larry's house was big, maybe four or five times the size of our house, but except for the enormous front lawn and the indoor swimming pool and the sauna, really not that much different, just crammed full of better brand name versions of all of the same crap that we had. Larry's parents left us pretty much alone, although Dr. Franklin would make the rounds every half-hour or so, presumably to make sure that no one was humping on his living room carpet. He dressed like he was going to the beach, but with a white cardigan tied around his neck. I'd never seen a man with a sweater tied around his neck before. Whenever he made an appearance, there was an oversized cocktail glass in his right hand filled with tinkling ice cubes and some kind of dark, almost black, purple liquid.

We drank pop and ate cake and listened to the records that Larry kept putting on and taking off—Queen, ELO, Styx—until somebody cannonballed into the pool and then everybody else hurried into their swimsuits and jumped in and then everybody was in the pool. All of the girls wore one-piece bathing suits and none of them looked as good with her clothes off as you'd imagined she would. Every time Dr. Franklin popped in to check on us, his eyelids were drooping a little lower, the smile at the corners of his mouth propped up a little higher. His purple tinkling drink was still in his right hand. The white cardigan was still hanging around his neck.

When my dad came to pick me up, he gave the Franklins' huge front lawn a long look before he restarted the car. It had to be the size of three football fields, easy.

If you didn't have a good riding mower, it'd take you all day to cut this thing, he said. He said it like that was a good thing.

On the ride home I switched the radio to FM from CFCO, the AM Chatham station where my mother kept it, and tuned it to WRIF, the rock station out of Detroit that everybody at school listened to. "Don't Stop Believin'" by Journey. I left it on. There wasn't anything else to listen to.

Yes, sir, my dad said, his arm hanging out the window while he drove, *that's why you need to get an education, boy. You remember what you saw there tonight, you don't forget it. You look at Dr. Franklin. He used his head, he used his brains. Now look at him.*

Maine bars Lowell bars plain bars red velvet plush lush bars — no matter where or what, the same people doing the same things that each of them could be doing at a quarter of the cost they're doing them at but that they'd have to do at home, alone. Instead, they're here, at the Mercury Lounge, Smithfield, Maine, all alone with all of the other people who don't want to be at home tonight, who also don't want to be all alone.

It doesn't take Jack long to become the centre of attention. The truckers sitting at the bar and the scattered locals slouching at the tables and the bored waitress and the balding bartender watching the fight on TV don't mind his standing at the jukebox and shouting over his shoulder at no one and everyone, *Cowboy music, hey? The soul cannot commune with cowboy music. Where is it written that the saddle is the proper destination of man?* just like a few of them even grin at each other when Jack says to Marie, the waitress (after she serves Joe and him their drinks and Jack can't coax her into saying much more than the *Yes* and *No* and *Thank you, sirs* that she says to everyone she serves), *Beauty itself doth of itself persuade / The eyes of men without an orator* because Marie isn't beautiful and poetry sounds funny coming from a grown man and the eyes of the guy sitting next to the guy shooting off his mouth say, *He's okay, folks, he's harmless, don't worry, he just wants to be friends.*

Besides, what the hell, it's Saturday night, nobody wants any trouble, a stranger is just a friend you don't know yet. And the one in the red-check lumberjack shirt, the loud one, he's a good tipper, and Marie gets into a good-waitress groove of knowing his and Joe's sipping rhythm and brings the two of them their next round of whiskey sodas before either one has to ask, and before too long Jack and Joe aren't much different than the Faron Young and Hank Snow songs floating from the glowing jukebox and ghosting around the room.

My people used to drink caribou blood.

Jack said it like a challenge. A challenge Joe wouldn't meet. Which was one more reason why Jack loved Joe.

The first North American Kerouac was Baron Alexandre Louis Lebris de Kerouac of Cornwall, Brittany.

So you said.

I did?

You did.

Jack took a long drink. *Well, I just said it again.*

Joe knew that if he didn't get Jack's mind off itself and onto something else soon, things could get messy. Consistently generous gratuities alone weren't nearly sufficient insurance against the threat of the actions and words of a man who'd nursed a bottle of brandy all day and was now jacked up on enough speed to keep the entire world awake.

What have you been reading these days, Jack?

Joe knew. Jack knew Joe knew. So:

So tell me all about Jacques Maritain, Jack said. *Impress me. He's the new white knight of all the college professors, isn't he?*

You might be surprised, Joe said. *You never know, you just might like him. He's got a lot to say about your boy Pascal.*

My boy, as you so glibly, so vulgarly, refer to him, doesn't need anything said about him by anybody, least of all by any pipe-poking tweedy dum-dum who's got a tenure track mind instead of a head full of bleeding angels. Blaise Pascal said all that was needed to be said about la condition humaine three-hundred-and-then-some years ago, all in that delicious holy prosody of his that will not and cannot be improved upon in spite of the best efforts of all of your B.F. Skinners and Marshall McLuhans and all the other naysaying mooks working with their pocket calculators against God's benign and almighty saving grace.

This was the Jack that Joe loved. Tonight, he thought, finishing his drink, was going to be just fine. Marie appeared at their table, set their tinkling fresh whiskey sodas down in front of them. Jack—fat, stoplight red eyes, jack-in-the-box hair—took Marie's hand.

I doth protest this much beauty.

Marie giggled. *You're not from around here, are you?*
Jack stood up, bowed.

Let me begin at the beginning. The first North American Kerouac was Baron Alexandre Louis Lebris de Kerouac of Cornwall, Brittany. He was a soldier, you see, a loyal man loyal to the King of France . . .

I liked Grandma and Grandpa Robertson best. I liked going to their house better than I did Grandma and Grandpa Authier's, anyway. My dad's parents' house was what a grandparents' house was supposed to be like. There were hard candies in a glass dish in the living room that had all melted together and attached themselves permanently to the bottom of the dish. Grandpa Robertson always wore a fedora whenever he went outside and he called me Lad, the same thing his father, a Scottish immigrant, had called my dad when he was a boy. The basement smelled like mothballs, and my grandma always made a fuss over me whenever I'd come by, would save me the prizes from inside their cereal boxes and never forgot my birthday and usually gave me a toy for Christmas that I'd asked for. The shades were half drawn in the summer to keep the house cooler, and the thermostat was kept low throughout the winter. When we'd come home from visiting, my mother would complain in the car, *I thought I was going to freeze to death. I swear, I've never met a man so cheap in my entire life.*

I didn't mind. I liked it, actually. The coolness felt clean to me. It felt like what I imagined Scotland felt like.

My dad and his seven brothers and sisters grew up in a rotting three-storey Victorian in Chatham's east end that not that long before had been part of one of the town's favoured neighbourhoods but by the mid-fifties had become the exile of not-by-choice of the town's squeezed-out working poor and most of its black population. By the time he left home, Grandma and Grandpa Robertson had escaped to one of Chatham's first shiny suburbs, lots of nice white neighbours, a rose garden in the front, and a ceiling that didn't rain. We'd lived in the east end too, just down the street from my dad's old place, until I was six and my parents had saved up enough money to graduate us to a brand new subdivision of our own that only twelve months before had been a farmer's soya bean field. Grandma and Grandpa Authier, though, still lived in the east end, in a house one-storey tiny and tarpaper black, only one lot removed from the railroad tracks, just on the other side of the cemetery.

Grandma Authier was fat, wore floral print cotton house-dresses the size of my pup tent, and always with a white apron tied around the front, and when she walked, which was rare—from her chair at the kitchen table, say, to her easy chair in front of the television set in the living room—it was like Godzilla on the move, rocking slightly side to side as she thumped along and you had to better look out down below if you didn't want to get crushed. Grandma wore hand-knit pink slippers over her pantyhose, and one time she stepped on my hand when I was playing with my Hot Wheels cars on the floor. *Oh, Raymond,* she said, laughing, *be careful, Grandma didn't see you there.* Grandma and Grandpa Authier always seemed to be laughing, Grandma especially. She reminded me of a circus fat lady whose job is to simply sit there and be her enormous laughing self.

Grandma and Grandpa Authier were both born in Quebec and they both called me Raymond. My dad called Grandpa Mike, but Grandma called him Mede. Mom called Grandma Mem. When Grandma and Grandpa didn't want anyone else to know what they were saying to each other they'd speak in French, although it didn't sound much like the *Pitou!-Pitou!-Où-est-le-poulet?* French I was learning at school. My mom would understand the gist of it, the swear words, for sure, but wouldn't ever tell me what they were. When she was younger she'd understood more, but at fifteen had moved out to live with my Aunt Yvonne and her new husband so she didn't have to hear any swear words in French anymore.

By the time I was crawling around with my Hot Wheels, Grandma didn't drink anymore and Grandpa no more than anyone else, but when I got a little older my dad would tell me stories of what it was like for my mom growing up. Waking up for school on Monday morning and the cupboards empty, all of the money Grandpa had made the week before cutting bush already spent. The singing, the yelling, the crying—the unholy trinity of non-stop Canadian Club drunkenness. My dad showing up to pick my mom up for a date and Grandpa asking him to first drive him over to the bootlegger's, his car out of gas and him too drunk to make it there by himself even if it wasn't.

The story went that my mother told her parents that they weren't going to be invited to her wedding if they were going to drink, and from that day forward Grandma went one step further, never touched alcohol again. For as long as I knew her, Grandma always drank coffee, heavy on the cream and especially on the sugar, no matter what the weather. Instead of the living room, all of the grown-ups would sit around the cigarette-scarred Formica kitchen table and drink and smoke and talk, country and western music coming from Grandpa's eight-track machine in the back room. Grandpa smoked his own cigarettes made from a rolling machine with a big silver crank, kept them in a white plastic container that bulged his shirt pocket. There was a warm bottle of Coke on the kitchen counter for mix that my dad would pour into a glass for me when we'd get there, but I was used to root beer or black cherry or C-Plus, anything but just Coke. If it was earlier in the evening he'd find a couple of ice cubes for me, but as the night went on it was room-temperature Coke or nothing.

I'd sit on the thick shag orange living room carpet and watch TV, the fizz from the bubbles in my glass of Coke making my nose twitch. Grandma and Grandpa Authier didn't have an antenna on their roof like we did, and at best the picture was fuzzy, murky, like watching *Happy Days* through a fishbowl. There was a cuckoo clock on the wall, and a squawking bird popped out of his house on the hour. The couches and the chairs all had a hard, clear plastic wrap draped over them, and if you sat down, your legs and your back got cold. There weren't vents in the floor where the heat came out like at our house or at Grandma and Grandpa Robertson's, but instead a large gas heater mounted to the wall of the living room that made you feel hot and nauseous if you stood too close to it for too long.

Most of the time I was the only kid there, except for my cousin Bradley. Bradley's father was my mother's brother, his mother my father's sister, but he'd lived with Grandma and Grandpa Authier ever since his parents got divorced, not long after he was born. Bradley slept on the bottom bunk bed in the only other bedroom besides Grandma and Grandpa's— the top bed if his dad, a roofer, happened to be working in town. Bradley and I looked about the same, but he was chubby and seemed older than the two years that separated us, worked with Grandpa getting greasy out in the garage on the weekends, drank coffee with Grandma at the kitchen table, knew when to laugh at the jokes passed around among the grown-ups that never made any sense to me.

Christmas at Grandma and Grandpa Authier's was never much fun because all I ever got was stuff that Grandma knitted me — mittens I wasn't going to wear because no one wore mittens, only gloves, and sweaters and scarves, and one year even a toque that there was no way anyone at school was ever going to see me in. One year my mom asked Grandma to buy me one of the toys I was asking for so that I wouldn't spend half of Christmas Eve moping around the kitchen table in my itchy new sweater asking when we were going to go home. On the ride over, my mom said I might be surprised at what was under the tree for me this year.

My usual gift from Grandma and Grandpa Authier was soft and spongy; this time, whatever was under the wrapping paper was hard and square. This was encouraging. Hand-knit scarves and mittens didn't come in cardboard boxes. I ripped off the paper and couldn't believe my luck. Not only had Grandma actually come through, got me an A1 gift for a change, another G.I. Joe for my growing army of combat guys, Action Jacksons, and Johnny Wests, but it was the absolute latest G.I. Joe, the one where you pulled his dog tag and he spoke one of six different commands. *Thanks Grandma, thanks Grandpa,* I said, tearing Johnny free from his box.

You're welcome, Raymond, Grandma answered. Grandpa was in the other room, changing eight-tracks.

I pulled Joe's dog tag and waited for his first command, watched the string attached to it slither back inside his throat.

Je suis prêt à aller.

I didn't understand. I pulled the dog tag again.

La mission est accomplie.

Something was wrong. I picked up the discarded box, studied it for a clue. Jesus Christ, she'd bought me a French G.I. Joe. She'd bought me a goddamn French G.I. Joe.

I carried Joe and the torn-open box to the table. *Listen,* I insisted, standing beside my mom. I yanked the string again.

La nuit tombe, nous devons faire le camp.

I looked from my mother's face to my dad's. *He's French,* I said.

Everybody laughed, no one more than Grandma. *Grandma, she thought she got you what you wanted, Raymond,* she said. Everybody laughed some more.

I turned to my mom.

We'll see if we can exchange it, she said, hand on my head.

But Grandma hadn't kept the receipt and I was stuck with Joe d'GI. My friends and I made the best of it. Grandma's G.I. Joe became all of the other action figures' solitary prisoner. We called him The Foreigner. We made sure he was always under heavily armed guard.

The back of his throat like a plugged-up toilet, he rolled off his back and turned onto his side, allowed the contents of his coming-on cold, his still-lingering strep throat, and whatever other gagging evidence there was of the damage he'd done to himself over the past twenty-four hours to gooey-gather in his cheek; opened his eyes, spotted an empty water glass on the motel room floor, and leaned over the side of the bed, spat. If it had just been spit, it probably would have made it. Instead: a long green string of phlegm, one end attached to his lower lip and chin, the other inching down the side of the mattress, a morning-after umbilical cord, late night last night's way of saying it wasn't quite ready to turn into today just yet.

But it was today, it had to be, for sure that's all that's ever been for sure. And even that—ticky-tock time and all the rest of that mechanistic materialistic monotheistic company line we expertly sell ourselves so as to dream ourselves a nice big fluffy hallucination of actually existing existence so as to keep ourselves distracted in the holy lonely Void—pah!

Write or not write, drink or not drink, be hungover to one's very marrow or not, all of it—*all of it*—just both sides of the same never-not-spinning coin, up, up, and away in the Nirvana of one's mind which, of course, isn't really one's mind at all but only one more comfy delusion to keep us deep asleep and from recognizing the Four Noble Truths, from following the Eightfold Noble Path.

Buddhism was a nice anaesthetic. It wasn't the second day of a three-day drunk or the cranial clear-cutting that results from the silver kiss of a shot of sweet, sweet morphine, but wordy wisdom doesn't give you the DTs or make you a dead-eyed junkie, either. Jack discovered Dwight Goddard's *A Buddhist Bible* at the San Jose library in 1954 while out west visiting Cassady and his family. Jack had been trying to suffocate his ego for years, almost from the time he'd discovered he had one—playing his homemade dice baseball game for hours alone in his bedroom, writing and illustrating and acting out his own Dr. Sax comic books, lying on the grass in his parents' backyard and looking up at the stars in the cold Atlantic sky and feeling so free, feeling so small, just a speck on another speck drifting through an everlasting universe of specks. To be *and* not to be—that was the answer to the question, the only question.

He wiped his chin on his shirt front and leaned back on his elbows. Joe in the other bed was still asleep—Let him sleep, Jack thought—Joe in his matching pyjama top and bottom snuggled deep underneath his sheets, Joe with his brushed teeth and with a conscientious wake-up call left with room service before they'd crashed into unconsciousness. Jack was still wearing the clothes he'd put on the day before, shoes included, before they'd set out from Lowell. He eased back down on top of the blankets with his head in the middle of the pillow.

He took a deep breath and stared at the ceiling and told himself that there was no self, there was no me, there wasn't any Jean-Louis Kerouac. He forced his mind to think the unthinkable, the boundlessness of space and time, the kotis of chiliocosms and kalpas. He reminded himself of his favourite Buddhist truisms: to repose beyond fate; that the true Tathagaata is never coming from anywhere nor is he going anywhere; that from the beginning not a thing was. He took another, deeper breath, and felt as if his skull was going to crack in half. He picked up the bottle on the side table and nursed down the fingertip of cognac left inside.

Sitting on the side of the bed, empty bottle hanging from his hand, *Joe*, he said softly, as much for his sake as for Joe's.

Jack looked at the other bed. Joe was sleeping with one of his pillows over his head. *Joe*, he said again, louder.

From underneath his pillow, *I'm up*, Joe said, but didn't move. Jack counted until thirty and got to eighteen, as long as he could wait.

We have to go, Joe.

Joe peeked out from underneath the pillow on his head. Since his wife had died, he'd found that it was the only way he could sleep. Better to open your eyes to nothing than to her not being there. He pulled off the sheets and stepped into his slippers, passed by Jack on the way to the bathroom. *I'll be ready in a minute,* he said.

Jack nodded to the floor. A minute, an eternity, what's one more eternity more?

Jack set the bottle down on the carpet. And where was his watch? Not another lost watch. He knew he was wearing it last night . . .

All philosophy is a footnote to a jelly-filled donut.

Just wait until we get home, my dad said.

Why can't I have it now?

Because you'll just get it all over the upholstery.

No I won't.

Wait until we get home, then you can have it with a glass of milk. That's the way you want to eat a donut.

Being old enough, nine, to be in charge of holding the paper bag of half a dozen donuts upright on my lap on the drive home from Wiersma's Bakery didn't seem like such a great thing anymore. A Saturday afternoon of Canadian Tire and Pop Shoppe and beer store errands finally over, Wiersma's Bakery was our last stop. More and more we got our donuts from the Tim Hortons that had just opened up. They had plain and chocolate and sprinkled and jelly-filled just like Wiersma's, but also Dutchies and eclairs and fritters, donuts I'd only seen on television ads for Dunkin' Donuts which we didn't have in Canada, plus a whole other section just for Timbits. I didn't think that even Dunkin' Donuts had Timbits. Wiersma's definitely didn't.

There were two donuts for each of us—plain for Mom, who liked to dunk hers in her tea after dinner, chocolate for my dad, for his lunch box for work, and jelly-filled for me—and my two were on top. It was August, so the car windows were rolled all the way down, but all I could smell was the smell of the donuts. My mind could taste them—sugary, cakey flesh until the first breakthrough bite of sweet strawberry gush—but it wasn't enough, my stomach didn't believe it, had to have proof of its own.

I'd be careful, I said.

My dad didn't answer, which at least meant he was thinking about it. CFCO was playing on the car radio, the quarter-after noon sports report, and the announcer said something about the Red Wings, and my dad's hand flew to the volume dial and then he flipped up his finger in the air for silence. Hockey news in the summertime—never mind about the Red Wings, my dad's favourite team—was like waking up to a warm melting morning in winter. When the announcer started talking about the Tigers' baseball game that night against the Indians, *Is Thommie Bergman Gary Bergman's brother?* I said.

Although I would usually fall asleep by the third period any time they played on TV, I'd inherited the Red Wings as my favourite team, and I liked the idea of us having brothers who were teammates. The Canadiens had Frank and Pete Mahovlich and they'd won the Stanley Cup last year. The Red Wings hadn't even made the playoffs.

No, he's just a kid, they just signed him out of Sweden. It sounds like he should help them with their power play. He was defenceman of the year over there.

They play hockey in Sweden? I said. I'd thought only the Russians and us played hockey.

Some of them do, he said. My dad flipped on the turn signal. *If you're gonna eat that now, eat it over your lap. And keep your legs together. I don't want you getting any of that on the seat.*

I waited a moment to show I was serious about not making a mess. I lifted the top donut out of the bag and carefully guided it to my mouth. I took a small bite, kept my thighs and knees squeezed tight together. My dad started humming a song he always hummed when he was happy. I took another bite, this time a little bigger. I hadn't hit jam yet, but that was part of the joy of eating a jelly-filled, working toward the middle, toward what you knew was coming.

Hhm hhm hhmhmm, hhm hhm hhmhmm, hhm hhm hhmmhhmmmm.

If you were too much in a hurry to get to the jelly, if you chewed like you were chomping on a pork chop or a hamburger, chances were some of the middle would miss your mouth and squeeze out either side and leak down your hands, or worse. Even though I was near enough to the jam by now I was able to extend my tongue and bring back a jellied appetizer on its tip, I knew this was the real test, that I had to go slow and be careful and not get greedy.

Hhm hhm hhmhmm, hhm hhm hhmhmm, hhm hhm hhmmhhmmmm.

I did. And I was. And I wasn't. Made no difference, though. A small glob of jelly shot from my donut and soared over my hand and plopped on the front seat between my father and me. My father stopped humming.

Jesus Christ, what did I say? he said. *I told you to be careful, didn't I?*

I was, I was being—

He looked at the jelly stain on the seat. It looked like a mountain of jam, like if we took a right corner too quickly it might topple over and bury me.

Eyes back on the road, both hands on the wheel although he usually only drove with one, the other arm hanging out the window, *Do you try to make me mad?* he said. *Do you want me to be mad at you?*

I didn't want to look at the jelly, and I was afraid to look at him—I didn't even want to look where he was looking—so I lowered my eyes to the donut still in my left hand, the paper bag of unspoiled five others in my right.

No, I said.

Then do as you're told when I ask you to.

I— I stopped myself from saying that I had. *I will,* I said.

My dad didn't say anything else the rest of the ride home and neither did I. When that song that had been on the radio all summer came on, the one that went *My name is Michael, I've got a nickel,* my dad snapped it off and we drove home in silence.

If only the radio hadn't been on, I thought. If it hadn't, my dad wouldn't have heard about the Red Wings getting that Swedish guy who wasn't Gary Bergman's brother and wouldn't have gotten in a good mood and changed his mind and said I could eat the donut in the car when he'd already said I couldn't and now there wouldn't be jelly on the car seat and he wouldn't be mad at me and everything would be all right, just like it was before.

The simplicity of it destroyed me. An avalanche of *ifs* buried me.

We turned into the driveway.

Before the car had even stopped, *I want you to bring those donuts in the house and give them to your mother,* my dad said, *and ask her for a clean rag and to fill up the blue pail halfway to the top with hot water and to put in three good squirts of dish soap, then I want you to bring it out to me without spilling any of it. Can you do that?*

Yes.

Then don't just sit there, go.

Watching my mom panic into action in the kitchen — rag, pail, hot water, dish soap; doing everything she could and as quickly as she could do it to help save the front seat of the Buick from the indignity of my jellied assault — *If, if, if,* I thought.

If.

And just where is he supposed to find that? Where, Joe, is this unhappy man we're hypothetically speaking of—it being agreed that unhappy man is the natural condition of man—supposed to find that? On the material plane I mean, where on the material plane?

If—if, now, I'm only saying if—if it could be located on the material plane, where would this unhappy man we're considering go searching for it in these United States of Amnesia in the year of our Lord nineteen hundred and sixty-seven, a country mad—mad, Joe, maaaddd—with going nowhere just as quickly as it can, awfulomobiles and murdercycles and taxi crabs and nobody walking anywhere anymore except maybe across a parking lot or maybe a two-lane highway like a poor cornered squirrel trying to stay unsquishy squirrelly. Aristotle—Aristotle 2,500 years ago, Joe, 2,500 years before candy red convertibles—Aristotle said, All imperfect things must travel. *The Greeks, my God, the Greeks, Joe! The Greeks knew—they knew the thing, they knew the very thing—they knew it and wrote it down and walked away to their date with the dust and ça s'en va, ça s'en va.*

Jack raised the bottle of Rémy Martin to his lips, drank.

And television's the same, television's no different, one's just parked out in the garage, the other one's just parked in the living room, what's the point of either of them but to avoid the point, Joe — the *point. Channel after channel calmly reassuring you that you're really not just a great big bag of sagging flesh with one end to blow sweet-breath kisses with and the other end to crap out of. All of it, all of it* — *peeling out at sixty miles an hour in your brand new Buick to impress the pair of tits in the passenger seat or staying home alone and watching* The Fugitive *or being the vice president of the United States or sucking on a bottle of Thunderbird with your belly in the Bowery or winning at croquet or knowing the names of all the fauna and flora and minerals or falling in love or failing in love or betting on the horses or fighting for freedom or learning a new chess move or riding to the top of the Empire State Building or flying off to China or talking on the telephone or hitting a home run or not laughing at the funny papers or going to the moon or deciding to stay inside and watch it rain all day* — *all of it, Joe, all of it, ugh: diversions, diversions, diversions.*

Pascal, Joe said.

Jack didn't answer. He took another slug of cognac, looked out the car window; squinted past his reflection in the glass.

The drooping telephone wires in the moonlight could have been the drooping telephone wires of forty years before, when Jack and his sister in the back seat of one of their father's friends' cars were rushed off to their Aunt Buckley's house in New Hampshire because, their brother Gerard's rheumatic fever not getting any better—getting much worse, in fact— Mémère decided it was best for the children to stay at her sister's house in New Hampshire until . . . that the children should stay at her sister Buckley's house.

Sometimes when Ti Jean rode in his parents' car, cramped between Gerard and Nin in the back seat, he pretended he was holding the biggest, most powerful scythe in the world, which he'd use to slice down the hills and the trees and anything else he wanted cut down, always careful to lift it out of the way at the last minute when a building or a bridge or anything else unbreakable got in the way. Sometimes he pretended there was a phantom horse running alongside the car, galloping through the rain or the snow and leaping over any obstacles it had to get around for as long as they rode, stopping only when they did.

Ti Jean and his older brother had always shared a bedroom, even when Gerard came home sick from school for the last time. From the other side of the room Ti Jean would hear Gerard struggling to breathe, gagging on his own breath, whimpering in the middle of the night, asking God, *Why do I hurt so much? I confessed like I was supposed to.*

And always Mémère in her thick brown bathrobe would rush into their room and sit down on Gerard's bed without turning on the light and hold her first-born against her, *shhh* him back to sleep. When the crying became screaming and the doctors came to the house so often it seemed as if they lived there, Mémère packed Jack and his sister away to their Aunt Buckley's house. The horse that rode beside them the entire way there was a good horse, he never left their side. Jack would tell Gerard all about him when they came back home.

Compassion, maybe, Jack said, lifting the bottle of cognac.

Come again? Joe said. He was trying to light the cigarette in his mouth with the lighter from the dash and keep an eye on the road at the same time.

Jack kept looking at the telephone wires.

Sorry, I didn't catch that, Jack.

I said, "Can't this thing go any faster?"

Before television and hormones taught me to be embarrassed, my mom and I rode the bus together uptown every Friday afternoon to deposit my father's paycheque at the bank and I didn't even mind if anybody I knew saw us sitting beside each other. Jupiter restaurant was always our last stop. Not just because it was near the bus station, but because it had a lunch counter with white vinyl stools that you could swing all the way around on and a machine with a clear glass top full of gurgling purple pop. After we'd finished shopping we'd sit at the counter and I'd order a hamburger with no relish and a grape pop, my mom the same thing every time too, french fries and gravy and a Coke. Whatever kind of pop you got, it came inside a white paper cup shaped like an ice cream cone placed inside a silver metal cup shaped the same way. The pop was just pop, but somehow it tasted better. And my mom never ate all of her french fries, always left some for me to finish, fried potato canoes in a warm gravy lake.

The only books my mother ever read were the ones she read to me. Someone must have told her it was a good idea to read aloud to your child, even if they didn't understand everything you were saying, so she read to me all the time, especially when my dad was working nights and it was just the two of us. I liked the big red book the best, the one that had the story of the Little Red Hen. I always knew what was going to happen, and even what the next sentence was going to be, but I wanted to hear the story of the Little Red Hen again and again anyway. *There are other stories in here too,* she'd say, fluttering the pages with her thumb, but I'd shake my head and say *No,* point to the big red book and say I wanted to hear the Little Red Hen. When I was older, my mom told me that she came to hate the Little Red Hen, was never so sick of anything in her entire life, but that was what I always wanted to hear her read, so that was what she always read.

When I was six years old, I decided to run away. Not only that, I left my mom a note on her ironing board that made it perfectly clear that it was all her fault. *I HATE YOU,* it said. I went to my room to pack for my trip but got sidetracked by my G.I. Joes, who needed me if they were ever going to explore the deadly giant bat caves under my bed. An hour later, mission accomplished, my gym bag still wasn't packed, plus now I was hungry. The note I left on the ironing board didn't seem like such a good idea anymore.

I padded down the hall and peeked into the kitchen, hoping that the note would still be there, but it was gone, the ironing board too. On the kitchen table, though, there was a Kraft cheese slice and Miracle Whip and lettuce sandwich surrounded on every side of the plate by a couple handfuls of

Fritos. It was my all-time favourite sandwich. Sometimes I didn't get Fritos with it even when I asked, even when I remembered to say please, even when I'd done something good.

Maybe she hadn't read the note, I thought. But she must have, she must have seen it when she put the ironing board away. I sat down and took a bite out of my sandwich. Why would somebody do something nice for somebody else if they'd done something bad to them? I thought. I crunched a Frito. It just didn't make any sense.

They stopped for the night somewhere off the highway in northern Maine. If the weather held up, tomorrow they'd be in Rivière-du-Loup.

By the time Joe had taken a shower and changed his clothes, Jack had finished the bottle of cognac and popped a couple of bennies and was ready to roll all over again, was the all-city running back he once-upon-a-toned-time was, fidgety on his feet and waiting for the snap of the ball so he could tuck that thing in tight and hit that hole hard and head for open field.

Amphetamines used to be a tool, a weapon, a way to help him write his books: *On the Road* in three weeks, *The Dharma Bums* in a week, *The Subterraneans* in three straight nights. Old Angel Midnight and little white pills at a hundred words a minute and first thought best thought, no crafty craft, get it on and get it down before the mind can meddle around like you know the mind likes to do.

Don't look so gloomy, Joe, we're on holiday, let us refresh ourselves with meat and drink.

Sure, Jack.

Joe would have liked to have flipped on the TV, maybe caught *The Fugitive* or *The Honeymooners* if they were lucky, and hit the sack early, get a good start on tomorrow, but he knew that Jack wouldn't be sleeping much tonight and that to let him hit the local bars by himself wouldn't be being a friend, wouldn't be doing what he came along to do.

He'd already called Mrs. Johnson, the next-door neighbour who was collecting his mail and keeping an eye on his house for him while he was away but whose real job was to let Joe know if Billy, his fifteen-year-old son who'd run away from home five weeks before, had come back. He hadn't. The only thing Joe was thankful for was that his wife wasn't around to worry where their son had gone. If the cancer hadn't killed her, agonizing over where Billy had disappeared to probably would have.

Joe unpacked his London Fog windbreaker from his suitcase. It might have been August, but every mile they put between themselves and Lowell it seemed to grow cooler. Stella had packed Jack a jacket too, along with several days' worth of clothes and underwear and socks, but he was already waiting outside the motel room door, mosquitoes and other tiny black bugs circling above his head, eager for the heat of the bare bulb outside their room. Joe grabbed the room key off the small desk.

You got everything you need, Jack?

Doody-do, I doey-do, Joey Joe.

Jack whistled something Joe didn't recognize—could have been Dizzy, might have been Zoot Sims—and Joe locked the door, waved away a determined mosquito at his neck. One night after they'd shut down the Peppermint Lounge and gone back to Jack's place to sit around his attic studio and keep drinking and listen to Bird on his tape machine, Jack had told him about the time when, after *On the Road* had hit, three different record companies had been after him to cut an album and he'd picked Hanover because, although it was the smallest, they'd let him choose the musicians he wanted to back him up, Zoot and Al Cohn, long-time heroes of Jack's, of anybody's who knew anything about jazz.

They respected you, Joe had said.

When we were done, when we were all finished and I'd packed up my poems, they both left without saying anything, not a word, not even goodbye. Didn't even bother to stick around to listen to the playback.

They're musicians, Jack. To them it was probably just another gig. I'm sure it wasn't anything personal. I've heard that record and it sounds great. Really. You should be proud.

They drank by the light of Jack's desk lamp. Stella and Mémère were asleep downstairs. Joe watched the long shadow of Jack's arm rise, descend, with his glass. Sitting next to Jack's desk was the unlit GENIUS AT WORK lamp that Mémère had bought for him at Woolworth's.

They didn't even say goodbye, Joe.

Jack—

They didn't even say goodbye.

I owned all the records as soon as I could—had a part-time job working in the sporting goods department at Sears, so it didn't take long; plus, the Doors only made six albums during the five short years they were together. No Talmudic scholar ever knew his sacred shit so well.

In Mr. Rose's English class we were supposed to memorize ten lines from any play we'd read of Shakespeare's, five percent of our entire year's grade, and I wrote out the first twenty lines from "The Celebration of the Lizard" instead. I would have quoted something from *On the Road* if I'd had a copy to quote from, but made do with what I did have. Underneath the large, looping zero written in red ink on my paper, *Very interesting, but not what was required*, Mr. Rose wrote. I didn't mind. I took it as a compliment. I brought my paper home with me and cross-checked it with the lyrics printed inside the *Waiting for the Sun* album. I'd gotten every word right, every line break and every pause of punctuation too.

At parties, I'd always bring along a Doors mixed tape and slip it into the stereo after midnight when everyone was drunk and no one would notice. Someone would always notice. They'd just click it off and pop it out and put Journey or Billy Squier or Asia back on. It didn't matter. For five, ten, sometimes fifteen minutes Morrison's voice would boom out of the speakers set up on opposite ends of someone's parents' cedar deck, his words and the band's music flooding the dark backyard and almost drowning out all of the come-on chit-chat, all of the Friday night football game recaps, all of the usual all-too-usual usual crap. At least for a little while.

Besides all day Saturday, I worked one night a week at Sears after school. I'd go home, eat something, take a shower, change into my suit jacket and tie and dress pants, and lie on my bed and listen to the Doors and wait for my mother to knock on my bedroom door and shout over the music, *You're going to miss your bus unless you get out there right now!*

Okay, I'd say, and look at the clock radio. I had five more minutes, easy, before I had to actually get up. If my mother had had her way I'd have been standing at the bus stop in the rain fifteen minutes early. My mother was proud of me—the jacket and tie I wore to work, my laminated name tag, the way my boss, Mr. Rock, told her and my dad that I was a hard worker—and didn't want me to do anything to jeopardize what I had at Sears. She told me that the way he went on about me, she wouldn't be surprised if I ended up with Mr. Rock's job someday.

My mother would knock on my bedroom door again and tell me that I was going to be late for work unless I got out there right now, and "The End" would be coming to its end, coming to the part where the narrator walks on down the hall and kills his father and screws his mother and Morrison starts screaming and moaning and half sobbing and the guitar player tries to strangle his guitar and the organ player assaults his organ and the drummer hits everything there is to hit until the entire thing soothes itself down, it's time for the opening verse again, the one about how this is the end, my friend, this is the end. It was all about Oedipus, you see, Oedipus the Greek myth. I knew, because it said so in *No One Here Gets Out Alive*, Morrison's biography.

I'd stand up and shut off my stereo and put the album back in its sleeve. I'd take my name tag out of my suit pocket and drop it onto my dresser on my way out the door. If anybody asked, I'd say I forgot it at home.

Game number two, play number one, Jack ran back the opening kickoff ninety yards, just missing crossing the goal line. The next time he touched the ball, returning a punt, he felt something snap in his knee and hit the turf like he'd been shot. The trainers told him it was just a sprain and to run it off, to suck it up, to get back out there and be a man and play through the pain. He did—and limped through an entire week's worth of practice, knowing damn well it wasn't any damn sprain, Coach Little riding him every day for not giving 110 percent, for letting down his teammates by dogging it through drills—until he finally convinced one of the trainers to let him get an X-ray.

It was broken all right—turned out he'd cracked his right tibia—and when Jack wrote home to tell his parents what happened, Leo was furious but not surprised. *You wouldn't see that dago bastard Little treating one of his Italian players that way,* he wrote. *And didn't he keep you out of the season opener against Rutgers when it was obvious to everybody that you were the best freshman by far coming out of training camp? Take it from your old man, it's not what you know, it's who you know, your old man knows, he learned that lesson the hard way.* Mémère sent along a five-dollar bill and at the bottom of the page told him to be sure to wear that nice blue sweater she'd gotten for him at McQuade-Lowell. *New York winters are damp,* she wrote. *Jacky you make sure to take good care of yourself for me okay.*

Every night Jack would sit in front of the fireplace in the Lion's Den with his leg in a cast propped up on a pillow on a chair and eat a steak dinner followed by a chocolate fudge sundae which he'd charge to the Columbia athletic department and read Thomas Wolfe. He'd started off by sneaking in pages of *Look Homeward, Angel* between getting caught up with all of the required reading he'd let slide because of football, but soon didn't even bother pretending that after just one more chapter he'd get back to the periodic table at the back of his chemistry textbook—wasn't long before *all* he was reading was Wolfe, *all* of Wolfe. Reading Wolfe writing America as a place not just to grow up in and sweat in and die in, but as one long, tragic poem as deserving of tender, lyrical exalting as Balzac's Paris or Dickens' London or Dostoevsky's St. Petersburg.

The bone in his leg mended and healed and Jack went back to Lowell for the summer with only one failing grade, chemistry, and with a promise from Coach Little that he had as good a chance at being named starting wingback next season as anybody. Big man on campus back home again, he read in his room and went swimming and played baseball and drank beer with the guys. His mother and father were proud of him, of what he'd accomplished, of what he was going to go on to do.

But things were different. G.J. and Billy Chandler were both gone, were in the army, and Sammy was talking about enlisting whenever he and Jack weren't reading long passages of Wolfe aloud to one another. The United States wasn't at war, but England was, and everyone you talked to thought it was just a matter of time. Leo had finally gotten another full-time job after Sullivan Printers had let him go after Jack had decided not to attend Boston College, but it was in New Haven, Connecticut, and before Jack returned to Columbia in the fall, Leo and Mémère packed up Jack's past into a bunch of cardboard boxes and said goodbye to all of their old friends. The next time he came back home, it wasn't.

The first week of September 1941, Jack was a Columbia University sophomore studying trigonometry and *Hamlet* and getting ready for the season opener against Princeton. On September 11, 1941, FDR declared naval war on Germany and Jack packed a suitcase and got on a Greyhound bus moving toward neither war nor home but at least he was moving. He was nineteen years old. If the world was going to explode, he didn't want to miss the fireworks.

Over the next thirteen months: hiding out in a small room in some city in the south he didn't know and where no one knew him, feeling heroic feeling lonely, trying to write like Wolfe or, next best, like Saroyan and Hemingway; living with his disappointed mother and father and sister in New

Haven (*Do you know the sacrifices your mother and I have made for you and your future? Do you think you can just do whatever you feel like for the rest of your life?*) and getting a job in a rubber plant and quitting at noon his first day on the line; working as a grease monkey in Hartford and beginning a novel and giving it up and starting it up all over again; receiving a letter from his parents informing him that they were moving back to Lowell (his father had quarrelled with his new employers, that's all his mother would say, his father still too mad to talk about it) and him soon following suit, gaining a spot as a sports reporter on the *Lowell Sun* and writing about all of the games that not that long ago he himself had played; hooking up with G.J. in Washington and marking time as a burger flipper and a soda jerk and a paper shuffler at the Pentagon; securing his Coast Guard papers now that his country was officially at war and shipping out as a merchant marine on the SS *Dorchester*, it being common knowledge that, on average, two National Maritime Union ships a day were disappearing beneath the Atlantic, and while standing on deck at midnight one night staring out at the sea through the fog and not being able to refute the torpedo logic that said that all of it—the ship, the sea, the fog, him—could just as easily *not* be—my God, he *was* Thomas Wolfe, all he needed was his very own endless novel to prove it.

After the *Dorchester* returned from doing its duty in Greenland and docked a month and a half later in Boston, there was a telegram waiting for him at his parents' new address in Lowell from Coach Little saying *You're welcome to return to the team if you're willing to take the bull by the horns.* It killed Little to have to ask him back, but what could he do? War was hell on college football rosters. Jack knew it killed him to have to ask him back, too, which was one of the reasons he was actually considering doing it.

He went back. Worked out with the team for a week, stood on the sidelines for the entire Army game (Little said he'd lost too much weight at sea), and was sitting at his desk in his dorm room on a Tuesday afternoon watching the snow fall outside his window, realizing it was time to go to practice.

Dum dum dum dummmmmmm.

Beethoven, the Fifth, on the radio.

Realizing he didn't want to go to football practice, didn't want to be outside in the snow, in the cold, to hit, to be hit.

Dum dum dum dummmmmmm.

Realizing he wasn't going to be a football player anymore. Realizing he was going to be a writer.

Football had been my second chance, a way to be something more than just me when it became clear that I simply wasn't all-star hockey material, never mind a budding, if late-blooming, National Hockey League prospect. The summer before the beginning of high school I started getting ready, ran wind sprints in the backyard around improvised pylons made out of Frisbees and baseball mitts and red and yellow lawn darts; practised punting at my soon-to-be-old school-yard, retrieving my own wobbly kicks and booting them back the other way; kept *The Terry Bradshaw Story* and *Assassin: The Life and Times of Jack Tatum* and *Playing Football the Joe Thesiman Way* stacked beside my bed, the copy of the *Hockey News* that arrived every week in the mail for my dad and me usually left unread in favour of finding out how real NFL players really did it.

It turned out I didn't have the arm for quarterback or the size for linebacker, but I was quick and had decent hands and was big enough to tackle receivers in the open field, so I started the season opener at left defensive back, one of only four grade nine starters. I was a better football player than

I was a hockey player, would have made an all-star team if there had been such a thing, but even when I caught a key third-quarter interception in our playoff game against Tecumseh High School in my freshman year, it never felt like I'd thought it would. It only felt like I'd thought it would once.

The day we found out who'd made the team and were assigned our helmets we were instructed to keep them in our lockers until the dressing room was finished being renovated, but I smuggled mine home with me in my gym bag. On the bus ride home I unzipped my Adidas bag two or three times to make sure that the helmet was still inside. The house smelled funny when I opened the door, toxic; my parents were in the living room painting the walls, my mother holding on to the ladder with both hands while my dad on the fourth step strained to make white meet white where wall met ceiling. The living room carpet was covered in clear plastic sheets.

Hi, I said.

Hello, son, my mom said, looking at me but still holding on to the ladder. My dad didn't say anything, concentrated on steadying the paintbrush in his hand. There was no way they could have known what was in my bag, but it felt disappointing anyway that they weren't excited like I was. The clock radio on top of the fridge, as usual, was on CFCO, the Great Voice of the Great Southwest, Chatham's only radio station, "Breaking Up Is Hard to Do" by Neil Sedaka. I felt ashamed that I knew all the words.

I went to my bedroom, took out my football helmet, then ducked into the bathroom and locked the door. I eased my helmet on over my ears and clipped on the chinstrap. I looked like a football player. I undid the white plastic strap and let it hang down past my collar. I looked like a football player on the sideline or just coming off the field. I stared at myself from different angles and with the helmet in slightly different positions, and every time I still looked like a football player. In spite of the closed bathroom door I heard the music on the radio stop and an announcer's voice I didn't recognize come on and report that President Reagan had been shot and taken to hospital, no word yet on his condition.

I pulled my helmet up by the bars so that my face was uncovered, listened to what were now a bunch of different radio voices all discussing the shooting. I heard my father say, *Hand me that masking tape,* and my mom answer, *Where do you want it?* and my dad say, *Just hand it here, I'll do it myself.*

There wasn't any more music; the voices on the radio just kept talking, most of them at the same time, all of them very fast. I pulled my helmet back down and reattached my chinstrap. I looked like Jack Lambert, I thought, the Pittsburgh Steelers' All-Pro middle-linebacker. I looked like an actual NFLer. I looked like a football player.

A black benny breakfast washed down with bad truck stop coffee fortified with three sausage fingers of mediocre brandy and Jack was all set to go — looked like a rumpled outpatient being escorted back to whatever institution he'd managed to wander away from, but upright and alert in the passenger seat at least and looking around and talking to Joe. Talking to himself. Talking to himself talking to Joe.

Right, Joe said, although to what he wasn't sure, trying to watch the road and read the map spread across the steering wheel at the same time. Yesterday he wouldn't have hesitated to ask Jack to take the map from him and look for their cutoff. It seemed impossible that yesterday was really only yesterday. Every hour with Jack was like a week with anyone else. Which, obviously, was a wonderful thing — was why being with Jack was like being with no one else. Which was also why Joe felt ten years older than he had a little more than twenty-fours hours before. But it hadn't been a decade, only a day. Otherwise, Billy might have come home by now.

And I want to mail this—Jack waved the postcard he'd bought at the truck stop—*the next chance we get.* He kept fanning it in front of his face like he was trying to cool himself off, but the morning was wonderfully clear and bright and pleasantly cool all on its own. A hangover on a morning like this is a sin, Joe thought. He pulled a Chesterfield from the pack in his shirt pocket and stuck it in the side of his mouth without bothering to light it.

Sure, he said.

After they'd finally found an open liquor store and sat down in a window booth at the truck stop and Joe had ordered for both of them—eggs over easy and bacon and home fries for him; coffee, black, with a side order of dry wheat toast for Jack—Jack had excused himself to the men's room after first managing to get down and keep down his inaugural cup of good-morning nourishment. When he returned to the table his hair was freshly wet and neatly, severely, parted to the right and he was carrying the postcard.

For Mémère, he said, holding it up, sitting back down. He took another sip of coffee, took the pen from his pocket, wrote.

Sometimes people would ask Joe—not Lowell people, but people he'd gone to college with, say—what Jack Kerouac was like. *He's a great bunch of guys,* he'd always answer.

How many 46-year-old men think to write their mother a postcard on their second full day away from home, delirium tremens wake-up call notwithstanding? Jack was a good son. How many vampire journalists lurking around Lowell looking for the real lowdown dope on the King of the Beats ever wrote about that?

Did you get one for Stella? Joe said.

Jack held up a forefinger, kept writing. There was a scab on the knuckle. *Hold on*, he said.

Joe allowed himself to read what he could. *Maine est beau, Ma, vous l'aimeriez.*

Okay, Jack said, flipping over the postcard, sticking the pen back in the same right-hand pocket he always kept his little red spiral notebook.

Did you get a card for Stella too? She'd probably like it if you said hello.

Mémère's postcard sat on the table between them. An oversized lobster wearing bright yellow swim trunks and black sunglasses stood on a bright white beach, waving hello with one of its claws. Across the top, WELCOME TO MAINE! it said. Jack meditated on the grinning lobster for a moment; turned the card over, took out his pen again.

Underneath *Love, Jacky XXX*

Hey Stella, Joe says hello! he wrote.

Mostly it had been just my mom and me, my dad at work or working around the house when he wasn't, cutting the grass or washing the car or fixing whatever needed to be fixed. Sometimes he'd be at home, but it would still be just the two of us, *Remember to be quiet now, your father's sleeping, he has to go in to work tonight.* So: keep the television turned low, no friends over to the house to play after school, my mom always running to the ringing telephone and picking it up no later than halfway through the second ring.

Being the man of the house had its benefits. If my dad was working afternoons, the four-until-midnight shift, I sometimes got to choose what I felt like having for supper—wiener wraps dipped in mustard, fish sticks and french fries, salmon sandwiches with plenty of cut-up sweet pickles mixed up with the Miracle Whip—and I always got to eat in front of the television as long as I made sure to use a TV table. We had a set of four, each one a different colour and with a different saying on it. Orange was GROOVY, purple was FAR OUT, yellow was WOW, blue was YEAH. I always used the purple tray. My mom, who'd watch TV with me while she ate her supper too, didn't have a favourite table.

My mom would let me watch what I wanted. We'd eat our supper and watch *Gilligan's Island*, *Hogan's Heroes*, *Green Acres*, *The Partridge Family*, *The Brady Bunch*. Whichever one we were watching, we never laughed, just like you never laughed when you read the coloured funny pages in Saturday's *Windsor Star*, but it was better than looking at your food while you ate. The TV stations were all American and sometimes it was frustrating. I'd had a Snickers bar and a Mars bar and a Milky Way before, but the ad on TV said that Hershey's was the Great American Chocolate Bar and I'd never even seen one, let alone tried it to see if it was true.

Mom, how come we can't get Hershey's?

It's American.

But so is a lot of other ones and we can get them.

You can only get Hershey bars in the States, she'd say, and that was that, I was never going to know what the Great American Chocolate Bar tasted like.

I'd drag a french fry through the blob of ketchup on my plate and watch Gilligan fall out of a coconut tree on top of the Skipper and wish that we lived in the United States, where all of the good stuff was.

These weren't *his* children — he hadn't rearranged the alphabet and blood-let his soul to spawn this, a generation of proud spiritual scoffers and moral and political malcontents, sneering intellectuals eager to critique falling stars and burning sunsets and various other ordinary miracles. Clearing their throats and pushing their horn-rimmed glasses up their noses and finding it extremely curious why any grown man would want to live with his aging mother. Ginsberg, for instance, Ginsberg who threw his own mother to the dogs of eternity by dumping her in an insane asylum to die because he wasn't willing to love her enough. Or the Hippies and the Yippies and the dropouts and the runaways. Runaways like Joe's own son, just fifteen and already — go on, say it, *say it* — on the road.

Did these people even read his books, even understand anything he'd ever said? Well, no. And take a look in the mirror, don't be so fucking stupid, how can you be so fucking naive? *Mademoiselle* magazine doesn't devote a three-page spread to the San Francisco Poetry Renaissance because the gals in Editorial think that Jack and the boys' expertly placed em-dashes really swing or because their collective manifestation of Olson's conception of Projective Verse is just real swell. Dove dish detergent, one of the many fine, fine sponsors of CBS's nightly news, wants lively discussions of current events and/or cultural trends, not deranged guobly-gook spewed out all over the airwaves during the pivotal dinner-hour national broadcast.

I'm here with Jack Kerouac, author of the controversial bestselling novel On the Road. *Jack, could you please tell our listeners what exactly it is you mean when you say that someone is* Beat? *Is there, for instance, any age limit to being* Beat? *Or, for example, could a person be identified as* Beat *just by the way that he dresses?*

Beat *means beatific, to be in a state of beatitude. It means accepting — loving — all of life, being sincere, practising kindness, cultivating joy of heart.*

Tell me, Jack: do you ride a motorcycle?

His mother understood.

His mother who only made it as far as page 34 of *On the Road* and whom Jack wouldn't let read *The Subterraneans* because he knew she wouldn't approve of the narrator's love affair with a Negro woman. His mother who wouldn't allow Ginsberg and Orlovsky into the house when they came out to visit Jack in Northport because they were bad boys who wanted to get her good boy Jacky in trouble, *You go home you bad boys and stay away from my good boy.* His mother who distrusted Jews and all those other dirty foreigners no more than she did blacks, Communists, and people who wore beards. His mother who, after his father died of cancer of the spleen when Jack was twenty-one (on his deathbed asking his only son only one thing, *Please take care of your mother*), set her alarm for 6:15 six mornings a week and rode the subway thirty minutes to her job at the shoe factory while Jack slept until noon after working halfway through the night on his first novel, always waking up to his favourite cereal bowl and his orange juice glass right there on the kitchen table right beside today's unfurled *Times* and a box of Corn Flakes.

Twenty years and fourteen books later, after Mémère had suffered a stroke and couldn't take care of herself anymore much less look after Ti Jean, Jack made a phone call to Stella Sampas back in Lowell. They'd dated for a couple of weeks when they were both teenagers, and she was the sister of Sammy, his best boyhood buddy. Jack used to tell his New York friends that there was a nice Greek girl waiting for him back in Lowell for when he got old and it was time to settle down. He was only forty-four, but it was time.

Stella wore thick black plastic glasses and was a little on the heavy side and had never lived anywhere other than Lowell, but she had a good heart. Drunk, Jack had called John Clellon Holmes long-distance from the wedding reception and told him so.

Over the noise, over the loud Greek music, *I just married a girl with a heart of gold, John,* he said. *You'll see, you're gonna like Stella. I'm telling you, John, she's got a real good heart, she's gonna take real good care of my mother.*

I didn't go to the mall on Friday nights with my parents as much as I used to, but I went with them this time. The guy behind the counter at Coles was old, but not as old as the woman at the store downtown. He had hair down to his collar and sideburns and a droopy moustache, looked like some body off *Saturday Night Live*.

Do you have the book On the Road? I said. I was hoping there wasn't more than one book called *On the Road*.

I don't think so, but let me check.

I followed him to the small shelf of books filed under Literature.

Sorry, no, I didn't think so, he said.

Wouldn't it be under Fiction if you had it? I said. *It's a novel.*

No, I know the book you're looking for, if we had anything by Kerouac it'd be here.

Care-Oh-Whack, Care-Oh-Whack, Care-Oh-Whack, Care-Oh-Whack.

Okay, I said.

The guy pulled a paperback from the shelf. *We've got* Naked Lunch *by William Burroughs*, he said. *He and Kerouac were friends, you might want to try this.*

I looked at the book in his hand. *Thanks, but I want* On the Road.

You might want to check the library, he said.

Okay. Thanks.

Good luck, he said, and I left the store to meet my parents at the other end of the mall, in Woolco. My mom would be wandering around women's wear, my dad would be in the automotive department, probably talking to somebody he ran into that he knew.

I was already seventeen, two years older than Morrison was when he'd read *On the Road*.

Care-Oh-Whack, Care-Oh-Whack, Care-Oh-Whack, Care-Oh-Whack.

I didn't have a lot of time.

There were two ways of looking at it.

Either: soul-stoking sunshine and gentle relieving breezes and hurry up, don't forget to slow down and look out the window at all that God has given us to comfort us, to calm us, to remind us why we're here.

Or: an idiot dying star not knowing any better than broiling us alive while the wind carries the stench from the west just like it does from the east just like it does from every direction else. And God is a conceptual proposition formulated out of a psychological necessity. And don't double-check your math, you just might end up adding it up right.

There were two ways of looking at everything, everybody knew that. Inside equals outside. You see what you feel. Chemistry colours perception. And Jack's chemistry wasn't so good. Not just today, back in the passenger seat of Joe's Chrysler Newport, not more than half an hour, finally, from the Canadian/Quebec border, but every day. Spend enough time in front of the television set drinking Johnnie Walker Red Label Scotch and Schlitz malt liquor boilermakers and there does come a point when simply being in a good mood is a highly improbable physical act. Study Emerson on self-reliance or the Buddha on self-annihilation or Whitman on singing one's own sweet self until your eyes burn burgundy, but if the body is sick, chances are the mind is sick too. Jack, of all people—a three-sport high school all-star— should have understood that. Did understand that. Wanted, in fact, nothing more than that.

Wanted: eager mornings; deep sleeps; tired muscles; earned sweat; happy fatigue; easy joy; dumb health; honest awe; small excitements; calm lust; quiet faith; clear thoughts. Clear thoughts, yes.

Thoughts like the ones he'd thought walking home at night from the Lowell Public Library (the librarian having to ask him not once, not twice, but three times to please bring whatever materials he wanted to the checkout counter because the library was closing now), thoughts so clear, so true, so undeniably, obviously *there* that it almost seemed pointless to bother writing them down they seemed so real, as real as the cold of the snowflakes colliding with his face, as the sound of the soles of his shoes slapping along the frozen sidewalk, as the feel of the weight of the library books bundled underneath his arm.

He had to write them down, though, because what if he forgot even one of them when he met up with Sammy later for their usual end-of-the-day hot fudge sundae or couple glasses of soapy ten-cent beer? An unthought thought doesn't exist. Love, for instance, needs lovers to live; God, believers to breathe. Eighteen years old and the tragedy of an unborn idea; worse, an idea aborted. Eighteen years old and an over-cast Tuesday afternoon in February is tragic.

Jack had been home for the summer after graduating from Horace Mann, sleeping late and beering with the boys and reading Jack London and Thomas Hardy straight through the night—tucked in tight underneath his favourite Mémère-made quilt and eating peanut butter and Ritz crackers and waiting for the freshman fall call of Columbia and his promising future to finally begin as promised—when, from underneath his window overlooking Gershorn Avenue: *Jack-eeee, Jack-eeee.*

Sammy was the guy who didn't flip to the sports section first, who wanted to know what happened yesterday halfway across the world in some country nobody had ever heard of. The one who would stand up in restaurants and recite Shelley and Byron from memory. The one who'd walk around Lowell with the gang on Saturday night outfitted in his father's too-long black overcoat and use a cigarette holder for his Chesterfield. The one who announced to Jack the first day they met that he was going to go to Emerson College and study drama and write his own plays and someday star in them and direct them and be a big Hollywood auteur. The one Jack's father called *That pansy Greek kid, Sampas,* the one the other guys put up with because he was Jack's buddy but who could be a real pain in the ass, that Sampas guy.

Jack-eeee, Jack-eeee.

If we're lucky, we meet the friends we need to meet, meet them when we need to meet them. Jack was lucky. A few years before, at Bartlett Junior High, he'd stopped some older kids from beating Sammy up on the playground, and Sammy remembered him, had heard from somebody that Jack was a reader now too, wrote long letters to his girlfriends that were like great big poems.

Sure, I know who you are, Jack said, leaning on his elbows, leaning on the windowsill. The French in Lowell tended to stick with the French, but everybody knew the Sampases; the Sampas brothers were all good athletes, all had the same curly black hair, were always smiling. Everybody liked the Sampas brothers.

Who are you reading? Sammy said.

Hardy. London. Whitman. Thoreau. Dickinson. Jack surprised himself, was impressed with his roll call.

Not bad, not bad.

This crazy Greek, he's crazy, Jack thought. Who stands around on the sidewalk shouting up four floors about what books you're reading?

Have you read Saroyan yet? Sammy said.

Never heard of him.

Oh boy, you're in for a treat, I'll lend him to you, The Daring Young Man on the Flying Trapeze, *I'll lend you my own copy. Let me tell you, Jack, I envy you, I really truly envy you, you're in for a real treat.*

After Sammy did go to Emerson College just like he said he would—before he enlisted in the Army Medical Corps two years later and died of gangrene in a hospital in Tangiers after being shot by the Germans on the beach at Anzio, and after Jack married Sammy's sister Stella twenty-four years later—Jack would tell his wife that he remembered two things best about her brother.

One, that he'd sing "Begin the Beguine" for no reason at all, the best reason there is for doing anything. Sitting in a restaurant, standing in a doorway, walking across a bridge, saying good night in the street . . . any time, and for no reason at all.

Two, that he couldn't recall a line, not one single line, of any of the plays or poems that Sammy had ever shown him, but Jack could still remember how when he'd read them they'd made him feel brave, made him want to think and say and do brave things. He'd read a lot of books since that summer evening when Sammy had stood underneath his window calling out his name—written a lot, too—but it had been a long, long time since he'd felt like he wanted to be brave.

What is that? Joe said. *I know that song.*

Jack stopped humming, slumped down further in his seat. *I forget,* Jack said.

No, I know it, I know I know it. Is it "Begin the Beguine"? Wow, I haven't heard that tune in years.

I told you, Jack said. *I forget.*

My first best friend was Sean. I was six and he was black and it didn't matter. I don't remember what I liked about him or how he became my best friend, but he was.

Until I was seven and we moved to the suburbs, we lived on Park Street, in the east end, the poor part of town, where the majority of Chatham's black people lived, and even if neither of my parents nor anyone on the playground at school came right out and said it, blacks were bad news, were to be avoided, were always the ones getting the strap at school or swearing at each other on the walk home or standing around together in front of Sterling Variety after it got dark in the summertime. Looking out the back window of our car on our way to wherever it was we were going, I'd see them standing there and no one had to tell me anything, I *knew* they were bad.

Sean and I always played at my house. I had a tabletop hockey game and every kind of sports ball there was and my mother would give us cookies and milk and sometimes Wagon Wheels and orange pop, but even if she would have let me go, Sean never invited me over to his house. My mom was actually the one who told me that Sean didn't have a dad, that his mom was the only one around to look after Sean and his older brothers and sisters.

Where's his dad? I said.

He's gone.

Did he die?

No, she said. *He's just gone.*

I had other friends — Hector, who lived across the street; Bill, who was in the same class as me and whose dad had played hockey with my dad — but my mom liked Sean the most. He was my best friend, so I was glad, but sometimes I wasn't so sure. Whenever she'd serve us our treats, Sean would always say, *Thank you, Mrs. Robertson,* and I'd just take mine and start eating and my mom would always have to say, *What do you say, Ray?*

Thanks, I'd say, chewing.

And then there was the way he said it — *Thaaaank you, Mrs. Robertson!* — and the way his eyes would get bigger, rounder, whiter when he'd see what she had brought us. C'mon, I'd think, it's just oatmeal cookies and milk, it's not chocolate cake and ice cream or pumpkin pie with Dream Whip or, my all-time favourite, Sara Lee cherry cheesecake, which I always got for my birthday and which my mom always served just a little bit frozen because that was the way I liked it.

He doesn't get all of the things that you do, my mother said once.

Why not? I said.

Because his mother doesn't buy them for him.

Why not? It wasn't like she had to make them for him, all she just had to do was go to the grocery store.

Because they can't afford them.

Why not?

Just because. And you should be more thankful that we can, like he is.

One year, for Mother's Day, our teacher Mrs. Jackson had us make Mother's Day cards we could take home with us to our moms. We cut the construction paper ourselves after first picking out the colour that we wanted and glued dry macaroni and silver stars and suns and moons all over the front. After we finished decorating the cover we were supposed to write on the inside in different-coloured Magic Markers why we loved our moms. I couldn't think of anything, so I just wrote *I LOVE YOU RAY.* All in all, though, I was pretty pleased with the way things worked out. There was macaroni all the way around the edges of the front of the card, and a different line of suns, stars, and moons separating *Happy* from *Mother's* from *Day.*

Sean and I walked home from school together, stopped off at my house to play tabletop hockey. I not only had the Toronto and Montreal players that came with the game, but also the players from every other team that I'd gotten separately for Christmas the year before, including Vancouver and Buffalo, the two brand new NHL teams. After we got the game out from underneath my bed, I gave my mom her card.

Well, isn't that nice, she said, reading it, closing it, looking at the cover one more time. *Thank you very much, Ray.*

Seizing the moment, *Can we have some cookies?* I said.

Oh, I think so, she said. *Just let me put this on the fridge first for your father to see when he gets home from work tonight.*

I made one too, Sean said.

Well, let me see, my mom said.

Sean pulled his card from his jacket pocket. He didn't have a lunch pail like I did to carry his school stuff and his lunch around in.

My mom made a point of admiring Sean's cover although it wasn't halfway as good as mine, was just a bunch of macaroni and stars and moons and suns stuck all over the place. Then she opened up the card and read what was inside, looking at it longer than it felt like it should have taken to read it.

Finally, *You're a very good son, Sean,* my mother said, handing it back. *Your mother should be very, very proud of you. I'm going to get you a plastic bag to put your card in so that when she sees it it'll be just the way you made it.*

Sean sat down cross-legged beside me and started helping me take off the Detroit players from when my dad and I were playing last time. We were going to play Vancouver against Buffalo. The Canucks and Sabres goalies were cool. Unlike all the other goalies, they both wore white plastic masks.

Let me see your card, I said. He handed it to me without looking up from plucking off the Detroit players.

I love you mom because you make me grilled cheese sand-wiches, it said.

Grilled cheese sandwiches, I thought. That's so dumb. Who cares about stupid grilled cheese sandwiches?

He could be good. He wanted to be good. He knew how to be alone.

Not that long ago, after all, that he couldn't still remember that particular Jack Kerouac, such a disciplined dumb-saint-of-the-mind that one, gagging on a young man's greed to see hear touch taste understand everything, the unspeakable visions of the individual spoken as spewed in countless little red notebooks of secret scribbled joy, visionary tics shivering in the chest for anyone willing to sit still long enough to confess his life to himself for all of the empty universe to hear. World without end within word: a pen, paper, silence.

Or Symphony Sid on the radio after midnight after a good day's work all done; a candle, a half a joint, and let Dizzy or Bird or Lester take the wheel for a while, let one of them make life worth living; or else, if tired of living, big Bach chorales or booming Ludwig B. symphonies or crashing St. Matthew Passions roaring from the hi-fi speakers to disappear inside of and wander around in and stride out of when all is sung and done, reborn and ready to be alive again, to really, truly be alive.

No need to be an artsy-fartsy shit about it, either—step into the backyard at three o'clock in the morning and eaves-drop on the trees; lift your eyes and admit the stars; recognize that the neighbour's cat tiptoeing along your fence is perfect, unchanging art; go to bed early for a change, get everything on the grocery list on the fridge, clear the neighbour's sidewalk of snow when you're done shovelling yours, double the mortgage payment when you can and still have enough left over to surprise your mother with that electric blender she saw on TV.

Be at home with Mémère and the cats. Nearsighted Mémère mending old socks and city-torn shirts—sad souvenirs of a New York weekend's silly empty frenzy—by dirty kitchen-window sunlight, a pot of peeled potatoes bubbling on the stove and Tyke meowing for his dinner from underneath the kitchen table. And Jack's bedroom—Jack's work-room—just that very day dusted by Mémère and carefully tidied and with the bedsheets changed and a clean batch of his laundry tucked into the correct dresser drawer. Later, evening, and Mémère settles into her easy chair and watches her stories on television while Jack reads the Diamond Sutra or rereads Proust in his room or sits down at his desk and feeds another page into the typewriter and covers it with the little black marks of his life. And tomorrow, and tomorrow night after that, the same, amen.

After *On the Road* made him a speed-dial celebrity, an editor asked Jack for a statement on his poetics, and he composed

"Belief and Technique for Modern Prose," a list of thirty essentials of good writing. Number three read: *Try never to get drunk outside yr own house.*

He knew. He knew.

Everybody was wrong. You *could* get blood from a stone. Might not be the type you wanted, but you could get blood.

Every time we went to the mall I ended up back at the bookstore looking for *On the Road*. Maybe someone had seen the light and cleared the shelves of all the hardcover picture books of kittens and muscle cars and restocked them with copies of *On the Road*. Yeah, right. It never occurred to me that I could just order it, and no one told me they'd be happy to take my money and place my order for me, to just keep checking back and be patient because these things take time. But every time we went to the mall I ended up back at the bookstore looking for *On the Road*.

Near the bookstore exit, near the cash register, was a large bin brimming with marked-down books: two-year-old hockey and football and baseball yearbooks, popular diet books that weren't so popular anymore, even books that were worth digging around for, like the one I'd gotten on the Grateful Dead, a real deal at $2.98, the only thing wrong with it as far as I could tell being the black Magic Marker slash across the top of its pages and the fact that I'd never actually heard any of the band's music. Sam the Record Man had section dividers for Grand Funk Railroad and Bobby Goldsboro, but not for the Grateful Dead.

Up to my elbows in a lake of reduced-to-clears, fighting my way through wave after wave of absolutely-final-sales: *Jack's Book: An Oral Biography of Jack Kerouac*. I'd never seen a picture of him before, only knew what little I knew from what it said in my Jim Morrison biography, but the shot of him on the cover standing in front of a dirty brick wall with a cigarette in his mouth and a brakeman's guide sticking out of his windbreaker pocket was exactly what I'd imagined he'd look like. He looked like he knew things it had cost him to know. Like wherever he was, he needed to be somewhere else. Like he knew he was the sort of person who'd end up on the cover of a Penguin paperback biography of himself someday. He looked like James Dean with genius.

Did you find everything you were looking for? the guy behind the counter said.

Yes, I said.

Apples and oranges and close only counts in horseshoes and hand grenades. He never said they were novels—just the opposite, actually—so what was all the fussy fuss? Only a fool or a book reviewer asks a fork to do a spoon's job.

So, okay, not novels—picaresque narratives, he called them; spiritual weather reports, really—but whatever they are, are they any good? Because making it new isn't enough. Newer and gooder, that's what really matters.

The novel is dead, Jack said. *I should know, I helped write the corpse cold years ago.* And the reason it was dead was because *Life hasn't got a plot, so honest art shouldn't have one either.* Take that, James Michener. You too, Arthur Hailey. Up yours, Herman Wouk.

Plus, he was a cradle Catholic taught well to automatic his sins in an unbroken blah blah blah because you don't dare get all clever and crafty when confessing your ethical imperfections to the Man Upstairs.

Plus, riding shotgun across the country and back with brand new best pal Cassady at the wheel gabbing his golden Okie patter from dusk to dawn and Jack realizing Oh my

God, *this* is what literature is supposed to sound like—one man simply telling another man the simple humiliations and agonies and always-too-late epiphanies that add up to his and everybody else's life—and not a sack of tricky tropes to be toted out and professionally employed in order to expertly con the reader into imagining a pretty little Book Club–approved daydream.

Plus, jazz, blowing and blowing and barely stopping long enough to catch your breath because otherwise you'll lose the tune and miss the point and don't worry about making any off-note uh-ohs, just the price you pay for paying attention to what's most important, the music.

Plus, not all books are equal, actual mileage of influence may differ. In Jack's case, *Look Homeward, Angel's* elegiac swooning, *Leaves of Grass's* ecstatic yawping, *Journey to the End of the Night's* endless raving: all three (and others) carrying him down the road of his own uninhibited inventing the furthest, each book's lasting impact the inimitable expression of each author's egomaniacal shouting self, each dead man most alive on the page when writing from the foggy inward I's cloudy eye outward, the unspeakable vision of the individual clearly spoken. Honest solipsism, in other words, as the only truly universal language. Wild heart equals wild form.

And yet, and yet . . .

Maybe because life doesn't have a plot, maybe that's precisely why a novel needs one. Maybe not one of Proust's or Joyce's wild scribbling children but just an arty moron too

loose in the head and not disciplined enough at the typewriter to do the job right. Maybe first thought isn't best
thought after all, is just sloppy firsts. Maybe—dark night of
the soul at high noon, when even your worst enemies might
have a point, when even snotty rejection slips and critical
ego slaps seem almost fair—*My God, how have I managed
to fool as many people as I have for even this long?*

Maybe.

But maybe if you kill the crabgrass you also kill the grass.
Maybe imperfect prayers still make it to heaven. Maybe a
heart is always a heart if it really is a heart.

I am what I am.

Thus Spake Popeye et al.

My father kept his porn stash on the top shelf of the hall linen closet. It didn't feel like I was into something I shouldn't be because why else unless he didn't mind me finding it was it sitting right there among the clean pillowcases and sheets and the Monopoly board and the extra vacuum cleaner bags? I hadn't even known the stack of magazines was there until I was eleven, when I was finally tall enough to spot them for the first time, so it seemed inevitable, like I'd earned the right to see what I saw, like I'd graduated somehow.

Besides, it wasn't as if I was actively on the make for pictures of naked women. I knew girls were different, knew it as far back as six or seven — the matching Henry twins (four big blue eyes, two identical long yellow ponytails, perfect penmanship both) a grade-A grade two example of something to be looked at, admired, ogled even, but never spoken to, not unless one of them spoke to you first — but whenever a perfumed pretty stood in front of me in line at the pencil sharpener or the water fountain, the washing-machine stomach I got wasn't the sound of sudsy sex going around and around, no matter how loud it tossed and turned and spun. Even the late movies on the French channel you'd suffer through on Saturday night, not knowing what the actors were saying or what the hell was going on, all on the chance of spying a naked breast or spotting a flash of pubic hair, were more about saying you saw things you weren't supposed to see rather than seeing things really you wanted to have seen.

But I had to look at those magazines. If I'd known what to do with them I would have smuggled them behind the bathroom door and done it, but no one had ever told me that my penis was good for anything besides pissing with and protecting behind a hockey cup, and my parents had never warned me about what not to do with it, which at least would have been something. So I'd wait until I was in the house alone and just turn the pages standing up in front of the opened closet, which was also handy in case someone happened to come home and I had to hide the evidence in a hurry. But I *had* to look at those magazines.

Not that it was the first time I'd ever seen a picture of a naked woman. Corn fields and soybean fields surrounded our new subdivision, to me and Mike Howell and his younger brother Chris, and Ted Young and his younger brother Simon, not prime development property to be sooner rather than later smothered under gravel driveways and newly tarred roads and fenced-in backyards overpopulated with above-ground swimming pools and shiny lawn furniture and brightly coloured broken children's toys, but the fields and streams and mountains that Grizzly Adams roamed on

Thursday nights at 8:30 on channel seven, right after *Baretta*. Even the appearance of a freshly backhoed basement of a house in progress was okay, became a World War II dirt bomb shelter or an after-supper meeting place to spit in and tell lies in and look at the magazines that Ted had discovered while searching the corn field behind his house for the golf balls he'd lost while practising his chip shot.

Ted was the only one of us who played golf. He said his dad said if he practised hard enough he had a chance at turning pro one day. Mr. Young was all right, gave us Mr. Freezies in the summertime that gave us headaches if we ate them too fast, but he worked at a different factory, Fram, than my dad did, and his favourite hockey player was Bobby Hull, not Gordie Howe, who my dad said was the greatest hockey player who ever lived. My dad said that Bobby Hull had a good shot but that that was about it, he was lazy and wasn't willing to get his nose dirty to win, wasn't willing to pay the price. When we played road hockey, Ted used a stick with a banana blade curve on it just like Bobby Hull's. I asked my dad if we could curve my stick too—Ted and his dad had warped his blade over the flame on their kitchen stove—but my dad said no, not only could you not control your shot with a big curve, how could you make a good, accurate pass with a blade like that?

I was disappointed—Ted's slapshot would whiz by your nose faster than anybody else's, sometimes even take sudden strange turns or drop off altogether like a baseball pitcher's sinker ball—but I knew my dad was right. What he said wouldn't have mattered much to Ted, though. Ted seemed almost as happy when one of his shots would scream by the net and disappear down the street as when he'd beat the goalie glove-side high and bulge the twine. And he hardly ever passed the ball to anybody anyway, usually hung around just outside the action, cherry-picking, waiting for someone to pass him the ball so he could go in all alone on a breakaway.

This one's okay.

She's all right.

Like you'd know the difference, Howell.

Like you would, Young.

Good comeback, Howell.

Eat me, Young.

I want a meal, not a snack.

The Howells and Simon Young and I were squatting in the corner of a half-built basement, waiting for Ted to turn the page of the magazine he was holding. He'd found it, so he got to hold it. It was after-dinner darkening, but there was still enough light in the sky that we could see. In the summertime I had to go home when the street lights came on.

This one would need a bag over her head before I'd screw her, Ted said.

I wouldn't screw her with your dick, Chris said.

You'd have to use my dick, Howell, 'cause yours wouldn't be big enough.

I would use yours, Young, but I'd need to borrow a microscope to find it.

Ted and Mike were the same age, were in the same grade, and their brothers were the same two years younger, but Ted and Chris were the ones who did most of the talking, the ones who called each other by their last names. I was a year younger than the older brothers and a year older than the younger ones.

Just turn the page, Ted, Mike said. Ted waited just long enough to make it seem like it was his idea, then turned the page. We all leaned in to look.

Jesus Christ, Ted said. *This one better start wearing an over-the-shoulder boulder holder or they're going to be hanging down past her knees by the time she's forty.*

Over-the-shoulder boulder holder—I had to admit, that was pretty good. Ted always had to be in charge and had a tendency to go home if he didn't get things exactly his way, but he did come up with some good lines once in a while, even if he probably did get most of them from his dad.

Hey, Howell, he said, *you ever sniff your sister's bra when she's not around?* He smiled at all of us as he said it, even at Mike.

Only when your mother doesn't let me smell hers, Young.

Shut your little mouth, Howell.

Shut your big mouth, Young.

I'll kick your ass, Howell.

Yeah, Young, you and whose army?

Everybody just shut up, Mike said. *Just turn the page, Ted.*

Ted glared at Chris, and Chris glared back at Ted, and then Ted turned the page. It was getting darker, getting harder to see, and we had a magazine full of pictures of naked women to get through. We all leaned in.

But the magazines in my parents' linen closet were different.

Ted's magazines were called *Beaver* and *Swank* and *Jugs*, and even though they'd been inside a white plastic grocery bag when he'd found them, there was dried mud caked across the fronts and backs and even on some of the inside pages. And the women in Ted's magazines were all either lying on their back prying their legs apart for the camera and usually attempting to jam one of their breasts into their mouth or else were on their hands and knees sticking their rear end in the air like Pepilou, our cat, did whenever she'd stretch out after a really long nap.

The women in *Penthouse* and *Oui*, my dad's magazines, were just as naked as in Ted's, but didn't seem as eager to prove it. They wandered the beach or lounged on a couch or, if they were in bed, seemed almost surprised to find a photographer discovering them there. Not shocked, not excited, just surprised. The pictures felt good on your eyes, too, soft and warm and welcoming, not like the ones in Ted's magazines, which felt as if they'd been taken using the same hard bright lights they used to light up the aisles of Kmart. And my dad's magazines smelled good, smelled like everything else in the linen closet, like the clothes softener my mother used on all of our pillowcases and sheets and extra blankets.

Sometimes at night, especially if my mother had just put fresh sheets on my bed, I'd want to get up and look at the magazines. I wasn't sure why, and of course I couldn't—the linen closet was at the end of the hallway, right between my bedroom and my parents'—but the longer I'd lie there not being able to fall asleep, the more I wanted to get up and look.

The only thing that would help me eventually doze off was trying to remember which teams were in each of the NHL's four divisions. Problem was, I knew where every team played, frontwards and backwards, and my mind would always go back to the closet and the magazines. Sometimes I'd be so tired in the morning I wouldn't feel like going to hockey practice. And when I'd finally get up and remember the reason why I was so wiped out, instead of feeling stupid or even embarrassed, I'd feel excited, like when my dad would announce we were eating out that night at Ponderosa or A&W, and I'd think, *Maybe I'll be able to be home alone tonight. Maybe I'll be able to look at the magazines then.*

He was no fag. He was no queer. Some of his friends were faggots—Ginsberg, Burroughs, Orlovsky after Ginsberg got done corrupting him—and sometimes it seemed as if the entire New York publishing scene was so pansied pink that if you ever wanted to see your words in black type you needed to pay for it on your knees, but Jack was no fag. Especially as he got older; just like as he got older he wasn't a flag-burning radical or a four-eyed intellectual or an America-hating Communist. Except if he was especially sloppy drunk.

In that case, *Everything is the Holy Ghost*—hetero, homo, and everything doing-onto-others or having-done-onto-you in between.

And *All the girls that perfect Proust was writing about, they were all boys anyway.*

And Christ, was he lonely. Would show up at Ginsberg and Orlovsky's Lower East Side apartment at four o'clock in the morning after five or six days of pointless, punishing spreeing himself all over the city, exhausted and filthy and gurgling drunk, blustering his way through the door and collapsing on the couch and pleading for a blow job.

C'mon, I'm old and red-faced and pot-bellied and nobody loves me, c'mon and somebody love me, for God's sake somebody love me.

Ten years before—five years before—square-jawed, clear-eyed Jack was the sweet-smelling, hard-bodied lover Ginsberg knew he could never have. And now that he could, he didn't want him. Him wasn't him anymore. Biology never remembers.

We do, though. Can, anyway. Allen and Peter unfastened Jack's belt and tugged down his dirty jeans to his ankles and took turns sucking his cock because he was Jack and he was their friend and he really was red-faced and pot-bellied and obviously lonely and most of all he was Jack, their friend.

Five minutes later, *What are you doing?* Jack said. *I'm not a fag, I'm not queer.*

We know, Jack, Peter said, *we know you're not. We're just trying to make you happy.*

The answer seemed to satisfy him. Jack closed his eyes and sunk himself deeper into the couch.

Ten minutes later they stopped trying. He couldn't come. He couldn't even get hard.

FM radio was a cock tease too.

The toys you tore open Christmas morning that never looked even halfway as good as they did when you'd seen them for the first time on television as toy commercials and knew that the remainder of your life would lack all meaning and joy if you didn't get them, and get them for Christmas *this* year. A wintertime daydream of summer vacation liberation that by August, suffocatingly humid and endlessly eventless, always turned into a summertime daydream of cooling September and the reprieve of school starting up again. Even — as much as you didn't want to believe it — all of the unbelievably amazing things for sale at the back of every comic book that somehow somewhere inside you you nonetheless knew could never be anywhere nearly as amazing as they claimed to be, especially the one-man fully operational submarine for only $5.98 plus shipping and handling or your very own Sea Monkey family with a Sea Monkey dad in his underwater easy chair puffing on his pipe while Sea Monkey mom happily set the kitchen table for herself and him and their two Sea Monkey children.

All of it, all of them: a con, a rip-off, lies. All of which was fine because you were just a kid then and now you were fifteen and weren't anymore, and besides, you'd discovered FM radio and the fucking heavens had finally broken wide fucking open, finally.

I was so up against it, no one had even told me that such a thing as the FM band existed. I'd had to discover it all by myself, like masturbation, like the idea of the Holy. I'd been working out, doing bench presses and arm curls and leg squats in the basement, trying to bulk up just like Coach Carivou said I should if I wanted to make the move from defensive back to linebacker, and had set up my entire stereo system from my bedroom upstairs. I'd bought the *Rocky* album for inspiration and it had worked, but only for the first song, the one that's playing during the famous scene when Rocky finally makes it jogging all the way up the Philadelphia Museum of Art stairs. For just under four minutes I was a happy maniac, felt like I could press and pump and grunt forever. Then the record player needle would slide into the second song and a sad horn solo would blow through the basement and I'd feel like lying down on the cold cement floor and taking a nap beside my dumbbells. If only the entire record had been as good as that first song. If only life came with a soundtrack.

It was too much of a hassle to keep putting the needle back to the first song, so I started listening to CKLW while I worked out, the AM station out of Windsor that everybody listened to. It was top-forty, and almost everything they played

sounded like it just missed out on being an ad for a brand
new breakfast cereal, but that's what everybody listened to.
I tried to make the best of it by always keeping an eight-track
tape in the tape deck just in case a song came on that I liked
so that I could tape it and play it back whenever I wanted.
Except for missing the song's first few seconds or having the
deejay blab through its opening, usually about what time
it was or what the temperature was, it was all right, at least
I ended up with an entire eight-track of personally chosen
songs that weren't as bad as some of the other ones.

Sometimes you'd think you'd really gotten lucky, would
hear a song come on that you liked while sitting on the
weight bench between forearm curls, and therefore would
jump right up and run right over, careful to push the Play
and Record buttons at the same time. The next time you'd
hear it, on the tape, you'd lower the barbell, careful to extend
your arms all the way down to get the full ripping effect on
the biceps, and think how smart you'd been to have gotten
a good one down on tape. A few reps later, you'd realize it
wasn't a good one at all, that it was just as bad as all the other
ones, you'd just heard it so many times on the radio it just
seemed like you liked it.

The FM switch on the stereo was no different than the
UHF knob on the television: maybe there was something out
there, but it wasn't anything I was supposed to know about. If
it was, why hadn't anyone told me about it? But I was in my
five-minute cool-down period, making the transition from

chest and shoulders to legs and abs, and I flipped the little black switch because I was killing time and bored. Most revolutions and love affairs begin the same way.

"Twilight Zone" by Golden Earring: you never forget your very first time. It wasn't the song, though, it was the sound. It was as if I'd been walking around my entire life with cotton balls jammed in my ears, like when I'd gotten glasses in grade eight because Mrs. Palmer in French class noticed that I kept squinting up at the blackboard, and all of a sudden the world was right there in front of my eyes, hard, sharp, intense. I dragged the weight bench over to the stereo and sat down and slid through the dial. Incredible. It was like being able to listen in 3-D. Even the lousy songs on the soft rock stations, the same junk I'd been listening to on CKLW, sounded better. Even the indistinguishable morons spelling out their radio station's call letters and blathering through the beginnings of the records they were spinning almost seemed alive.

But after every two or three songs, always the same advertisements for beer companies, for car dealerships, for burger places, for hair replacement and wart removal clinics, for autobody repair shops, for banks, for insurance companies, for women's clothing stores, for exotic animal shops, for home renovators, for men's large and tall shops, for furriers, for grocery stores, for landscapers, for pawnshops, for pizzerias, for window repairers, for TV antenna installers, for steak houses, for . . . After a while it seemed like the only reason the songs themselves existed was to give the listeners a break between ads.

It sure sounded good, though. When that ad for Speedy Muffler came on, it sounded as if that busted muffler was right there in the same room as you.

Canada didn't seem much different than America, seemed like there was just a whole lot more of it. A couple of hours into Quebec, following the St. Lawrence River east all the way to Rivière-du-Loup, sky and trees and fields and barns and cows and more cows and *this* was why he was travelling a thousand miles away from at least the familiar gentle sorrow of his own bed at home?

What's that smell? Jack said.

I don't smell anything, Joe said.

Jack stuck his nose out the window. *I smell something funny.*

Joe looked at the road, then did the same. Nose back inside, *Clean air,* he said.

What?

What you're smelling, it's clean air.

Jack lifted, tipped the bottle of Chivas Regal, washed down another benny. The cognac would make things more interesting. The speed would make sure he was still awake once they were.

In the meantime, he clicked on the radio—it'd be nice to hear some French voices besides the same ones always echoing around inside his head for a change. Joe would talk French with him if he wanted him to, but Jack had yakked his ear raw all morning, give the guy a break. Besides, once the benny kicked in, he wouldn't have any choice. The radio was mostly angry static—no towns around, just farms so far, maybe ten other cars the entire four hours they'd been on the road—so he stopped the dial at the first station that came in clearly.

Rock and roll, ugh. Some idiot shouting about wanting some other idiot to light his fire, come on, baby, light his fire, baby. How could something so monotonous still sound so abrasive? How could people fork over hard-earned money just to have their eardrums raped like this? I feel like I'm living on a foreign fucking planet, he thought, turning the dial.

S'matter, Jack, not digging what the kids are calling groovy these days?

Jack didn't answer, didn't even bother counterfeiting a smile, just kept trolling the radio waves. It wasn't as if he was looking for something good, for something he liked; just something not entirely terrible, something that wouldn't make him too upset. He took his fingers off the dial. Aretha Franklin, "Do Right Woman," okay, not bad, no Lady Day, no, this broad couldn't even carry the big red corsage Billie Holiday always used to have pinned to her dress when he and Edie would sometimes sit with her between sets whenever she'd play the little clubs around Harlem, but at least she was speaking the same language. Jack and Edie's song had been Billie's "I Cover the Waterfront."

Edie was a rich kid from Grosse Pointe, Michigan, who knew which fork to use and who was studying art someplace downtown whenever she felt like getting out of bed in the morning but who basically kept busy being young and well off in New York during the war. Like all the forward-looking, good-looking Village girls, she had short hair, a smart mouth, and a hair-trigger clit. Jack barely had to breathe on her to make her shake and shiver and quiver and quake and call out his name like she was drowning and Jack was the only one who could save her. It was a long, long way from sitting on the swing on Mary Carney's front porch back in Lowell drinking lemonade and holding hands and hoping to get a kiss at the end of the night.

Edie paid her rent and everybody else's who crashed at her sixth-floor walk-up on 118th Street—Jack included—with the allowance she collected every month from her parents and whatever else she could squeeze out of her grandmother who lived just around the corner and who was supposed to keep an eye on her daughter's fast daughter but who was deaf and so undone by arthritis that she never set foot in the apartment. Jack's old Horace Mann classmate Henri Cru was in the navy now and giving Edie gooey underpants with his crisp officer's uniform and well-rehearsed routines about growing up an orphan in Paris, and when it was time for him to ship out he introduced her to his Columbia football-star buddy, Jack.

Edie didn't discriminate when it came to good-looking men: Henri was a tragic French aristocrat going off to this terrible war in this oh so most terrible of centuries, Jack was a big brooding secret sensitive athlete who was going to be a great writer someday just like his hero Thomas Wolfe, and who, post–moochy moochy, liked Edie to cook him up a big plateful of eggs sunny side up at three o'clock in the morning with real slabs of peameal bacon on the side just like Mémère used to make, not that plastic-wrapped kind you got at the supermarket in scrawny little strips.

Edie liked the way Jack would emerge from her steaming bathroom with a white towel wrapped around his neck, his shoulders and chest and arms and legs still wet and warm and peasant strong. Jack liked Edie because she was alive, liked to laugh and drink and eat and fuck almost as much as any guy he knew. Jack said he fell in love with her when, on their very first date, she ordered and ate six hot dogs with sauerkraut in steady succession, something they never served as an entree at the Grosse Pointe Country Club. Sometimes, after Jack had dropped out of Columbia and was waiting around for his merchant marine papers to arrive, they'd spend all day in the apartment doing nothing but screwing and smoking in bed and eating big meals that Edie would throw together. Jack called her Frankie, she called him Johnnie.

And how silly it all seemed now. All of that effort just to scratch an itch that always comes back. We were Shakespeare and Jesus Christ on the Cross and a man on the moon, but mostly we were just dust who wouldn't admit it, just a couple of sweaty animals sniffing each other's dirty assholes in the park in the dark and not having any fucking clue why.

The first electric shiver of the drugs and the booze coming together to do their thing tingled his brain, inflated his chest, tickled his tongue. Jack looked out his door window. A small herd of bull oxen were standing around in the middle of a field doing nothing but looking like a thousand pounds of black steel with ball-bearing testicles and hot red blood.

Sometimes I feel like one of those, Jack said.

Joe looked up from the road. Jack raised his bottle, drank.

Sometimes I feel like I'm ready to croak, he said. *But sometimes I still feel like one of those.*

I never had a bible until I had *Jack's Book*. Not one that I read and reread and could recite from. Not a real bible.

I did have a small red copy of the New Testament that the Gideons had given us at school back in grade eight that we were supposed to write the date and our name in and read from every day if we wanted to be happy. Who didn't want to be happy? The only bibles I'd ever seen before were in hotels, like the ones we'd stay in every summer when we'd visit my Uncle Ronny and Aunt Margaret in Niagara Falls. You'd find them when you were looking for free matches and pens and hotel stationery.

I tried to read my little red copy of the New Testament—from the beginning, like the man who'd handed them out to us in the gymnasium had told us to—but I always got bored. I wanted to be happy, but reading the Word of God, as the man in the gymnasium called it, felt too much like school. The only difference was that, if you didn't feel like studying this particular book, there wasn't anybody there to make sure you read it, and no way for anyone to know that you hadn't. I'd put the New Testament back in the top drawer of my night table and click on the black-and-white television set that shared space on top of my dresser with my Candle stereo.

But no one had to threaten me with hell to make me read *Jack's Book*. *Jack's Book* was every book I'd ever wanted to read plus a whole library of illicit others I hadn't even known existed. *Jack's Book* was small-town, working-class kid rises and falls, the coming down almost as glorious as the going up, even me knowing that no one can resist a good train wreck, the faster the crash and the bigger the body count the better. *Jack's Book* was an atlas of places I needed to go, a phone book of people I needed to meet, a textbook of feelings I needed to feel. *Jack's Book* was a how-to book, except instead of outlining how to build your own backyard deck or install a television antenna on your rooftop, it told you to live your life like life is worth dying for, to burn, burn, burn just like Sal and Dean in *On the Road* because four seconds of lightning is better than a decade's worth of cloudless skies.) wow! 6

Some guy in *Jack's Book* described how, the first time he saw 25-year-old Jack, the first thing he noticed were his hands. Hands, he remembered, that could have belonged to a football player or a lyric poet or both, whatever those hands wanted to do.

Reading *Jack's Book* lying on my bed, the Doors playing on the stereo, the bedroom door shut to everyone and everything else; setting the book down on the bed and looking at my own hands. Looking, and wondering, wondering . . .

The car hit a pothole.

Half asleep, Jack shifted in his seat, elbow brushing pot-belly as he readjusted his heavy body, clasped his hands and prayed a pillow for his head. He thought of his father and the big healthy gut he'd had. Of the dinners his mother had made every night when he was growing up in Lowell. The homemade pea soups and long loaves of crusty white bread for dipping, the grease-glistening pork chops and overloaded bowls of mashed potatoes and fresh green peas, the all-day-simmering, entire-house-overheating Sunday night pot roasts, the pork ball stews and fresh cut tomatoes and just-husked corn on the cob. And always at least two glasses of ice-cold milk with maybe a third later with dessert, dessert never less than a big slice of chocolate cake or a big piece of date pie or a couple of big scoops of vanilla ice cream with an entire cut-up peach plopped on top. And no matter the sea-son, a pot of strong black coffee always brewing on the stove, the best coffee he'd ever tasted, had still ever tasted.

You are what you ate when you were eleven and a half years old. Go to Paris and gobble down the brains of cows and the entrails of snails and the ass-ends of frogs and act like you really like it, that you're finally really living, but you can't lie to your stomach. You can try, but your stomach won't listen.

He thought of his father dying of stomach cancer in the tiny apartment in Ozone Park, Jack's mother off to her job as a leather cutter every morning, Jack staying behind to do whatever he could to make his father as comfortable as possible. Leo spent all day, every day, in his bathrobe with a blanket across his knees, the highlight of every week when the doctor came to visit and drained the fluid from his rotting stomach. Jack would listen to his father in the other room wince, then groan, then softly weep.

The last day of his life, his father and Jack argued about how to properly brew the coffee. The second-to-last thing his father said to him was *Beware of the niggers and the Communists*. The last thing his father said to him was *Please take care of your mother.* Jack thought he heard his father snoring in the other room. A few minutes later, when he came in to check on him, he realized it had been the sound of his last breaths. The ink stains on his father's hands a stigmata.

He thought of how at the funeral it had seemed impossible that this was the same man who'd once been walking down the sidewalk on the Lower East Side with his wife, Jack's mother, and a group of rabbis walking arm in arm down the same sidewalk in the opposite direction wouldn't part for them, and Jack's father, not saying a word, not even removing the cigar from his mouth, stuck out his stomach and *poom* knocked a rabbi right into the gutter. He took back his wife's hand and they kept on walking.

Over the casket, *For dust thou art and unto dust shalt thou return*, the priest had said.

The car ran over another pothole. *You sure got that right*, Jack thought he thought.

What's that? Joe said. *I thought you were sleeping.*

I am, Jack said.

Alvin's dad wasn't just a mortician, he also let us drink his booze. We didn't do it very often — once the thrill of being asked if you wanted a beer, *Help yourself, the cold ones are at the back of the fridge,* wore off, who really wanted to chugalug a John Labatt Classic in the ten minutes you had to kill waiting around for Alvin to get ready before having to rush off to catch the nine o'clock movie? — but the fact that we could if we wanted to was what was important. No one else's parents opened up their liquor cabinet to us, just like no one else's father ever described himself as, variously, a born-again atheist, a political libertarian, and a sexual non-interventionist. I wasn't sure what the second thing was, and was even less sure I wanted to have the third one explained to me, but I liked the idea, at least, that whatever they were, there were people in the world who were such things. As far as I could tell, the fail-safe recipe for a fully functioning, well-adjusted Chatham, Ontario, adult was equal parts non-practising Christian, vote-by-rote citizen, and till-death-or-an-ugly-divorce-do-you-part husband or wife. It was nice to know there were other items on the menu. It was nice to know there was an entirely different menu.

Alvin's record collection sucked—prog rock mostly, rock and roll imposters like Marillion, the Alan Parsons Project, and ELP, overproduced, over-the-top pomposities performed by latter-day hippies who'd somehow managed to read a few books without pictures and listen to a few pieces of music recorded before Elvis was born and who therefore thought they were far too sophisticated to just shut the fuck up and play their instruments loud and fast, the way they were intended to be played—and he wanted to become an optometrist, something no seventeen-year-old should ever decide they want to do with their one and only life. Not when they're seventeen, anyway.

But Alvin was all right. He was the only student in the history of Chatham Collegiate Institute to get a note from his parents excusing him from all phys. ed. classes, as easy an A as there was. He took baths *(He's in the bathtub, Ray, I'll get him to call you when he's out)* instead of showers. He lived overtop of a funeral home. He read books he didn't have to, most of them borrowed from the shelves built into the living room wall over the fireplace (the funeral home was downtown, the three-storey, red-brick house it was housed in nearly a century old), paperback souvenirs of his father's long-gone long-haired years—Albee, Sontag, Mailer, James Baldwin—all published, it seemed, by one of the same three publishers: Grove, Avon, New Directions. I recognized a couple of the names on the spines from *Jack's Book*, and Mr. Samson encouraged me to take home with me whatever books I wanted. I settled on Baldwin's novel *Giovanni's Room* and finished it in two days, feeling pretty smart, feeling pretty surprised, actually, that this literary stuff wasn't all that heavy-going after all. It wasn't until a couple of days later that I realized the book was about a guy who was in love with another guy. I'd have to read slower next time. I'd have to learn how to pay closer attention.

When Alvin made a new friend, he'd give them an after-hours tour of the funeral home. You'd travel back down the long set of stairs that had brought you to the front foyer of his house, and then, back at the bottom, go through a door to the immediate left of the door where you had first come in (the Samsons' door was never locked, day or night, you didn't bother knocking or ringing, you just came in). Even though the upstairs, where Alvin and his mom and dad and sister lived, wasn't anything like the suburban rancher homes where the rest of us grew up—hardwood floors, fifteen-foot ceilings, wooden chair rails all around the kitchen, push-button light fixtures—walking into the funeral home was like stepping into a different century.

Upstairs was old-world antiquey too, but there were framed Picasso and Cézanne prints and family photos hanging on the walls, a VCR blinking alive in the TV den (we still rented ours from the only video store in town: two movies and twenty-four hours' use of the machine that they'd slip into a black plastic carrying case for you, all for $9.95), the massive Apple computer (the first I'd ever seen) in the family workroom beside Alvin's bedroom, the wonderfully slick, cool-to-the-touch copies of *Harper's* and *The Economist* and *The New Yorker* fanned out across the top of the toilet tank. Downstairs, though, there wasn't any reason to believe it wasn't 1922. Downstairs, it was all heavy Victorian furniture and thick blood-red carpeting and low-lit table lamps soaking everything they touched in a gaslight yellow fog. And it was quiet, quieter than anywhere I'd ever been: no street sounds, no radio playing in the background, no ringing or beeping telephones. Because of the carpet, even the evidence of your own feet moving you from room to room was non-existent. It felt like you had wandered upon the deserted set of an old Vincent Price movie, one of those British Hammer films from the early sixties adapted from an Edgar Allan Poe story, everything just a little too throbbing Technicolor to be true, everything just a little too still to be safe.

And then there were the dead bodies.

First Alvin would walk you through the viewing rooms. There were three of them, and in each there was usually an old man or old woman laid out in their eternity best with his or her wrinkled hands neatly folded above their crotch. It actually wasn't that scary. Actually, it was sort of disappointing. If it weren't for the orchard of flowers surrounding the casket and the fact that you knew you were in a funeral home, it could have been anybody's gussied-up grandparent who'd dozed off on the sofa after too much Thanksgiving turkey.

The embalming room was different. Through yet another door you made your way down cold cement steps to the scaldingly bright basement, where the naked body laid out on the steel examination table and the shiny tools of dissection and the chemical stink of preservation reminded you of Mrs. Smith's grade ten biology class, except that instead of a pinned-in-place, gutted frog on display there was a recently deceased human being. But that wasn't what was different. And the after-autopsy worm of stitching nearly stretching from neck to navel on every freshly carved corpse wasn't what was different either. You got used to that, just like you got used to seeing dead people. It seemed as if you could get used to anything.

But sometimes some old guy would have a faded, almost indiscernible blue tattoo of some woman's name stencilled on his withered bicep, *Betty*, or *Mary*, or *Kathy*. Or sometimes there would be somebody younger, a woman in her early fifties, say, who'd brought along her own scar tissue to the table, testimony of a recent failed mastectomy or a long-ago C-section. And once there was a little girl, she couldn't have been older than six or seven, who had shoulder-length blonde hair and unblemished, somehow still creamy white skin and bright red fingernail polish on all ten little fingers and toes.

How did she die? I said. *She looks like there's nothing wrong with her.* Even the nail polish was perfect, not a single chip or scratch.

My dad said a fire, Alvin said. *He said there was a big fire on Williams Street two nights ago.*

You'd think she'd have some kind of burn marks on her or something.

My dad says most people who die in fires die because of the smoke, because they suffocate.

But still . . .

But still, it didn't seem right. At the very least, the red nail polish didn't seem right. I wondered if it was her or her mom or maybe one of her sisters or a girlfriend who'd put it on. I wondered if she was the only one who'd died in the fire. If she was, I wondered how her parents must have been feeling. I wondered who she was.

Science doesn't make sense. No way does science make sense.

A cat is 116 different kinds of bones. Also, 500 skeletal muscles. Also, all of its internal organs. Also, its 62-point nervous system. And that's not even everything that's just on the inside.

While visiting Ferlinghetti in San Francisco—footsteps following the familiar travelling logic of: if he was there, then he wouldn't be here; and if he wasn't here, then maybe he wouldn't be who he was when he was here—there was a letter for Jack from Mémère care of City Lights Bookstore.

I don't know how to say this son but sit down and listen to me anyway honey. Our little Tyke is gone. One minute he was ok and then he started throwing up and then he just wouldn't stop. And he wouldn't stop shivering like he was frezzing so I rapped him in a towel but to no availe. He just kept throwing up and wouldn't stop I've never seen anything like it. And then he just stopped breathing and then he was out of his misery.

Jack would kiss his kitten Tyke's soft white belly. Would feed Tyke in the morning, Tyke rubbing against Jack's leg, purring him thank you. Jack would stand in the backyard and hold Tyke up to the moon.

Look at the moon, Tyke, look!

How can science explain that? How?

No way.

No one had told me that the world was going to end. I forget how I found out—television, probably—but when I did, I felt betrayed almost as much as I was upset. Why hadn't my parents or one of my teachers or even somebody from the government told me that between the Americans and the Soviets alone there were enough nuclear weapons in existence to destroy every person on earth twenty-five times over? More than that: that the likelihood of it happening sooner rather than later was very, very likely, what with the President of the United States reportedly saying that while a nuclear holocaust would be an undeniably tragic event, it was somewhat comforting to know that it would also be a fulfillment of the apocalyptic firestorm as foretold in the Bible that would herald the return of our Lord and Saviour, Jesus Christ himself. I mean, come on.

I took the bus downtown to Coles on a Saturday afternoon. I didn't know what I was looking for, but it was the only place I could think of where I might find it. There, or the library. Whatever it turned out to be, though, I wanted to own it, it had to be mine.

An hour and a half later, I was back on the bus. I removed today's first purchase, a book, out of the plastic bag. I had no idea why I'd had to have it, only that I did. It was a coffee-table-sized book that my mother was never going to allow me to leave on our coffee table. It was called *Horrors of the Twentieth Century* and it had nothing to do with Dracula or Frankenstein or anything else I'd ever seen on Sir Graves Ghastly's Saturday afternoon horror show. It was divided into several different sections—murders, suicides, child abuse, war atrocities—and was basically just large black-and-white photos with short captions underneath explaining what you were looking at. The caption would read something like *Chicago, 1962: A six-year-old girl is taken into the custody of Illinois State Children's Aid workers. Her right hand has been severed at the wrist by her stepfather with a butcher knife. The man later told police that the child had been warned several times about "playing too loud" while he was attempting to watch television in an adjoining room.*

You didn't need to read the captions to understand the pictures. Every time you looked at a picture was like every time you got a canker sore in your mouth and you couldn't stop running your tongue across it even though you knew it would hurt—it would burn—every time you did. I managed to put the book back inside the bag.

The map that I'd bought made more sense. I took it out, unfolded it across my knees. Except for the driver and a couple of old ladies sitting together near the front, there wasn't anyone else on the bus. Except for after school, the bus was nearly always empty.

The map was of Canada, although once I figured out that I needed a map, what I'd really wanted was one just of Ontario. I placed my finger on Chatham and carefully traced a path upward, bypassing Toronto, North Bay, and not stopping until I hit Thunder Bay, by my calculation twenty-three hours north of my hometown. The key, I figured, was to plan out an escape route that would carry us far enough north that the nuclear fallout would be as minimal as possible yet deliver us not so deep into the Arctic that we'd have to live in an igloo and survive on whale blubber.

By the time I pulled the cord over my head and the bus slowed down at the stop near my house, I'd figured out our ultimate destination: Fort William. Gauging by my thumb and the scale at the bottom of the map, it was a good twenty hours north of the likely most northerly nuclear target, Toronto, yet, being some kind of former or maybe even still active minor military post, must have had a grocery store or two and motels and maybe even a hockey rink, for the off-duty soldiers. I slid the map back inside the bag, beside my new book.

When I got home I stuck the map up on my bedroom wall with the adhesive gum my mom made me use. The gum didn't leave any marks, but in the summertime, when it got really humid, the corners of your posters tended to peel off, would droop from the walls until one day you'd walk into your bedroom and find them all lying on the floor, as if someone had torn them down. After a while I quit trying, didn't bother anymore, just left my walls bare.

I used a red pen to carefully mark out our escape route. I wasn't going to say anything to my parents until it was absolutely necessary. They wouldn't understand what we were up against, had never experienced anything even remotely like *Horrors of the Twentieth Century*.

That was okay. I knew what was going on now. I had my eyes wide open enough for all of us.

He settled on the Red Sox game, electric fuzzy and echocy fainter with every empty country mile they moved closer to Rivière-du-Loup, but it was better than spending ten minutes making love to the radio dial hoping to come up with maybe a minute and a half of uninterrupted something sounding not unlike actual music. Boston was up on the Yankees five-two, bottom of the fourth. Everybody said this was probably Mickey Mantle's last year, his knees just couldn't take it anymore, the left one so bad it was literally just bone on bone, not even a shred of a thread of cartilage to cushion the pounding anymore. For athletes, it's always the legs that go first. For writers, it's always the never-ebbing capacity for worldly wonder and the resultant cager rage to tear it free from the overexcited brain and slam it down on the unsuspecting page and keep it pinned there in an expertly executed hold of holy brawling poesy so that the good and the bad and the happy and the sad and the ugly and the lovely all get trapped on the mat for now and later and maybe even forever.

Jesus Christ, he was tired. Writers just get tired. Being awake is hard work.

If anybody's got a shot at the Triple Crown these days, I think it's Yastrzemski, Joe said. Jack drinking either ranted or moped. Joe preferred the former. Jack hadn't spoken a word since he'd started fiddling around with the radio.

Jack nodded. Joe waited a moment; waited a moment more. Cleared his throat. Continued:

The only thing I wonder about is if he's got enough power.

Mantle's got enough power, Jack said.

Mantle? He can hardly stand up anymore.

I didn't say he could or he couldn't, I said he's got the power. People forget, when Maris hit those sixty-one home runs and broke Ruth's record, Mantle hit fifty-four. One hot week for the Mick and one cold one for Maris and that could have been Mantle's name in the record book.

Yeah, but that was seven years ago, Jack.

It wasn't seven years ago.

It was, it was 1961.

It wasn't 1961.

It was. You know how I remember? I remember because I can remember thinking how funny it was that Maris hit sixty-one home runs in the year 1961. I remember thinking that it seemed like it was destiny.

They let the radio talk for a while. Noyes was at the plate, a two-and-two count.

Who's this Noyes? Jack said. He still read the box scores every morning, whether he started the day with a mug of Cutty Sark or not.

Just some kid they just called up, he's supposed to be their new centre fielder.

Why isn't the Mick in centre?

Joe knew better than to tell the truth. No way was he going to check into a motel in Rivière-du-Loup with Jack in a mood, not if he could help it. *Mantle must be tired,* he said. *They must have decided to give him a day off.*

Jack considered this; slid down in his seat and turned on his side, pushed his face into his bicep.

That's smart, he said. *Rest him now because they're going to need him down the stretch. You want your big guns ready when the games start to really matter.*

Sure.

I'm taking a nap, Joe.

Sure, go ahead.

Just don't forget to wake me up when we get there. I don't want to miss anything. I've got research to do, you know.

T-ball was as close as I ever got to playing real baseball. Not playing hockey wasn't an option. Only the handful of bused-in farm boys and the kids at school whose parents were first-generation Italian- or Portuguese-Canadians were excused for being not quite normal — not quite as normal as the rest of us, anyway, who, every August, stood in line with our fathers at the Moose Hall Lodge sweating and waiting to hand over our parents' $125 for the privilege of being an Atom or a Pee-wee or a Midget for the next seven months. There was also always the same man, we just called him The Jacket Man, who year after year sat behind a long wooden table covered with samples of the hockey jackets he took orders for. Any-body who had the money could get a jacket, but only the guys who were on the All-Star team were allowed to buy leather jackets.

Nobody wore a baseball jacket. Baseball was just a game, something to do in the summertime when we got tired of playing road hockey. No one ever pretended they were Reggie Jackson or Steve Carlton when we got a baseball game going at the schoolyard, not like they pretended they were Darryl Sittler or Larry Robinson when we dragged our hockey nets into the street. Everybody knew who Fergie Jenkins was—the most famous person to ever come from Chatham—but he was still just a baseball player. It meant more that Ken Houston, who was born in Dresden but who played for the Maroons for two years, beat up Dave "The Hammer" Schultz in his first NHL season. Grandpa Robertson had the article about it from the *Chatham Daily News* taped to the wall of his shed, left it up there even after it got yellow and brittle and the Scotch tape at the corners began to fall off.

My dad had stopped playing sports by the time I'd started, but he'd been good at all of them and wanted me to be good too. He'd hit ground balls to me in the backyard and coach me how to catch them. At first it was fun, they'd just roll my way across the thick green grass, barely even making it there, and then a quick scoop and the ball snug in the web of my glove and I'd toss it back like an outfielder to the second baseman after shagging a lazy fly ball. The bat still in his right hand, my dad would catch the baseball bare-handed and hit me another grounder, this time a little harder than the time before. After about five minutes the balls would start whizzing past me, ricocheting off my glove if I was lucky, usually bulleting by me altogether and coming to a stop only when they'd *thud* against the wooden fence.

You gotta get in front of it, he'd say.

I know.

Bend your knees and get in front of it, like a goalie.

I'd nod and he'd hit me another one, this time taking a little heat off so I could do what he'd said. Sometimes I'd catch it, would square myself to the ball and lean into it and try not to act surprised when there it would be, miraculously in the bottom of my mitt. And then the next ball would come faster than the last one, then the next one even faster than that, until *thud*, I'd jump out of the way and the ball would shoot past me again.

What's wrong, you afraid of that thing? You're only going to get hurt if you're afraid of it.

I know.

If you turn sideways, it's gonna hit you, you are going to get hurt. Plant your feet and stick your glove out there like a man, get mad at it, eat it up.

I'd end up mad, but it wouldn't be at the baseball. I'd end up wishing I was the one with the bat and he was the one wearing the glove and he could be the one dancing around for his life for a change. The tears in the corners of my eyes that I wasn't going to let get any further felt like the tears I wasn't going to cry whenever I was supposed to be helping my dad fix something and he'd send me to the basement for a screwdriver, and no matter how hard I looked or how long I spent searching I wouldn't be able to find it, only to have him storm past me to the basement and the tool box, and when he came back up a minute later with the elusive screwdriver, his not saying anything a hundred times louder than any words he could have ever spoken.

After we were done and came inside the house, first me, then him, my mother would say, *What's wrong?*

Nothing, I'd say. My dad wouldn't say anything. I'd go downstairs to get my cold pop, he'd get his beer from the refrigerator in the kitchen.

Baseball was stupid, everybody knew it was stupid. That sonofabitch, I'd show him. Just wait until hockey started up again. I'd show him what I could do then. And when I did, I wouldn't even care.

You don't need Freud for this one.

Joan Haverty was Jack's second wife. He knew he needed a wife because he realized he'd wasted four years of his life writing *The Town and the City*, his first novel, spinning silly tales instead of tearing the entire thing down in order to build it all back up, all in order to communicate the incommunicable, a single red rose in the rain in the middle of the night and no one watching. He'd been smoking bomber after bomber in Mexico and reading and rereading Cassady's long locomotive letters describing dwarf cab drivers and being bored in bus stations and getting his cock sucked and losing game after game of pool and everything else you weren't supposed to write about if you were serious about writing serious literature.

But giving yourself amnesia as a means to remembering something new is hard work, and it's nice to have a homey wife to cook and to clean and to help keep your ass in your chair typing and typing until the tap runs hot and you can finally say what you didn't know you had to say. Jack asked Joan to marry him two days after their first date. Joan's previous lover had recently had his head amputated by a subway pillar and she was living in his Greenwich Village loft lighting candles in his memory and trying to decide if he'd made a fatal mistake or a final decision. When Jack proposed, it was either say yes or move back in with her mother in Albany. At the wedding reception held in her dead lover's loft, everyone got drunk but nothing went right. The beer keg leaked all over the living room floor. The toilet got clogged and people pissed in the sink and the bathtub. A platter of sausages fell behind the refrigerator and no one bothered to pick them up.

Jack moved his rolltop desk from his mother's house out in Richmond Hill into the loft and sat down to write *On the Road*, but after Joan got a job in a department store during Christmas rush, Jack found he was lonely when he wasn't writing and insisted they move in with his mother. Besides, even with the part-time job Joan made him take synopsizing movie scripts for Twentieth Century-Fox, they weren't even close to making the rent on time. And Joan thought it was sweet the way he didn't want his mother to be alone in her old age.

Every morning Joan would wake up to *Jacky! Here's your juice!* and Mémère in her bathrobe standing over Jack's and her bed, holding out a glass of cold orange juice for her boy to begin his busy day with. Every day Mémère would correct Joan on the proper way to do the dishes or make potato salad or to clean under a bed so there weren't any dust bunnies. Every night at supper Joan would watch Jack happily inhale his mother's pork chops and mashed potatoes and the slices of bread she'd pre-butter for him and listen to Mémère complain about the foreigners who were ruining this country and how the Communists were going to poison the water supply and that if her husband Leo, Jacky's father, were still alive, that Allen Ginsberg, that dirty Jewboy Ginsberg, he wouldn't dare come around here trying to get her good boy Jacky in trouble.

Ma, is there any more milk? Jack would say, holding up the empty bottle.

Because their living expenses were so low now, Jack was able to quit his job. Joan kept hers, though, and one night came home late from work to find Jack just finishing off a good day at his desk and in the mood for some celebratory spice cake. It was almost midnight and she had to get back on the subway in less than eight hours to open up the store in the morning. She knew Mémère was sleeping, so didn't want an argument, just said she was exhausted and was going to bed.

You should never deny your son anything, Jack said.

Joan didn't have to ask him if he knew what he'd just said.

You know what I mean, he said. *You make your husband grouchy when you deny him the things he needs.*

Even if she hadn't been so tired she wouldn't have known what to say. Joan went to their room and left her clothes where she stepped out of them, didn't even bother to brush her teeth before she pulled back the sheets and laid down her head.

She woke up to the sound of Mémère and Jack speaking French in the kitchen, the smell of spice cake baking in the oven.

The closest I came to having a blood sibling was my cousin Bradley. Because his dad was my mom's brother, his mom my dad's sister, our DNA was cooked in the same juices, did double duty shaking and baking both of us. The only way we looked different was that I was skinny and he was fat. If we lined up side by side, me on the left, we looked like that before-and-after picture at the back of my comic books, the one in the ad for *Gain Weight! Grow Muscles!* where the guy gets sand kicked in his face at the beach and all the girls laugh, except that in our ad it went from rib-showing scrawny right to triple-chin chubby, bypassing what it looked like to *Be a Real Man!* altogether. And Bradley didn't live with his parents, he lived with Grandma and Grandpa Authier.

Before Bradley hit teenagehood—and would always be out in the garage driving the grease deep underneath his fingernails overhauling his mini-bike or building a new go-cart made out of old lawn mower motors and wood that he and his friends would steal from construction sites—whenever I'd go with my parents to visit Grandma and Grandpa Authier there was always stuff we could do together: trade hockey cards, bounce a tennis ball against the side of the garage, watch television, a horror movie if we got lucky. Whatever we did, though, we were on our own. Unlike at Grandma and Grandpa Robertson's, where even if my dad and I just dropped by for five minutes to fix the leaky bathroom sink I was the main show, the candy-eating, dollar-bill-taking, number-one grandson attraction. At Grandma and Grandpa Authier's, Bradley and I would sit with our glasses of warm Coca-Cola on the orange shag-carpeted living room rug and *rat-rat-rat* crank the dial around and around trying to outrun the snowstorm of static on the TV and attempt to ignore the loud voices and the country and western music coming from the kitchen. Whenever we'd visit, my mom and dad and my grandma and grandpa and whoever else was there would sit around the kitchen table and talk, the women at one end and the men at the other, the room always warmed by the always-on stove, always a pot of something rolling-boiling on top or something else baking or roasting in the oven.

When I was old enough to see that some things were normal—everybody did them, they had to be—and some things weren't, I asked my mom why Bradley didn't live with his mom or his dad. *Because they got divorced,* she said. *But why does he live with Grandma and Grandpa?* I said. *Didn't Uncle Jim or Aunt Norma want him?* It took her a moment to answer that one. *Uncle Jim goes away a lot for his work so it's better that Bradley lives with Grandma and Grandpa. And when Aunt Norma met her new husband she wanted to start a new family.* Things my dad would say to my mom on the drive home from visiting made more sense.

That poor kid, you can see he eats too much because no one pays any attention to him.

Mom and Dad do their best.

I didn't say it was their fault, they're his grandparents, not his parents.

Mom said he's visiting your sister next weekend.

My sister, shit . . . All that does is make him feel worse when she ships him back to your parents.

Well, what can you do.

I don't know, but it's still a goddamn shame.

My dad did do things. Enrolled Bradley in Little League baseball until he discovered that tearing an engine apart so he could put it back together was more fun than grounding into double plays and striking out with the bases loaded. Took him with us for a week in August one year when we rented a cottage at Erieau. Brought him along sometimes to watch when I had a Friday night hockey game. My mom did things too. My grandma cut Bradley's hair every Saturday afternoon, the same brush cut she'd given her sons, but my mom stepped in when he turned eleven. *Take him to a barber, Mem,* she told her mother. *Il est bon,* Grandma said. *Take him to a barber or the other kids will make fun of him.* Grandma gave him the money to go to the barber.

I felt most sorry for Bradley at Christmastime. My parents would always make sure he got something good—a Boston Bruins sweater, a deluxe ratchet set, ten dollars in an envelope — but compared to the haul I'd wake up to every December 25 it was just appetizer-sized stuff, nothing compared to the Christmas-morning main entree I could count on being served: a new ten-speed bicycle; a two-man tent; an eight-track-tape-equipped Simpson-Sears stereo. We'd bring Bradley's present with us when we'd visit both sets of grandparents on Christmas Eve. Last stop would be Grandma and Grandpa Authier's, and I wanted to leave almost as soon as we got there so I could go home and go to bed and go to sleep and get up and open my gifts. Somebody, Eddie Webster or Gary Bechard or Brad Skipper, would call me in the morning and we'd go over our lists, compare what we'd got.

Christmas Eve when I was ten we showed up at Grandma and Grandpa Authier's as usual around nine o'clock, and Bradley opened his gift from us, a hand-held transistor radio, I opened mine from Grandma and Grandpa, a scarf that Grandma had knit, and Bradley and I watched television while the grown-ups drank and talked and listened to country and western music in the kitchen. I waited half an hour before I started showing up in the kitchen every fifteen minutes to stand beside my mother and let her know I wanted to go home. I always put the pressure on her because my mom didn't drink and I knew she didn't like it when my dad drank too much like everyone else usually did at Grandma and Grandpa's, especially at Christmastime. By ten-thirty I'd had enough, stood closer, whispered into her ear, *When are we going?*

Soon, she said. Her breath smelt funny. I looked at the

cluttered kitchen table. Her coffee cup had turned into a beer bottle.

Do you want some more Coke, Raymond? Grandma said.

No.

Do you want some more Coke too, Bradley? she called into the living room.

Yes, please, he said.

Bradley was watching Rudolph save Christmas on television at the same time that he was listening to his Christmas gift from my parents through the white earplug that had come with it. He was wearing the brown sweater with a white reindeer on it that Grandma had knitted for him for Christmas, and was wetting his fingers to pick up the last potato chip crumbs left at the bottom of the bowl we'd been given to share. I'd only had a few because the chips were regular and I liked barbecue, but now I was hungry and wished I'd had more.

I carried two heavy whiskey glasses of warm Coke back with me into the living room and sat down on the carpet beside Bradley. The chip bowl was empty, picked clean. I could hear a song playing inside his earplug although I couldn't tell what it was.

Do you want to try it? he said, pulling out the plug.

It's all right. I'd had a transistor radio for a couple of years already.

You can if you want, he said, offering me the earplug. It was already smudged with yellow ear wax.

No, it's all right.

Bradley shrugged and stuck the plug back inside his ear, turned back to the TV. I took a sip of Coke, sneezed. *Bless you*, Bradley said, without looking away from the television. I looked into the kitchen. My dad was smoking his cigarette with the tips of his thumb and his forefinger pinched tight to the filter like he did whenever he'd been drinking a lot. His tie was loosened and he was laughing at something somebody had said. Everyone was laughing, even my mom, who hardly ever laughed at anything. I saw her hurry to put her beer bottle down and to cover her mouth like if she took her hand away all the beer would come spurting out.

I went back into the kitchen a couple more times and didn't even bother whispering it anymore, just said, *When are we going home?* — even said it to my dad once — but either he or my mom would just say, *We're going soon, son, we're going soon.* And each time, *Raymond, why don't you go lie down on Grandma's bed if you're tired?* Grandma would say. *I'm not tired*, I would answer, and for some reason everybody would laugh, thought that what I'd said was somehow very, very funny.

I fell asleep on the rug. The shag was itchy, and bursts of laughter from the kitchen would sometimes jolt me awake. But before I could get up and march into the kitchen and tell my mom it was way past time we went home, I'd fall back asleep. Sometimes the sounds from the television would slip inside my dreams, become part of what I was dreaming. I knew I was dreaming but I still couldn't force myself to wake up.

Bradley shook me awake.

What do you want on the pizza? He was on his knees beside me, like he was praying. He looked more excited now than when he'd ripped the wrapping paper from the box his radio had come in.

What pizza? I said.

We're getting a pizza, extra-large, whatever we want on it, anything.

Why are we getting a pizza?

Bradley gave up on me and got to his feet and went into the kitchen. I looked at Grandma's cuckoo clock hanging on the wall over the television. It was after one o'clock in the morning. Was it still Christmas Eve, or was it Christmas now? I couldn't tell. Either way, you weren't supposed to be ordering a pizza. Whatever right now was, this wasn't what we were supposed to be doing.

Not quite four o'clock in the afternoon by the time they got to Rivière-du-Loup, plenty of time for Jack to at least get a start looking through the civic or the parish records. After paying for the room and getting their key, though, Jack insisted they visit the motel lounge for a quick whiskey and soda.

Are you sure? Joe said. *This is what we came all this way for, isn't it?*

Just one quick one, Jack said.

Joe shrugged. *It's your trip.* . . .

Just one quick one.

Joe knew that, for Jack, there was no such thing as one quick drink. For Jack, there was either sobriety or oblivion; otherwise, only the long, steady fumble of getting there. But give the guy credit, Jack knew it too. Before setting off on a spree he'd always tell Mémère where he was going and when he thought he'd be back and would only take enough money with him to get him started, borrowing however much else he needed along the way and keeping strict accounts of how much he owed and to whom. There's wisdom in knowing you can't trust yourself. It's a conscientious suicide who's careful to carry two pieces of identification with him at all times.

The lounge wasn't much — wasn't even much for a motel lounge — just a small plywood-panelled addition to the main building with a moose head mounted on one wall and an out-of-order cigarette machine mingling with a few scattered, unoccupied tables, and after they sat down at what passed for the bar they were surprised to see the same man standing behind the Formica counter who'd helped them check in. There was a door connecting the motel office to the lounge, and a bell over the lounge door that told him when he had thirsty guests.

Ah, we meet again! Jack said, tossing a cigarette into his mouth. When Jack had addressed the man in French when they'd checked in, the man had answered in English. When Jack asked the man if he didn't speak French, *Yes,* the man had replied. *And how many nights will you be staying?*

Unlit cigarette dangling from his mouth, *Either that or I've got déjà vu stuck in my ears again,* Jack said. He pushed a pinky into his ear and energetically rubbed it around; pulled it out and flicked it, a few drops of post-shower wet dribbling across the countertop. A white rag hung from one of the man's big hands, but he didn't bother using it.

Joe had agreed to go for the drink Jack wanted, but only if Jack first agreed to freshen up in their room. This was the only motel they'd seen on the way in, and Joe didn't feel like being forced to vacate it within their first hour there and having to climb back in the car and start looking for another one. Now he wasn't so sure he'd made the right call. All he'd hoped was that Jack would change his sweaty shirt and splash some water on his greasy face and maybe try to comb down his hair, but Jack had surprised him, made Joe wait while he showered, shaved, and even slipped on his checkered sports jacket that until now had been hanging from a coat hanger in the back seat. What for, Joe didn't know. From what they'd seen so far, there didn't seem to be much reason to worry about fashion etiquette. Most of the traffic, what little there was, had been tractors and pickup trucks.

The shower and the shave and the fact he'd run out of cognac a half an hour before they'd stopped at the motel only postponed what had to happen; fresh reinforcements in the form of two quick whiskey and sodas picked up the pace, flushed his face phony healthy, straightened his posture on his stool, itched his tongue to talk or it would surely grow fat in his mouth and choke him with heavy silence. Jack looked around the lounge. There was no one there but him and Joe. His sports jacket felt tight across his chest. He could feel his heart beating.

Does that cigarette machine work? he called out to the man on the other side of the door, knowing that it didn't. The man had served them their drinks and gone back to his post at the front desk. Joe pulled his pack of Marlboros out of his shirt pocket and pushed it toward Jack. Jack ignored it.

Pardon? the man said, appearing in the doorway.

Do you know any Kerouacs who live around here? Jack said.

No.

I'm a Kerouac — Jean-Louis Kerouac — and this is my good friend, Mr. Joseph Chaput. My grandfather was born here.

Okay. The man crossed his arms.

Jack lifted, finished his drink; shook the empty glass, an ice cube maraca.

Does that mean you'd like another whiskey soda? the man said.

Oui. Deux, he said, pointing to Joe's still-full glass.

The man went behind the counter and took down the bottle, slowly unscrewed the plastic cap, silently splashed two clean glasses with Canadian Club.

Talking to the man's back, *Why won't you speak French with me?* Jack said.

Without turning around, *You're American, aren't you?*

My first North American ancestor was Baron Alexandre Louis Lebris de Kerouac of Cornwall, Brittany, a brave soldier who fought for France in —

You've got Massachusetts licence plates. You're from Boston?

Lowell, Joe said helpfully. *About half an hour north of Boston. Thanks,* he said as the man placed the fresh drinks on the counter.

You're Americans, the man said, addressing Jack.

North Americans, Jack said. Pointing at the man then back at himself, *Our blood is the same blood. The language of my forefathers was the same language of yours. All three of us —* he swung an arm around Joe's shoulder — *are sons of France.*

The man wiped his hands on his towel. *We get lots of Americans up here this time of year,* he said. *They come to kill the caribou.* He shut the door to the motel lobby behind him.

It only took Jack one swift drink to piece together why the man had been so cold. Of course. It was obvious.

We're not Jewish! he yelled. *It's the Jews, I know, who've corrupted your language — my language — the French language, our French tongue. That's exactly why we Frenchmen need to stick together. Come back in here, my friend, let a blood brother buy his blood brother a drink.*

The lounge door reopened. This time speaking to Joe, *The bar is now closed,* the man said.

I'd enjoyed the three-beer giggles, graduated to six-pack bliss, and had even gone on to experience the profounder pleasures of chugalugging Brador, teenybopper consciousness expander of choice, like sucking an ice-cold distilled pork chop from a beer bottle but with a leg-rubbering alcohol content of 6.1 percent. But now I wanted to get drunk. Jim Morrison drunk. Take-a-fire-extinguisher-to-the-keyboardist's-harpsichord-because-the-band-doesn't-mean-it-enough drunk. Hang-from-a-fifth-floor-window-because-the-party-going-on-inside-is-so-boring drunk. Tell-ten-thousand-people-to-go-fuck-themselves-because-we're-not-playing-*Light-My-Fire*-tonight-because-we-don't-fucking-feel-like-it drunk. Now I wanted to get Jack Kerouac drunk. Stay-up-all-night-tale-telling drunk. Grow-a-golden-gibbering-tongue drunk. See-hear-taste-smell-things-never-seen-heard-tasted-smelled-before drunk.

According to both *No One Here Gets Out Alive* and *Jack's Book*, Jim and Jack at their most alluringly irrepressible normally ran around with the same accomplice, Jack Daniels, and I set out to make Mr. Daniels' acquaintance. It wasn't as easy as buying beer, though, as Jamie, our usual go-to guy because he was big, over six feet, more than two hundred pounds, and the centre on our senior football team, refused to even try his luck at the liquor store because his father, the Reverend Dalzell, was a Scotch and water man and Jamie couldn't run the risk of being recognized at the counter as the minister's son. Our usual fallback plan—lurking around the side of the beer store and waiting for somebody sufficiently scruffy to be heading inside and politely asking them if they wouldn't mind buying us a twelve-pack because we'd, uhm, forgotten our ID at home—was also out. People like my dad drank beer; people like the Reverend drank liquor and wine. A guy in dirty work clothes might tell you to get lost, to buy your own goddamn beer, but a guy in a suit and tie might tell the liquor store guy inside who might call the cops who might . . . No one ever said transcendence was easy. Break on through to the other side, yeah.

Let's just get beer, then, Jamie said. We were sitting across from one another in the nearly empty cafeteria, Friday lunch hour almost over. Jamie'd agreed to take a bourbon holiday with me, but this was cutting it too close. The dance was tonight and we still didn't have anything to drink. And you couldn't show up at the dance without having had something to drink. Even the preppies who actually liked the lousy music the deejays played—Soft Cell, Human League, Flock of Seagulls—sat around one or the other's parents' posh living room fortifying themselves pre-dance with John Labatt Classic and Schooner and wine spritzers.

This is so lame, I said.

Yeah, well, lame or not, it's all we're going to get.

I still don't know why you just don't try the liquor store.

I told you why.

I know, but—

Passing by our table, *Try what at the liquor store?* Pete Farrell said.

Pete was on the football team like us but never got to play, was a reserve left offensive tackle, only a pair of shoulder pads and a helmet higher on the depth chart than the water boy. He wasn't stupid, but he wasn't smart either; asked me once in English class when he saw me thumbing through my copy of *Jack's Book* before the bell rang why I was reading a book that we weren't being tested on. He seemed to be able to borrow his dad's pickup truck whenever he wanted, though, so sometimes he was a handy guy to let hang around.

I want to get some Jack, I said. Jack. I liked the way that sounded. Like when narcs in the know on TV said *blow* instead of *cocaine, horse* instead of *heroin.*

My sister drinks Jack Daniels sometimes, Pete said.

Oh, yeah?

That shit'll fuck you up.

I smiled at Jamie. *Oh yeah, I know,* I said. Jamie bit into his apple.

She'd probably sell you some of hers, Pete said.

Really? Why?

Because she's my sister. If I tell her you guys are friends, she'll probably do it.

That would be cool, I said. *That would be very cool.*

Why don't I pick you guys up tonight and we'll go to my sister's place before the dance and we can party there?

That sounds great, I said, nodding several times, mostly for Jamie's benefit. I knew what he was thinking—that people who use the word *party* as a verb are precisely the sort of people you don't want to party with—but a sure-thing ride and easy access to hard liquor were worth putting up with almost anything, even Pete.

Whatever, Jamie said. *Just as long as we stop at the beer store.*

No problemo, Pete said.

Jamie crunched a final chunk out of his apple, aimed and arced the core toward one of the several metal garbage pails bisecting the boys' side of the cafeteria. Two points. *At least I don't have to chip in for your whiskey now,* he said.

It's not whiskey, I said. *It's bourbon.*

Whatever.

There's a difference.

How would you know?

Believe me, I know.

Pete's sister Ann lived in a fourplex near the community college. On the ride over, Pete said she lived with her boyfriend, whose name was also Pete, but if she did, he wasn't around when we got there. She looked like Pete would look if he were a woman in her mid-twenties who never washed her hair, and after she'd unhooked the gold chain on the door and led us into the living room we noticed she dragged her right foot on the linoleum floor. Every time she did, her slipper made a *ssshing* sound like somebody telling somebody over and over again to be quiet.

Jamie and I sat on the couch, Pete in one of the armchairs. The couch and all of the chairs were covered in hand-knit yarn shawls. Two different sticks of incense smouldered in separate sandalwood incense burners. A single table lamp smudged a dirty yellow glow. No matter how hard you tried to focus, it still seemed like you'd suddenly contracted jaundice.

Here, Jamie said, poking me in the ribs with a beer, *start with this.* He pulled another bottle out of his box of twelve and tossed it to Pete. He placed one more on the glass coffee table beside a bunch of old magazines, the kind you'd find in an unsuccessful dentist's office. *Does your sister want a beer?* he asked Pete.

Pete twisted the cap off his Blue. *Ann's got a cold,* he said.

Jamie waited for more.

She's always got a cold. Pete shook his head, smiled.

Jamie slid the bottle back in the box.

We could hear the *shhh* pause *shhh* pause of Ann coming out of the kitchen and into the living room, but neither Jamie nor I looked up. When she clinked the bottle of Jack Daniels and some glasses to the coffee table we both acted surprised to see her standing there.

She coughed, covered her mouth. *Are we shooting, or are we sipping?* she said. Although the furnace was rattling the heat vents and it must have been eighty degrees inside the apartment, she pulled her unbuttoned cardigan together like she was freezing. She looked at Jamie, then at me.

Not me, he said, leaning back on the couch with his beer. *I'm not my old man.*

Your dad drinks Scotch, I said.

Close enough.

I looked at Pete. *I'm driving,* he said. Pointing to the bottle in his other hand, *I better stick to beer.* I saw Jamie roll his eyes and take a drink from his Blue.

Ann coughed again, one hand going to her mouth, the other still holding her cardigan together. Jesus Christ, why don't you just do the damn thing up, I wanted to say.

Well, it looks like it's just me and you, Roy, she said. It was the first time she'd smiled since we'd been there, including when Pete had introduced us. One of her bottom teeth was missing.

Ray, I said.

She was already filling two stubby shot glasses with brown liquor. *Petey says you're a man who likes his Jack,* she said. I heard Jamie snort. *If you're a Jack man, you probably like it straight up like I do.*

She handed me a full shot glass and clinked hers to mine just enough to make a pinprick of sound. The bourbon shimmered like the surface of a lake on an almost windless day.

Cheers, she said.

Cheers, I said.

It didn't make sense—drinking but not tasting—but I

followed her lead, swallowed down the liquor while trying not to let it touch my tongue. The smell was enough to let me know what I was getting into, anyway: sweet gasoline, razor blade smooth. I set the shot glass down carefully on the coffee table and leaned back on the couch beside Jamie.

What's it like? he said.

It's good.

What's it taste like?

It tastes good.

Ann limped to a side table and stuck a homemade tape inside a cheap cassette recorder, limped back and poured out two more shots. James Taylor bleated through the single black plastic speaker, fire and rain and sunny days he thought would never end.

Cheers, she said.

Cheers, I said.

Let's go.

We really better go. They don't let anyone into the dance after ten o'clock.

Fuck off, I said.

Just get his coat and let's go.

Thanks, Ann.

Yeah, thanks.

Fuck all of you, I said.

Someone bundled my coat underneath my arm and pushed me down the hallway like a shopping cart with only three good wheels. I stopped and turned around and tossed the coat over Jamie's head, spun him around and jumped on his back.

Hey, c'mon, guys, I've got neighbours.

Ray, c'mon.

Ray.

Fuck all of you, I said. *Fucking . . . bourgeois pigs.*

I looked up at the ceiling from my back. A brown water stain looked like a cloud that looked like a water stain on a ceiling. My back should have hurt, I knew, but it didn't.

Is he all right?

I didn't know he was such an a-hole, Jamie.

He's not. Usually.

I pointed up at Ann's, Pete's, and Jamie's faces looking down at me looking up at them from the floor.

You. You. And you, I said. I took a deep breath, dodged a tidal wave of vomit in the pit of my stomach. Recovered, still lying on my back, *The time to hesitate is through,* I said.

All right, Lizard King, get up.

What's he talking about, Jamie?

No time to wallow in the mire.

Just get him out of my house, guys, okay? Please?

It's just something from a song.

But what does it mean?

It means it looks like we're not going to the dance, Pete.

He could still remember when all he ever wanted to do was write one beautiful sentence.

Dear God, if only mastery — if only minor mastery — of my craft, of the form, of my mind. If only possession — if only partial possession — of all this handmade magic. If only to serve on the same team as Shakespeare, Cervantes, Rabelais, if only to qualify as a backup to a backup to a backup, honour of honours just to play on the same scribbling squad, century after century of playing together at the only game in Time worth winning.

But, of course, in time:

I mean, Dear God, if only publication — vindication, I mean, validation, absolution — if only my very own name on the actual spine of a dusty, dog-eared, long-out-of-print single volume sitting alone at the top of the shelf at a third-rate library somewhere in, I don't know, Idaho, say, that no one ever visits but there it is anyway — my book — phlebitis, toothaches, and inconclusive paternity tests inadmissible in a court of law meaning nothing, absolutely nothing, them and the ugly world they're puked from go straight to hell, instant immortality copyright © 1957 by Jack Kerouac, Library of Congress Catalog Number 57-9425.

But, of course, in time:

I mean, what I really mean, Dear God, is if only honest fame, some real recognition, I'm talking true appreciation here, not this spokesman for a bunch of juvenile delinquents shit. I mean, how come every Bernard Malamud and Herbert Gold and Saul Bellow gets his shiny little good-boy/good-book gold star, not to mention having his asshole personally slavered by every single member of the Jewish critical conspiracy in New York but I'm just a big tin-eared Canuck who don't know nothing about nothing, just ask the wise men at the Saturday Review *("adolescent blathering") or the* New York Herald Tribune *("slapdash and grossly sentimental") or the* New York Times *("garrulous hipster yapping").*

The world is such a big place. No matter how far you travel or what you do once you get there, always some good reason for pettiness, envy, resentment. The grass really is always greener. Just don't let the fresh paint job on the fence fool you. All those rusty nails, all that rotten, worm-ridden wood, it's all underneath there somewhere.

Walking downtown to the bus depot after school, I noticed a medium-sized, black Magic-Markered sign sitting by itself in the dirty front window of an empty storefront on King Street.

HEATHER CLUB BOOK SALE
ALL BOOKS .25 – $1.00
ALL PROCEEDS TO THE SISTERS OF
ST. JOSEPH'S HOSPITAL

Chances were I wasn't going to uncover a copy of *On the Road* at a book sale run by a bunch of nuns, but *Jack's Book* was an excellent road map to where my mind was supposed to be travelling, so I had plenty of other unpronounceable stops along the way besides Kerouac to be on the lookout for.

I'd never been to a second-hand book sale before. The room smelled like what it felt like to be inside in January while you watched it sleet and snow and the wind pushed around the trees outside. The long banquet tables that the books were neatly, if not alphabetically, arranged on were divided up just like a regular bookstore. There were sections for fiction (Irving Stone, Pearl S. Buck, and Arthur Hailey dominating in duplicates, often triplicates), psychology (*Norman Vincent Peale's Treasury of Joy and Enthusiasm*), history (*Edgar Cayce on Atlantis*), autobiography (Anita Bryant's *I've Seen the Glory*), and, of course, religion (plenty of large print New Testaments, *Good News Bibles*, and even some theology books with titles like *God Exists and Is Alive and Well and Living in Lockport, New York!*). And like that game on *Sesame Street*, one of these things is not like the others, one of these things just doesn't belong: *Why I Am Not a Christian* by Bertrand Russell.

Stamped in blue ink inside the front cover, CHATHAM UNITARIAN FELLOWSHIP it read. Know-thy-enemy reading material for the parishioners, I guessed. I grabbed both it and the battered green hardcover hiding beside it, *An Introduction to Philosophy* by G.T.W. Patrick, and brought them to the nun with the grey metal cash box at the front. I was afraid that when she saw the title of the first book she'd decide not to sell me either. She did, and both of them for one dollar. Even though I paid for them, when I walked out the door with the books in my gym bag I felt as if I'd stolen something.

It was May, May impersonating July, reminding everyone that summertime in southwestern Ontario is like stepping into a steamy bathroom only moments after someone else has just finished taking a long hot shower. But our house was autumn brisk due to our new central air conditioning.

I wasn't used to the house being cold when it was hot outside. My parents, my mother especially, were still saying how they couldn't believe how they managed to live like they did before, but I couldn't get used to putting on more clothes when I got home from school just so I wouldn't be cold. Plus, I had a sore throat from practically the first day the cool air came rushing through what used to only be the heat vents. I dropped my gym bag in my room and took my two new books with me out to the backyard.

I grabbed a lawn chair from the shed. The shed felt like a tin kiln, like if you messed around inside long enough and breathed too much of its air you'd end up searing your lungs. I unfolded the chair in the middle of the yard. Our subdivision was still being bulldozed when we'd moved in a decade before, and there still weren't any trees for shade, so the middle of the backyard was as good a place to sit as anywhere. I was close enough to the house, though, that I could hear the steady whirr of the air conditioning unit around the side. I could even hear the Eglins' air conditioner next door working away on their side of the fence.

I picked up *Why I Am Not a Christian* because it was a paperback and lighter. A lie to say that I understood what I read. A lie to say that I read.

Page 15, a refutation of something called the First Cause Argument. Page 36, the Christian Church as a source of moral intolerance. Page 95, the religious persecution of someone named Thomas Paine. Page 161, why religion can't cure society's ills. Page 139, a debate between Bertrand Russell and Father F.C. Copleston regarding the existence of God.

I was excited enough that every time I began reading an essay I never got past the first couple of pages out of fear that if I kept reading I might miss something going on somewhere else in the book, but I was also mad. Why hadn't anyone told me you were allowed to ask questions like this? How come I hadn't known there were people like philosophers in the world whose job it was to sit around all day wondering about the meaning of life and writing books telling people all about it?

Ray, why don't you come inside where it's cool?

My mother was at the back door, one foot on the cement step, one foot still inside.

I'm okay, I said. I could hear CFCO playing in the kitchen, "Sunday Morning" by the Commodores.

All right, but don't stay outside too long. You'll end up getting heatstroke if you stay outside in this muck for too long.

I won't. I was looking at the book resting on my knee. On its cover, underneath the title and Russell's name, a black cross with a big white X struck through it.

I don't know how you can stand it out there, she said, shutting the aluminum door then the wooden one, the whoosh of the last sucking up the sound of the radio. It was too hot for anybody to cut their lawn, so all I heard was the hum of the air conditioners.

I reopened *Why I Am Not a Christian*. It didn't matter where. Wherever it fell open, I'd just start there.

You won't find the word *religion* in the Bible. You can't use a slide rule and a ballpoint pen to prove that Jesus loves you. God doesn't give a shit that *The Journal for Existential Theology* is an influential quarterly with a wide and growing readership of prominent academics, clerics, and educated laypersons. Faith is at the bottom of the stairs, down in the basement, and don't bother with the light switch, the bulb is burned out, it's always been burned out.

Gerard was Jack's first teacher, when he was healthy enough to take his younger brother by the hand and lead him around the Stations of the Cross outside the Franco-American Orphanage on Pawtucket Street, stopping and patiently explaining the meaning of each one. Jack was four years old and the crucified Christ was life-sized and blood-ied and looked so sad. Ti Jean felt sorry for him. Ti Jean felt scared of him. Gerard told his brother not to be afraid, that after His resurrection Jesus lived forever in heaven and knew a happiness no one could even imagine. On their way home they'd have to pass by the Archambault Funeral Home.

Gerard would be laid out there less than a year later. Later still, Jack too.

In the school auditorium Ti Jean saw a movie in which the statue of Saint Thérèse turned its head. Sometimes he saw his own plaster statue of Saint Thérèse sitting on his dresser beside all of his track and field trophies turn its head too. Sometimes Jesus or the Virgin Mary would rattle his bed at night. The church basement where the children would gather on rainy afternoons after school to drink weak lemonade and listen to Bible stories was dark and musty-smelling and you never knew what was lurking around the corner of its twisting, stone-cold alcoves. Jacky knew Jesus was gentle as a lamb and was his sweet, sweet saviour because Gerard had taught him so, but sometimes the black-lacquered cross bearing a glowing white plastic Jesus would wake him up in the middle of the night, would be staring down at him, daring him to shut his eyes.

Gerard was a saint, Jack's mother often told him so. His meekness, his kindness, his otherworldly patience even while suffering his excruciating final earthly spasms—my God, the simple way he used to rescue mice from the traps his father would set around the house—all were good things for Ti Jean to remember when he was being a bad boy. How embarrassed his big brother would be of him if he could see how he was acting, Mémère would say. Gerard's former teachers, the sisters of the St. Louis de France Parochial School, who'd filed past his little coffin so deferentially while four-year-old

Ti Jean looked on, beat Jack when he became a student there whenever he needed to be disciplined. The welts he took home with him hurt, almost as much as the shame he carried with him for not being as good as Gerard.

Hopping hormones and after-school baseball practices and the paperback adventures of Jack London were good gloom beaters, though, God in His proper place as a Sunday morning exercise, something to talk about in religion class or during summertime riverbank bull sessions with G.J. and Scotty. Sunshine kills shadows. Even if it can't be daytime all the time.

One warm summer night when he was twelve, crossing the Moody Street Bridge with Mémère, a man walking ahead of them carrying a watermelon underneath one of his arms suddenly dropped dead. Jack and his mother ran to the man, but he was gone by the time he hit the ground. The dead man's sightless eyes stared into the water of the Merrimack River churning beneath them. His cracked watermelon slowly rolled away from him down the southern incline of the bridge.

Although he was twelve, Jack crawled into bed with his mother and his sister that night, his father for as long as he could remember sleeping alone in his own room. His sister, who always slept with Mémère, eventually abandoned them for Jack's empty bed because it was too crowded. As he fell asleep Jack felt embarrassed at having returned to his mother's bed because he was afraid, something he hadn't done in years. But when he woke up in the night to pee and found himself huddled against Mémère's warm flesh, he knew that death couldn't touch him as long as he stayed snuggled where he was. He couldn't see the crucifix he knew hung on the bedroom wall over the bed, but even if he had, he wouldn't have been scared. He knew Jesus was watching over him. He could feel it in his bones.

It didn't seem right from the very start. Eddie was the one I played with, not Robby. We took the bat and the ball and a glove and the T-ball stand with us to the park anyway. Robby was thirteen, two whole years older than me, so he carried the stand.

Mr. Webster worked with my dad at Ontario Steel, and sometimes he and Mrs. Webster and their sons Eddie, Robby, and Donny came to our house to visit, sometimes we visited theirs. My mom liked it better when they came to see us. The Websters had an old dog named Tammy, three cats, a bird, and a big, bubbling aquarium that took up most of their living room, and my mom said that their house smelled like a zoo. I liked the way the animals wandered around everywhere when you were watching TV, always something coming up to you wanting to be petted or just walking by ignoring you, but the rugs didn't smell as good as the ones at home — you could tell that Mrs. Webster didn't pour the white powder that was supposed to smell Springtime Fresh on her rugs before she vacuumed like my mom did. Sometimes when Mr. Webster was telling a story he'd use the F-word, even if I or his kids were in the same room. He had a tattoo on his right forearm that said *MOM*. One time when we were visiting at Christmas, Grandma Webster was there too. I watched her sitting on the couch eating potato salad and ham rolls off a paper plate, but I couldn't see anything special about her. Everybody knew your mother was your mother, so why would anybody bother to get her name branded into their skin forever?

The park was right behind our house—a tall metal fence separated the backyards of all the houses on our street, Park Street, from the park—but it was too high to climb, you had to walk around the block to get to it. Robby and I carried the equipment around the block. Both of us were too old to need the T-ball stand, but as soon as Robby saw it in our garage he'd wanted to use it.

Where'd you get this? he'd said. *D'you steal it?*

No.

Where then?

My dad made it.

What for?

So I could practise.

Must be nice, he said, taking out the steel pin and adjusting the height level, adjusting it to his level.

I shrugged. My dad made me lots of things: a steel puck to make my wrist shot harder; targets for my hockey net to improve my aim; even, later on, when we moved to our new house, installed a metal bar between two beams in the basement ceiling for me to do chin-ups from after I'd said I wanted to do ten of them every day because Terry Bradshaw in his book *The Terry Bradshaw Story* said that that was what he did when he was a kid.

Let's hit grounders off it, he'd said, throwing it over his shoulder.

You'll hit grounders off it, I thought. I'll end up chasing grounders.

Eddie was the same age as me, and if he had been there instead of Robby we would have taken turns at bat. Eddie was at home with the mumps, though, so I picked up the glove and the ball and the bat and told my dad we were going to the park. He and Mr. Webster were sitting in lawn chairs in the backyard drinking beer. My dad said okay but to play where he could see us.

Once we were on the sidewalk, *Why'd you tell him where we were going?* Robby said.

Whenever I leave the house I have to.

That's gay, he said.

I shrugged. Whatever gay was, it definitely wasn't something you wanted to be.

We got to the park and dumped the equipment close enough to the fence that my dad and Mr. Webster could still see us, but far enough away that they couldn't hear us. Robby placed the ball on top of the T-ball stand and practised his swing. I put on the glove and walked into the field. I turned around and put both hands on my knees, ready. On the other side of the park, another tall fence separated it from Ontario Steel. In the summertime, when the windows at home were wide open, you could hear the pounding of the steel presses from the factory day and night. You got used to it and didn't really even notice it, but waiting in the field for Robby to hit me the ball, I did.

Keep going, he said, waving me away.

I stood back up and did what he said.

When I was far enough out, he took a couple more practice swings and then finally swung at the ball. The ball shot from the tee and tore through the grass to my left, rocketing right by me. Even if I hadn't had to catch it backhanded it probably would have gotten past, but it looked better missing a ball while going to your backhand. Even the pros sometimes missed a ball trying to catch it backhanded.

Get in front of it, Robby yelled. *Plant your feet and stay square to the ball.*

I nodded and put my hands back on my knees. Robby was a jerk, I thought. Who did he think he was, my dad? Robby was gay.

Robby kept pounding the ball off the tee while I kept trying not to tell him not to hit it so hard because it wasn't much fun picking up dead balls in the grass lying fifty feet past me. There was no way I was going to do it, though. That's exactly what he would have wanted. You could tell by the way he smirked whenever I'd heave back another ball that had bulleted past. I let him keep smashing grounders and smirking at me for about ten minutes, then snapped a final dead ball into the palm of my glove and jogged in.

Tired already? he said.

Let me hit a few.

I've hardly hit any, just let me hit a couple more.

I kept coming, kept my eyes on the grass. I knew that if I looked up at him I'd give in.

Just a couple more, he said.

Let me have a turn.

Just a couple more.

I kept coming.

I'm going to hit one, get ready.

Let me have a turn.

I'm going to hit it, you better get ready.

If I looked up I knew it was all over. I kept coming.

I'm serious, he said, *I'm going to hit it.*

Don't be gay, I said.

You better get ready because I'm gonna swing now.

I still didn't look up. He wouldn't hit the ball at me. Nobody was that stupid.

Here I go, he said, *I'm swinging.*

I could see the metal base of the T-ball stand by now, so I knew it was all right to finally look up.

The first thing I saw when I got up off the ground was Robby running away. Then the blood splattered across the front of my T-shirt. The red of the blood seemed redder than red, probably because the T-shirt I was wearing was white, the one that my mom had ironed the I'M AN OSCAR MAYER WIENER patch onto that she'd sent away for for me from the back of a package of hot dogs. My head didn't hurt, but when I put my fingers to where Robby had hit it with the bat, over my right eye, I felt a mud puddle of blood and screamed.

Dad!

I kept my hand on my head and moved toward the fence and our backyard.

Dad!

I was close enough now that I could see Mr. Webster and my dad laughing about something. I couldn't hear them, but I could see. I was almost at the fence now. How could they be laughing?

Dad!

I heard myself scream, and I scared myself. I screamed again, and again, this time with all ten fingers wrapped tight around the mesh of the fence. I saw Mr. Webster stand up from his lawn chair and point, my dad drop his bottle of beer and take off running toward me.

Dad!

He never slowed down. When he got to the fence he jumped up on it at full speed, jammed his feet and stuck his fingers into the mesh holes, scrambled to the top like a monkey on *Wild Kingdom*. When he got to the top he hung there a moment straddling the metal bar, then shimmied down a few feet before dropping to the ground. I stopped screaming when he landed.

He placed both hands on the sides of my face and tilted my head upward and looked at where Robby had hit me. He put his arm around my shoulder and guided me toward the park entrance.

You're going to be okay, he said. *Let's get home and get you fixed up.*

I hadn't cried yet, but now I did.

It wasn't my fault, I managed.

It doesn't matter, he said. *Let's just get you home and get you fixed up.*

I . . . just . . . wanted to . . . hit, I said, hiccuping up the words between tears.

That's all right, he said. *You didn't do anything wrong. Let's get you home now. Let's get you fixed up.*

No matter how late he stayed out or how liquor-legged he was when he wobbled in, Jack always stuck his head in Mémère's room to let her know he got home all right. One night, stumbling in near dawn, he didn't bother knocking, just pushed open Mémère's closed bedroom door at the exact instant Mémère, birthday-suit nude, was getting out of bed. Mémère's hands flew to her breasts, she fell to the floor, began foaming at the mouth.

Nine days later, when she insisted she be discharged home from the hospital, the end result was a stroke that had left her right side untouched but affected her left side enough that she couldn't get out of bed on her own, let alone walk. Jack phoned Stash in Northport and kept repeating how he'd nearly killed his own mother.

Jack, it was an accident.

My own mother, Stash.

Jack, listen to me, I know you, the last thing in the world you'd ever do is anything to intentionally hurt Mémère.

Ma mère, ma mère.

A week of playing nurse later, he was back on the phone to Northport again.

The only things that still work right are her asshole and her mouth, she sure keeps that thing flapping twenty-four hours a day, I'll tell you. 'Jacky get me this, Jacky get me that, Jacky I need you to clean up my number one.' I'm fucked here, Stash, she needs someone to look after her, I'm in way over my head.

Can't you get a nurse to come by and look in on her?

You don't get it, she needs somebody here full-time.

Couldn't you hire—

You know what my total income was last year, Stash? Seven thousand eight hundred and ninety-seven dollars. What do you think?

A week after that, he called Stella in Lowell, asked her if she would please, please come to Hyannis to help him take care of Mémère. Seven weeks after that, he asked her to marry him. It wasn't just because he needed a nurse, he told Stash.

I can see Sammy's eyes in her eyes, he said. *I can hear Sammy speak from her lips.*

Stella hid Jack's whiskey bottles from him and did his and Mémère's laundry and sewed their clothes and cooked their meals and bathed Mémère and ignored it when they'd talk in French in front of her when they didn't want her to know what they were saying. Stella also convinced Jack to help her convince Mémère that they would only move south if she agreed to undergo regular physical therapy. Mémère didn't like strangers in her house, even registered therapists, and after Jack bought her two new cats, Timmy and Tuffy, to help cheer her up, she seemed content to lie in bed all day with one or both of them on her lap and ring the bell Stella had given her for whenever she needed something.

One afternoon not long after they'd moved to Florida, Jack looked up from his easy chair parked in front of the television screen to see the squat therapist they'd been told by the nuns at the hospital they'd been lucky to find dragging his mother around the house like a rag doll. Jack yelled at her to stop.

This is part of your mother's therapy, Mr. Kerouac. As difficult as it may seem to you right now, she needs to do these exercises if she's ever going to learn to walk on her own again.

Dammit, stop it, I said.

The therapist rolled her eyes and plopped Mémère down on the couch; hands on her hips, said that Gabrielle was simply going to have to work harder if she wanted to get the full benefit of her professional help.

Mémère's head fell forward on her chest. Just as Jack had thought—she'd passed out minutes ago. Stella ran to her, lightly slapped the back of her hand to attempt to resuscitate her. He had to get out of there.

Forsaking the air conditioning, something he rarely did in the middle of the day if he had any choice, he went out to the backyard and sat in the wooden lawn chair he'd bought for reading in on the rarer days it wasn't sweltering. Bracing himself for much worse, it wasn't actually that bad. Thought:

Sometimes it's enough for the rain to come and the humidity to break and the temperature to drop and to finally be able to breathe again.

He pulled his notebook out of his shirt pocket and was about to bon mot his thought down when a tangerine from an overhanging branch from the next-door neighbour's tree fell and hit him on top of the head.

He looked down at the piece of orange fruit lying on the green grass in the bright sun. Looked up at the still-swaying limb. Pressed pen to paper.

"Orlando Blues," that's what he'd call it. Of course he'd write a poem about it. When a fucking tangerine falls on your head, what other options do you really think you have?

It was funny. It had to be funny. What else could it have been?

My dad and a couple of his buddies who were on strike at the factory were going to help bring in a farmer's tobacco harvest for some extra cash. Immigrants and people who couldn't get real jobs worked on the farms around Chatham — not people like my dad and his friends — but he made it sound like Mr. Brown and Mr. Finch and him were planning on spending a couple of weeks at a day camp for adults more than they'd be going to work for the first time in months. And even though everyone was still collecting strike pay, my dad told my mom over supper that it was pure gravy money, cash payment at the end of every week.

Why don't you have to pay taxes? I said. I'd just finished my first summer of corn-detassling, my first paying job, so I knew all about what a decapitated paycheque looked like. We'd gotten a photocopied handout inside the envelope containing our first cheque explaining away all of the deductions: Federal Tax, Social Insurance, Unemployment Insurance. All of a sudden $3.25 an hour didn't seem like so much money anymore.

Any kid from Chatham who was thirteen years or older and at least five foot one could, if they wanted to, spend half of their summer vacation getting up at six-thirty in the morning and sleepwalking through the dawn to their assigned pickup site in order to wait around with thirty or so five-foot-one-and-over others to be delivered via a rented school bus to the first corn field of the day. Here, you pulled your green garbage bag over your head through the hole you'd already cut in it and walked up and down row after row of dewy cool corn, at every stalk tearing the tassel off its top, dropping it to the ground, then moving on to the next to do the exact same thing. Row done, you'd stand around until everyone else had finished with theirs, passing the time complaining about the wet and the cold (and, by late morning—garbage bag back-pocketed—the heat), talking about what you were going to do with all the money you were going to make, or making fun of whoever had emerged as that year's resident loser. Sometimes you'd wake up in the morning more tired than usual, would be getting dressed and realize you'd spent the last eight hours dreaming of detassling, one long night of over and over again only a warm-up to another long day of the real thing.

Most of the workers are Jamaicans that come over here to work just for the summers, so it's all under the table, he said, spreading some margarine on a slice of bread. Before the strike, we'd used butter. Either way, my dad was still the best at making sure it went on smooth and got right to the edges and didn't tear the bread when you spread it. He set the slice of bread on the edge of my plate, put the knife back to work on another piece for himself.

How much are you getting? I said.

Five bucks, he said. To my mom, *Is there any chili sauce, my dear?*

Yep, she said, getting up and going to the fridge.

My dad hummed while he painted his slice of bread yellow. He hadn't hummed or called my mom *my dear* for a while. He'd built the deck he'd always wanted when the strike had started and, before he'd started worrying about saving money, had fixed everything around the house that needed fixing while the strike dragged on, and had recently taken to re-vacuuming the floors my mother had just finished cleaning and to explaining to her what was wrong with her meals and what she could do to make them better. The week before, they'd had their first real argument in front of me. When I'd asked my mom what it had been about, she'd said, *It's just nerves and the strike.* After a summer of setting my alarm for 6:30 in the morning and coming home at the end of a long day of corn-detassling feeling like doing nothing but climbing back in bed, I would have thought it would be the other way around, that being on strike and *not* working would be when your nerves would be at their best.

Five bucks an hour and no taxes, I said. *That's forty bucks a day.*

That's right, my dad said, taking the jar of chili sauce from my mom. *Thank you, my dear.*

Every Labour Day weekend my mom and dad turned the kitchen into a canning factory, boiling tomatoes and slicing up peppers and onions and celery and filling Mason jar after Mason jar with the chili sauce that my mom and I didn't like because it tasted too hot but my dad put on nearly everything he ate. It was almost time for them to start bottling again.

Do you think I could get hired too? I said.

No, my mother said.

Why not? School doesn't start until next week.

All you've done is complain about how sick you were of working, and now you want to go and work in a tobacco field? I don't think so, no.

No I haven't. And it's five dollars an hour and no taxes. It's gravy money, Mom.

My dad finished covering his mashed potatoes with chili sauce, set the nearly empty Mason jar down on the table. *I could talk to Jim Brown, I guess,* he said. *He could ask Ferguson the farmer, they're old friends.*

All right, I said, pumping my fist.

No, Ken, my mom said. *I don't want him working with a bunch of foreigners.*

They're not foreigners, Mom, they're Jamaicans.

No, I said. *I don't like the sounds of it.*

Jesus Christ, my dad said, *it's not like he'd be there by himself, I'd be right there beside him the whole time.* He lifted a forkful of potatoes into his mouth.

See? I said to my mom.

No, she said, shaking her head.

He'll be fine, my dad said, and my mom and I both knew that that was the end of it, that I'd be going along if Mr. Brown got the farmer to say it was okay.

He'll be just fine, my dad said. *And if the boy wants to work, we should let him work.* He picked up the jar and held it upside down over his plate, tapped it firmly on its bottom over and over again like he was trying to keep rhythm to a song only he could hear. *It looks like it's getting to be chili-sauce-making time again*, he said.

Even getting there was funny.

Mr. Finch picked my dad and me up at 6:30 sharp. We were waiting in the dark on the front step with our lunches and our Coleman Thermos cooler. I'd only seen the cooler used for gin and Wink before, when we'd go to Grandma and Grandpa Authier's sometimes in the summertime for a barbecue. It was strange to see it filled with nothing but cold tap water. Mr. Brown was sitting in the passenger seat. He turned around, rested his furry forearm along its back.

Now, whose fucking idea was this again? he said.

Mr. Finch and my dad both laughed.

I think it was Diane's, my dad said. *To get you out of the fucking house for a change.* Diane was Mrs. Brown.

Mr. Finch and Mr. Brown both laughed.

That's strange, Mr. Brown said. *That's exactly what Jeanie said to me about you.* Jeanie was my mom.

Now I know you're full of shit, my dad said. *Jean only talks to you when she doesn't have any other fucking choice.*

This time everyone laughed, me included.

I'd only heard my dad use the F-word maybe five times, tops, in my entire life, and this morning he'd already said it twice in the first two minutes we were in the car. I'd have to remember to tell Mr. Brown thank you for getting his farmer friend to agree to let me come along. The first sports report of the day came on CFCO and Mr. Finch turned up the radio. We all listened to last night's baseball scores and watched Chatham turn into the country.

Highgate, where the farm was, was on the other side of Thamesville. When you came off the highway you had to drive through town to get to the farm. Town was a grocery store, a beer store, a post office, and a variety store that also rented VHS tapes. A long mud driveway snaked from the road to the farmer's big house. Mr. Finch parked the car beside a dirty white Cadillac and we all got out and stretched. If the Cadillac had belonged to my dad, it never would have gotten that dirty. My dad washed our car every Saturday afternoon, whether it needed it or not.

Mr. Brown knocked on the front door of the house while the rest of us waited by the car. An old woman—she must have been the farmer's wife—shielded her eyes from the hard, already hot morning sun and pointed over his shoulder. Mr. Brown turned around and looked in the same direction; all of us, too. A field, maybe a quarter of a mile away, was dotted with people who looked to be already at work. Mr. Brown walked back toward us.

The old lady says we're supposed to park beside the other workers.

Well, la de fucking da, said Mr. Finch.

We all got back in the car.

The farmer that Mr. Brown knew wasn't around. The foreman knew who we were, though, and told us what to do and put us right to work doing it. Red wooden slats were laid out every few feet down every row of chopped tobacco leaves, and we were each given a metal cap with a razor-blade-sharp point that you stuck on the end of every slat in order to slide the tobacco leaves onto it. That was it. Later on, a machine would come along and pick up the slats to be hung in a barn to dry. I worked in the row beside my dad; Mr. Brown and Mr. Finch in the two aisles next to him. The Jamaicans and some Mennonites from a community near Thamesville kept to themselves while they worked too. There wasn't anything to say to each other anyway. Everyone had their own metal cap and there were endless rows of red wooden sticks to fill up with endless chopped tobacco leaves.

Now, whose *fucking idea was this again?* Mr. Brown said, and my dad and I and Mr. Finch laughed.

We kept laughing up the first long row and all the way down the just-as-long second, my dad and Mr. Brown and Mr. Finch taking turns trying to break each other up while we all bent and capped and thumped the tobacco plants down the slats with the palms of our hands. By ten o'clock, though, the time of our morning water break, the August sun having arrived for the day for good, everyone's hands were hurting too much to laugh. The Jamaicans and the Mennonites pulled off their gloves to drink from their jugs of water. Because none of us had thought to bring gloves, our hands were pink, almost red, from pounding the tobacco plants and handling the coarse wooden slats, and all of us picked at at least one sliver. Most of the Jamaicans were drinking their water out of emptied pop bottles, but I didn't feel sorry for any of them. They and the Mennonites and we were spending the break sitting in the shade of three different trees on the edge of the field, and I drank the water my dad handed me and looked at the hands of the Jamaicans, black and soft and without any little pieces of wood stuck underneath their skin.

I finished my water and handed the green plastic cup that fit inside the Thermos cooler back to my dad. He took it and refilled it.

Here, drink some more, he said.

I'm not thirsty anymore, I said.

It doesn't matter. You don't want to get dehydrated.

I won't.

Just do as you're told, he said. I took the cup and drank.

Sonofabitch, Mr. Finch said. He was leaning against our tree and trying to pull a sliver out of one of his palms.

What's wrong? Baby got a boo-boo? Mr. Brown said. It was the first time anyone had made a joke in a while. I laughed. Mr. Finch and my dad didn't. I stopped.

Want me to kiss it and make it all better? Mr. Brown said.

Shut up, Jim, Mr. Finch said. He didn't say it like a joke. He said it like he wanted Mr. Brown to shut up.

Take it easy. It's not my fucking fault you've got a sliver.

Mr. Finch looked up from his hand. *No, it's only your fault you didn't have the fucking brains to tell us to bring gloves with us.*

How was I supposed to know we'd need gloves?

I don't know, you were the big shot who was friends with the farmer, weren't you? Motioning with his chin toward the Jamaicans, *Jesus Christ, even the niggers have more sense than us.*

My dad stood up and went behind the tree. I heard him unzip the fly of his work pants and piss in the weeds.

The foreman stepped out of his truck. You could hear the whoosh of its air conditioner when he opened the door. *All right,* he said. *Let's get back at it, boys.*

Everyone stood up. My lower back felt like it did the time I got checked from behind into the boards during hockey practice and I had to miss the next game. I remembered that song about tobacco picking, the one about how when the guy heard the name Tillsonburg his back still hurt. I'd always thought it was just supposed to be funny.

The Jamaicans and the Mennonites and Mr. Brown and Mr. Finch and I stayed in our three little groups, but we were all walking in the same direction, the field.

The foreman noticed my dad still peeing behind the tree. *Okay,* he said, *break's over, let's go, bud.*

I was nervous but also excited about what might happen. No one talked to my dad like that.

My dad did up his fly while he jogged to catch up to the rest of us. Passing the foreman, *Sorry*, he said.

My dad said something to me as we were walking, but I didn't know what. All I could think was, Why did you apologize? You were only finishing your pee. You shouldn't have had to apologize.

What was wrong with these people? I thought. Didn't they understand? Didn't they know we were better than them?

There wasn't much to see. There never is. Especially when you've already seen it all before and better, in your mind.

Turn left, Jack said.

I think we've already been down there. They'd been touring town for over an hour, had been up and down every street, paved and otherwise, ten times it seemed.

Nah, make a left.

That's the first street you hit once you come in off the main road, Joe said. He stopped the car at the empty intersection anyway, let Jack see for himself. Words, he knew, weren't going to convince him of anything.

Most of the houses in Rivière-du-Loup weren't much more than tarpaper shacks, just like the smallest, poorest houses in Little Canada back in Lowell. The few people they saw out on the streets—errand-slouching old women mostly—were blank-eyed and drudgery-stooped and wore the same fading flower-print housedresses that Mémère wore. A three-legged black dog drank out of a puddle in the middle of the dirt road; stopped, looked up at them.

Jack realized Joe was right, they had been here already, he remembered seeing the church steeple from this direction. Also just like back in Lowell, the brown brick church was Rivière-du-Loup's architectural centrepiece, easily its tallest, most imposing building. It stood over the rest of the town like a threat.

You're right, Jack said. He said it like he knew it but still didn't believe it.

That's okay, Joe said. *At least we know where the church and city hall are now. Let's go look at those archives.* He put the car in gear but kept his foot on the brake. There still wasn't anyone behind them waiting for them to move. Even the three-legged dog was gone.

No.

Jack reached into the back seat, grabbed the brown-bagged bottle of brandy he'd made such a big deal of telling Joe he wasn't going to touch until the work he had to do with his family records had been done and they were back at the motel celebrating his good-boy good-day's scholarly labours.

They're not going to let you near what you need if you go in there smelling like booze. You didn't tell Jack Kerouac what to do—not if you wanted him to do it—but for Christsake, this was why they'd come all this way, wasn't it? Wasn't this the reason they were here?

Twisting off the cap, *Let's just go,* Jack said.

Joe hesitated; took his foot off the brake. They coasted through the intersection. *Where to first?* he said. *The church or city hall? They're both about the same distance, it doesn't really matter.*

I'm serious, I need to get out of here, Joe.

Jack, we're already here. Let's just—

Joe, I need to go. Now.

The car picked up speed. Joe watched the church steeple get smaller and smaller in the rear-view mirror. Eventually, *So where do you want to go?* he said.

Jack took a drink. He took another drink.

I don't know, he said.

Officially, it was the Victoria Day long weekend, when every Chatham teenager whose parents would let them would head to Rondeau Provincial Park, although everybody at school just called it the May Two-Four weekend and understood that the fresh air and the campfires were just pleasant excuses to get as drunk and as naked with somebody besides yourself as possible. Two years running, I was still only batting .500. Between just him and me, Jamie and I could put away a case of Labatt Blue in twenty-four hours, but neither of us had yet showed up at school on a post–Rondeau Monday morning mosquito-ravaged and still hungover but ready and willing to kiss and tell to whoever was willing to listen.

You could see stars in the sky at night in the park. By nine-thirty, campfires, lanterns, and the headlights of the Jeeps the Yogis drove on their patrols around the parkground were the only light until morning. Unless it was somebody you knew really well, sometimes it would take five minutes of talking to someone to figure out who they were. It was like Halloween, but with booze, and you didn't have to bother with wearing a mask.

So far the old man has had to bury his brother, his grand-mother, and his old man.

Jamie was talking about his father, the Reverend Dalzell, who couldn't pick us up at the park Sunday afternoon—even though my dad had dropped us off—because after his Sunday sermon he was visiting cancer patients at the hospital. Unless he was sick, it was the only Sunday of the year that Jamie was allowed to miss church.

He didn't bury them, I said. *The gravediggers did.*

It's an expression.

We were sitting across the campfire from one another. Steve McKay and Joel Belanger, the two guys who were splitting the cost of the campsite with us, had taken off as soon as the sun had gone down. Each of them had a girlfriend with her own tent for two waiting for him somewhere out there in the darkness. We probably wouldn't see either of them again until it was time to leave on Sunday. It didn't seem fair. It wasn't that long ago that Steve McKay's sole redeeming social skill was being able to imitate the voice of Disco Duck.

It's an expression, I said, *but he still didn't bury anyone. The workers did.*

An Introduction to Philosophy was, admittedly, heavier-going stuff than Bertrand Russell's breezy drop kick to all things Christian, but I'd struggled through enough of it—and skimmed the sections that I hadn't or couldn't—to become an instant convert to both the religion of the syllogism (armed with two declarative sentences of the subject-predicate type and a clearly connected conclusion, it was, I happily deduced, now logically impossible for me to ever be wrong about any-thing again) and the fundamental philosophical virtue of being as intellectually uncomfortable as possible. Because the unexamined life wasn't worth living. Because better to be Socrates unsatisfied than a fool satisfied. Because, just like I read about Søren Kierkegaard courageously combatting the spiritual complacency of nineteenth-century Copenhagen's self-righteous, shot-calling bourgeois, the only possibility of owning any sort of authentic faith, religious or otherwise, was by leasing it upon a foundation of forever-doubting despair.

How about, "He performed the funeral oration," is that all right? Jamie said.

I poked a stick into the campfire, shoved a small log that hadn't caught fire yet closer to the flames. *If by "oration" you mean he spoke some mumbo-jumbo over the dead body to reassure people that the fairy tale they tell themselves that they're all going to sprout wings someday and fly up to heaven is true, sure, fine. I'm just saying that the guys doing the shov-elling are the ones providing the only actually useful societal service.*

The necessity of executing my recently self-assigned Socratic gadfly duties aside, once, when I was over at Jamie's house, I'd overheard his mother tell someone on the tele-phone, *Honestly, these unions, I'm telling you, they're ruining this country. These people, they don't know how good they've got it.* Some statements you don't need to run through a syllo-gism to determine whether or not they're bullshit. Some truths you're born into.

Take a pill, Karl Marx, Jamie said. *Keep it up and the Yogis'll hear you and drag you in for insubordination.*

Jamie wasn't just an honours student, he was also pretty smart. He could see the chip on my shoulder poking through my favourite powder-blue Adidas T-shirt better than I could, even in the dark. Besides, he always preferred hanging out at my house, seemed more comfortable there than he did at his own, liked yakking with my mom and dad about nothing a hell of a lot more than I ever did. My mother would smoke with him at the kitchen table if I was in the shower or getting ready to go out. Jamie wasn't allowed to smoke at home. His dad asked him how he thought it would look if one of his parishioners saw one of his own children smoking. Jamie and my mom smoked the same brand of cigarettes.

You ready for another one? I said, opening the cooler. My dad had given us an old Coleman cooler for bringing with us to parties because we didn't like trusting our beer stash to the host's refrigerator where anyone could just reach in and help themselves, and we'd painted the entire thing red with a fat black diagonal stripe across the top, the same design as on the cover of Neil Young's *Reactor* album. Neil's was the only music we voluntarily listened to besides the Doors. I'd made Jamie a fellow addict of both. Junkies like junkie company.

Jamie lifted his bottle of Blue, chugged what was left. *I am now,* he said.

Except for on the football field, drinking beer was the only time I envied his heft. We'd halved the cost of the case of beer, but I'd only end up drinking a third of it, no matter how hard I tried to keep up.

In the time it took me to stick my hand into the cooler and ignore the numbing cold of the two bags of ice cubes we'd used to carefully entomb the beer, inching it deeper and deeper, as close to the bottom of the chest as possible, where the really, really cold ones were—voices, girls' voices, and coming from somewhere on our own campsite, girls slurring their words and laughing loudly at things that didn't sound very funny, but saying our names so not just lost and passing by and looking for someone else.

The voices floated closer to the fire. Now there were bodies and faces too, Michelle Turnball's and Michelle Bartlet's and Stacey Larmner's.

Hey you guys, you guys got any beer? one of them said, too dark to tell which. Not that it mattered. Even Jamie and I knew that candy was dandy but liquor was quicker. After that, though, we didn't know anything, we were on our own.

Stacey Larmner was the best-looking one, so I manoeuvred myself closest to her by the fire. She also looked like she was the drunkest, so the decision was a no-brainer.

Did you guys hear about Joe? one of the Michelles said.

Holland? Jamie said.

Joe Holland, yeah.

No.

He got busted for drinking off his campsite? And when the Yogi asked him for his name and address and phone number he gave them a fake name and stuff? But then the Yogi called it in on his radio and then they checked up on it and found out he wasn't who he said he was? So they took him to the Yogi station and nobody's seem him since? Both of the Michelles tended to lift their voices at the end of their sentences, regardless of whether or not it was a question, so it was hard to know which one was telling the story.

Oh, man, Jamie said. *His old man's going to kick his ass tomorrow.*

The two Michelles squealed in unison like Jamie had just said something particularly amusing, and I used the cover of their cackling to say to Stacey, *Did you check out that book sale they had near the bus station?*

Everyone knew—because she made a point of telling everyone—that Stacey's ambition since she was thirteen years old was to be a page in the House of Commons once she graduated from high school, and that she was known to ask teachers for extra help if she didn't receive the highest grade on any given class test, so I thought she might be impressed. Plus, she seemed pretty loaded and not her usually annoying chatty self, so I figured the move was mine to make.

Jou, j'get anything good there . . . then? she said, swaying slightly on the log we were sitting on. If only the Prime Minister could see Ms. Keener now, I thought. Rich kids, who were usually the same as the smart kids, normally made me nervous. I wasn't nervous now.

Some quite excellent philosophy books, I said. *Have you ever read Bertrand Russell's* Why I Am Not a Christian? *It's really quite good.* I knew I sounded like the fucking Professor off *Gilligan's Island*, but screw it, it felt good to feel like the smart one for a change.

No, I'd . . . that sounds interesting.

I actually brought it with me, I said. *It's in my tent, do you want me to get it?*

No, she said, standing up, taking a final pull from her bottle of beer before letting it drop to the ground. *Let's look at it in there.*

I was excited but also worried; by the way she was speaking and acting, it seemed like she'd suddenly sobered up. I lifted the flap to the tent and let her crouch inside first. I didn't have to worry for long. I didn't even have time to light the lantern or get my book from my bag.

Her clothes smelled like campfire smoke, just like mine. A few minutes later we smelled like ourselves, our discarded jeans and T-shirts and socks and running shoes getting to know each other better on the sandy floor of the tent. Soon, her smells were my smells, mine hers. Kissing her, kissing her everywhere, I kissed my own naked shoulder once by mistake. But that was all right. That felt good too.

For twelve entire seconds in 1957, while *On the Road* sat on the *New York Times* bestseller list for almost as long, once a week there'd be at least one letter waiting for him in his mailbox composed by a female lover of the arts offering to suck his cock until his mouth went dry or to let Jack fuck her until she didn't know her own name anymore. Some of the letters included pictures. Frequently the women were wearing clothes.

They stopped making fan mail like that around the same time the newspapers and the magazines started running recent photos with their articles and not the one on the back of *On the Road*. Today, for instance, bills, bills, and overdue bills, plus some human excuse to hang a pair of glasses around his neck by a silver chain and with an entirely unearned attitude of societal and spiritual alienation he'd picked up from some snivelling paperback translated poorly from the French sending Jack a form letter asking him if he would please consider contributing to a survey he was undertaking about authorial influences for the small literary magazine he co-edited. Actual letters from actual people that his work actually meant something to, these he welcomed and still answered, but more typical was the request he'd received a couple of months back from the Black Panther Party asking him, if he wasn't just another white liberal hypocrite, for a contribution, no matter how big or small, to help fund the revolution. Jack burned the letter and put the ashes in an envelope but was talked out of mailing it back by Joe.

I'm no liberal, Jack said. *I've been Republican since '32.*

You were ten years old in 1932. And you told me you've never voted for anything in your life.

I bet Ginsberg's behind this, I bet he's the one who gave them my address. The Jews and the blacks and the Communists have all got a shared interest in seeing this country driven to its knees. This country gave my Canuck family a break and I see no good reason to denigrate said country now.

Joe knew there was no point in being rational around the irrational. The only way to get Jack off a sour subject was to change it. Since becoming Jack's friend, Joe had become an expert in the logic of elusion.

What if they trace the letter back to you? Joe said. *Think about Mémère.*

Jack thought about his mother. *You might be right,* he said, tearing up the envelope.

At least this request was only informational. Even if no one asked you what your literary influences were unless no one read you anymore. They don't keep cats and dogs in the zoo, only animals that are beginning to disappear. When the doctoral students started moving in, he'd know for sure he was American History.

Sure he'd drop the guy a line. The $125 reconditioned Smith-Corona typewriter he'd just bought but couldn't really afford needed something to do. Just because you were sick to your soul of writing didn't mean you weren't still a writer. A soldier who gets his leg shot off can still feel his leg.

"Books as influences you mean, I s'pose. — Early on books, let's see, *Catechism* (in French), *Holy Bible* (also in French), *The Little Shepherd of Kingdom Come*, *The Bobbsey Twins*, *Rebecca of Sunnybrook Farm*, plus don't forget *Shadow* magazine and *Phantom Detective* magazine and *Street and Smith's Star Western Magazine*, third-eye eye teeth cut on all of these. — Big boy reading that affected me most, Saroyan, Hemingway, Wolfe, Wolfe especially, waking me up to America itself as the ultimate narrative subject. — Words only go paper-cut deep tho, body and soul where the real divine directions get issued from. — So. — Introduced to natural storytelling by my mother, kitchen-table stories about Montreal and New Hampshire and our ancient Breton forbears — Jazz, too, the raciness and freedom and humour of music as opposed to all that dreary analytical nonsense they use with which to teach schoolchildren to hate literature. — And Cassady, Neal Cassady maybe most of all, not just the long, long (sometimes 40,000 words, no exaggeration) letters he'd write me describing, say, a single sad afternoon in a Denver hotel room, describing every single tragic detail, just like old

Dostoevsky, but also just listening to him talk his talk and all of a sudden realizing that of course that was the way to tell a story, just by telling it, no stopping, just keep going, you yourself the teller of the tale getting excited in the very act of telling, even Neal's slippery rhythm testifying to this, that Okie rhythm, that 'Now look here, me boy, I'm gonna tell you something now, something you gotta understand, so lissen closely to me now' rhythm that says there's a flesh-and-blood body on the other side of the book telling the story and not just a bunch of nouns and verbs and adjectives held together under house arrest by a bully bunch of rules of composition some mastermind mammon cooked up to keep everybody talking and thinking and living the exact same way. — Because ask yourself this, Mac: Were we born and do we suffer and do we die just so we can all sound the same? — What a spit in God's eye, that.

"All of this all about *how* though, not a word yet about *why*, the very reason there's a *how* in the first place. — Why? Because I love the world (I still love the world) and supplication is what lovers do.

"Sincerely,

"Jack Kerouac"

He removed the piece of paper from the typewriter, placed it face upward on his desk.

I do, he thought.

He read over the last line.

I really do.

Skin on skin was as good as advertised, everything all the songs said it was and then some. Seventeen years old and with my hand slid underneath Stacey Larmner's T-shirt, five self-determining fingers magneting across her hard white chest in search of whichever breast they managed to cling to first, not a question of whether or not this was what they called heaven but of how long I'd be allowed to hang around and what I needed to do to get some celestial more. The uninterrupted torture of adolescent horniness — basement couch bliss always *Just a little further, baby, just a little bit more* away.

Most of the time we spent together we spent together studying, usually at Stacey's house. I'd never studied with anyone before — studying as anything more than attempting to memorize a half semester's worth of half-assed notes the night before the big exam was still a novel concept to me — but to be a page in the House of Commons, just being an honours student wasn't enough, all of your grades had to be in the nineties. Even then, a strong scholastic record was important but not sufficient. It was also, Stacey explained, essential that she have a rich and varied resumé by the time she graduated, which was why she'd joined the re-election campaign of our Progressive Conservative Member of Parliament: she was hoping that the honourable member from Chatham–Kent would write her a nice letter of recommendation for her page application package. (When the time came, though, she said, swearing me to secrecy, she was going to vote Liberal.) It was also why she'd volunteered to become a Big Sister to a Native girl who'd lost both of her parents to drug overdoses. Being a Big Sister was important because Stacey really needed something substantial that was community oriented to beef up her resumé, but it wasn't easy. Sometimes we'd talk on the telephone after she'd gotten home from her weekly appointment.

My God, she's so depressing. I try to get her to talk, I do, but all she ever says is "I don't know," "I guess so," "Maybe." I mean, I know she's had a hard life, but c'mon, make an effort, at least try *to be happy.*

Stacey wasn't all academics all the time, though, she was a high achiever in other ways too. She had an older sister studying art history at Western and a brother who was in med school at McGill, and each of them made and mailed her cassette tapes of the music they were listening to at school, stuff that made Stacey the first person in Chatham who'd ever heard most of it. Most of it was gauzy-sounding, heavily synthesized stuff with stiff rhythms and emotionless vocals that didn't make me excited about being the second person in Chatham who'd ever heard of it. She'd play hand-labelled tape after tape while we'd study across from each other at the kitchen table or read together on the couch downstairs. I never asked her to change a tape because I didn't want to look like the kind of person who couldn't appreciate what university students listened to. Sometimes it was hard to concentrate, though, especially if I was studying calculus or chemistry, subjects that didn't make a whole lot of sense even when the room was quiet.

They're called Kraftwerk, she said. *They're from Germany.*

I nodded, watched the wheels of the tape turning around inside the cassette player, the black Maxell tape slowly spooling to the right.

It's meant to be this way, she said. *It's meant to be repetitive.*

It sounded like what it sounded like inside the factory where my father worked.

When I was thirteen, the company held an open house for the families of all the workers. I'd only known what Ontario Steel looked like from the outside. The company tried to make it as pleasant inside the factory as possible — free cans of pop chilling inside green plastic garbage pails full of ice, complimentary key chains and bottle openers with the company's name stamped on them handed out at every entrance — but they couldn't do much about the noise or the heat. Ontario Steel made automobile parts, car bumpers mostly, and there were several different machines of several different sizes and shapes blasting away doing all sorts of different jobs. No matter the machine, though, and no matter where you went in the factory, the slamming of metal to metal, the pounding of steel into steel, the crashing of iron onto iron. Each individual machine had its own smashing rhythm, but after a while it all began to sound like the same enormous engine, as if all of its different components had synchronized their individual clanking to create some sort of ear-stabbing, incomprehensible beat. Combined with the heat generated by the machines — the machines never stopped, the factory never shut down — it felt like we were taking a guided tour of hell as brought to you by the good people at Ontario Steel, the soundtrack to tonight's journey through miserable eternity provided by Satan's Heaviest Metal Orchestra.

It's supposed to reflect the dehumanizing nature of modern society, Stacey said.

I nodded again, stared down at my calculus textbook. Why would anyone want to listen to what it felt like to be dehumanized? I thought. Stacey's dad was an architect. I bet it didn't sound like Kraftwerk where he worked.

I tried to concentrate, looked harder at the numbers and the symbols in my book, but they still didn't make much sense. I pulled the small red notebook, the one I'd started carrying around with me since I'd read that that was what Kerouac had done, out of my bag on the floor. I'd replaced my Adidas gym bag with a tan canvas over-the-shoulder army bag that I'd gotten at the Salvation Army, the same kind that *Jack's Book* said that the characters in Kerouac's novel *The Dharma Bums* carried around.

I opened up my notebook and wrote down the date; pressed my pen to the lined page; waited. I wanted to say something. I wrote down the word *The* and then crossed it out. I wanted to have something to say.

Stacey stood up from her chair and came over and sat down on my lap, took my pen out of my hand and shut my notebook. She pulled up her shirt and directed a breast into my mouth. Stacey was also way ahead of all the other girls at our school at not wearing a bra. Her mother, who was a councillor for Chatham–Kent Mental Health and who had a master's degree in sociology, rarely wore a bra either.

I sucked and licked and sucked until she decided it was time I paid attention to the other one. When I'd finished with it and went back for seconds at the first, she got up from my lap and pulled down her shirt.

That's enough for now, she said, sitting back down. *I just needed a little pick-me-up. I really need to ace this test on Friday and I felt like I was going to fall asleep.* She clicked on her calculator and started punching in numbers.

I'd forgotten we had a test on Friday. I thought about pulling my textbook back out of my bag, but opened up my notebook instead. There was something I wanted to say, I thought, something I wanted to remember.

I traced the date that I'd already written. I pressed my pen to the lined page. I waited.

He made them take it. He made the sonofabitches take it.

It took five years of *No, thank yous*, of *I'm sorry to have to tell yous*, of *I'm afraid this isn't quite what we're looking fors*, but he finally made them take it. He signed the contract for the publication of *On the Road* at Viking's New York office on 118th Street on January 11, 1957. He'd done what he'd wanted to do and he'd done it like he'd wanted to do it and he made the sonofabitches take it.

The hard part was over now. All he had to do now was write.

And wait until they saw the sequel he was planning, the sequel to *On the Road*. He was going to call it *What Happened Later*. What a story that was going to be.

I pushed away my physics textbook, an unsatisfactory meal unfinished.

Alvin and I had abandoned his kitchen table for the living room coffee table, hoping for a little change-is-as-good-as-a-rest lift. Everywhere around us was delicate antique furniture and wick-lit glass lanterns and a harpsichord that took up the middle of the room. No one in Alvin's family could play, not even Alvin's father who'd bought it at some shop in Windsor, but it fit the feel of the room.

I picked up the paperback Alvin was carrying around with him these days, Anton LaVey's *The Satanic Bible*; flipped. *Don't you need to believe in God to be a Satanist?* I said.

Alvin put the finishing flourish on the careful figuring he'd been working on in his binder. He'd moved from the problem in the textbook to its neatly printed solution on the page before I'd had time to understand what was being asked.

I don't know, I don't think so. I haven't read all of it yet.

The inevitable bookmark stuck inside whichever paper-

back Alvin had borrowed from his father's shelves seldom
inched past the quarter-way mark. Because he wanted to
be an optometrist, Alvin had to study all the time, had to be
especially good at all of the courses where there was only one
right answer and you always had to show your work. I was
discouraged before I even picked up my pencil. Ten minutes
of intense calculation to come up with sometimes only a
single lonely digit seemed like pretty lousy odds. Even if you
knew what you were doing, just one botched line of simple
division, just once mistaking something squared for something cubed, and you were screwed. We didn't call them
questions anymore; now we called them *problems.*

I read aloud from Anton's new and improved holy book.

*"Open your eyes that you may see, Oh men of mildewed
minds, and listen to me ye bewildered millions!"*

Mildewed minds, I said. *That's not bad.*

I looked at the cover. Most of Mr. Samson's library was
composed of paperbacks circa the late 1960s, most of which,
regardless of whether a novel, an autobiography, or a hand-
book to Lucifer-assisted hedonism, had a half-dressed woman
on the front, usually in a miniskirt, and with an attractive yet
slightly menacing older man looming over her. *The Satanic
Bible* wasn't any different. A distinguished-looking silver-
haired gentleman in an expertly tailored black suit holding
a martini in one hand and a thick black book in the other—
Satan enjoying cocktail hour, apparently, just back from
Black Mass and goddamn thirsty—leered, mouth to ear, at a

very young blonde girl perched cross-legged on a high silver stool and attired in a black miniskirt and matching black bra and white stockings and black heels. Satan, it turned out, was a swinger.

"For I stand forth to challenge the wisdom of the world; to interrogate the laws of man and of God!"

That makes sense, I said. It was basically the same as what Jack said: Above all else, burn, burn, burn.

What did you get for 4a? Alvin said.

I haven't gotten there yet.

Alvin looked up from his textbook. *Do you want me to help you?*

It's okay, I said, shutting my own copy. *I should get going. I've got a ton of history to read before I go to bed.*

Plus, I was supposed to call Stacey at ten. Not before ten, not after ten, but ten. At ten she would have finished her own studying for the night but not yet sat down in front of the House of Commons proceedings on the French public television station. She didn't tune in for the politics but for the language practice. *I want my French to be so good by the time I'm a page that I'll be dreaming in French,* she'd said. She never mentioned what in French she wanted to be dreaming about.

Alvin slowly started packing up his books. *I wish that's what I had to do. I've got at least another hour of this and then probably two more of biology.*

Only to someone carrying an all-science full course load

would the prospect of studying the rise and fall of the Canadian fur trade sound appealing. Although at least in history and English class there weren't too many unconditional answers. When people and what they got up to were your only data, there was a lot of latitude when it came to what was considered right and wrong.

Don't forget this, I said, handing him *The Satanic Bible*. He stuck it in his back pocket.

I wish I had more time to read the things I want to read, Alvin said.

You will. That's why you're busting your balls now. Just wait until you're out of high school. You'll be free then. Whatever you want to do then, you'll be able to do. That's what Stacey kept telling me whenever I wanted to make out or listen to music or do anything else but study.

Alvin nodded, didn't seem convinced.

Who's downstairs? I said. What bodies were on display in the visiting room of the funeral home downstairs, I meant.

A woman. And a man, I think.

Old? I said. I'd seen enough dead bodies at Alvin's by now that shrivelled senior citizens didn't warrant the walk downstairs.

Yeah.

I picked up the album jacket belonging to the record playing on the turntable, *Tales of Mystery and Imagination* by the Alan Parsons Project. I'd mentioned to Alvin that the Doors had taken their name from Aldous Huxley's book *The*

Doors of Perception, and he'd taken off the perfectly fine Neil Young album we'd been listening to and replaced it with Alan Parsons.

It's based on the work of Edgar Allan Poe, he'd said. *His stories and poems. I think you might find it interesting.*

I'd felt like I was going to fall asleep. Somehow it managed to bore me and piss me off at the same time. This must be what it's like to have to suffer through church, I'd thought.

I guess I'm going to go, then, I said.

The woman's a nun, Alvin said.

What woman?

The woman downstairs.

You mean there's a nun down there?

Alvin nodded. *She came in yesterday. My dad actually finished with her just before my parents went out tonight. The visitation is tomorrow.*

Why an old dead woman who was a nun was interesting and an old dead woman who wasn't a nun wasn't, I didn't know. But she was. *Can we check it out?* I said.

Let's go.

Alvin's dad was the mortician, but it was his mother who was always on him about bringing friends downstairs. What if someone walking by on the street saw them, what if one of his friends tracked mud on the carpet, what if, what if, what if?

My mom was good that way. If I'd asked, she probably did mind that I would spend the money she'd trust me with for new clothes on Salvation Army-bought, second-hand blue jeans and old work shirts like the ones Jack wore in the pictures in *Jack's Book* and keep whatever was left over for albums and beer. It probably did make her uncomfortable that the Doors' "The End" was my usual morning aural pick-me-up, to be played the way Jim would have wanted, as loud as my cheap speakers would allow. She probably would have preferred that Alvin didn't carry his copy of *The Satanic Bible* with him when he'd come to pick me up. But probably because she was scraping dirty hospital cafeteria trays and washing dishes and mopping kitchen floors when she was fourteen instead of passing notes back and forth with her girlfriends at the back of math class about which cute guy she was hoping would ask her to go rocking around the clock on Friday night, I got handed just about all the adolescent slack I knew what to do with, had a homegrown head start at acting out black-cat Anton's numero uno instruction for all-around immoralism, *Do What Thou Will*. Nihilism begins at home.

Alvin led the way, clicking on a succession of table lamps. By the time the entire downstairs was alight, we stopped at one of the entrances and read the sign. SISTER PATRICIA MCCABE. We padded across the thick rug in our stocking feet. As a concession to Alvin's mother, we'd taken off our shoes. We stepped up to the coffin.

Cancer, Alvin said his dad had said, and she looked it. Her face had been whittled away to nearly head-shrinker size, her heavily white-powdered skin stretched drum tight across the sharp bones of her face, her thin, unpainted lips lemon-sucking pursed like she didn't approve one bit of finding herself dead.

I've never understood, I said, *why it is that Christians, who are always going on and on about how wonderful heaven is going to be, end up being just as sad as everybody else when somebody dies.*

Worse, Alvin said. *We had a Baptist funeral here last year and you wouldn't have believed it. I could hear people crying and moaning all the way upstairs, even with my stereo on. And then at the end, when they all sang, every song was about how happy they were that the person who'd died was going to meet Jesus.* Alvin traced a finger over the mass of rosaries wrapped around the nun's bony linked hands. *They were pretty good singers, though.*

Do you think she really believed she was going to heaven? I said. *I mean* really *believed, like even when she was probably in torture because of the cancer?*

She was *a nun.*

I guess.

I know what you mean, though. I mean, how could any sane human being believe that crap?

Given what he'd had to work with, Alvin's dad had done a good job. Except for two long black nose hairs sprouting out of the nun's right nostril, a great job. Someone should trim those, I thought.

Actually, it bugs me, you know? Alvin said.

What does?

Well, say she really did believe in heaven, had perfect faith right up until her last breath.

So?

So, she never had to face the fact she was going to end up as a hollowed-out corpse someday. We're the ones who know the truth, and we end up getting punished for it.

I never thought of it that way.

For someone who had such bad taste in music and who was going to end up as an optometrist, Alvin was all right. Living on top of a funeral home his entire life made up for a lot.

If she was so sure she was getting her wings one day, Alvin said, *then I bet it wouldn't bother her if she took this along for the ride.* He reached into his back pocket and pulled out his copy of *The Satanic Bible.*

What if somebody found out, though? I said. *Your dad would lose his job. Your mom would kill you.*

Who would find out? We could stick it underneath all those robes and nobody would be able to tell.

How could you be sure?

No one's going to start feeling around underneath her robe. She's already been embalmed and laid out. And after the funeral the day after tomorrow, she goes right to the cemetery.

We both looked down at the nun. Her mouth seemed even more scowlingly scrunched than before, like she knew what we were contemplating. Her fingers seemed grasped even tighter around her rosary. Each of us waited for the other one to say something.

Finally, *It's your only copy, though,* I said.

That's true.

It would kind of be a waste. In a way.

It's my dad's copy, too. What if he went to look for it?

And it's a neat copy. It's probably pretty rare. You probably can't even buy a copy like that anymore.

Without saying anything else we turned around and left the same way we came in, Alvin shutting off every light he'd clicked on until the funeral home was dark again and we were safely on our way back upstairs.

Milarepa. Mill-ah-rep-ah. A Tibetan monk, ninth century AD. Think about that. Stop looking at that fucking blonde and think about that. All there is to know and therefore to say, he said— Who said? Milarepa said. That's what I said— eleven centuries ago. Don't take my word for it, though, don't take anyone's word for anything anyway anywhere. That's what my father always said. Actually, my father never said any such thing. But that's exactly the sort of thing my father would have said, and if this was a novel I was writing instead of a simple conversation I was having with a new friend, that's just what I would have him say. If you're writing a novel, you see, you put in just enough facts to make what you're writing true. Facts are necessary, but they're not sufficient. That's a logical truism. An ontological nudism. An epistemological boohooism. But logic, that's not my job—that's Joe over there's job, he's the one who got straight As and has a Phi Beta so-and-so to prove it. Hello over there, Joe. Wave at Joe. Joe is a very lonely man but he bears his burden bravely, nobly even. Instead of picking at his scabby soul like I do, he worries whether his buddy Jack's shoelaces are tied and that he's got a clean hanky in his pocket and that there's milk not cream for the morning coffee. Ah, Joe, he's . . . Joe, Joe . . . Joe's the big brother I never had. Up your ass with Mobil gas, I'll cry if I want to. A man can cry for the selfless love of another man's love, why not? And fuck anyone who says fucking otherwise. Although I did have a big brother once. Gerard was my big brother, but Gerard died when I was four and he was eight, and the nuns, they swore he smelled of fresh rose petals the entire time he lay in his casket. Gerard taught me kindness and charity and forgiveness. Old Joe over there—ah, see, he's shy, he's lighting that broad's cigarette and pretending he doesn't hear me talking about him—Joe has taught me to always keep my hotel key on my key chain and that knowing where the North Star is at all times is as good a way to keep from getting lost as any and that every time you want to hear a song on your tape machine it's always on the other end of the tape, always. But even though my father never read Milarepa, he knew a few things too. Don't fool yourself: just because a man never sat meditating in the Himalayan snow or achieved silky nirvana on a mountaintop doesn't mean he didn't take good care of his family or wake up one day and wonder what the hell happened to his life or have sad thoughts about what's going to happen to all of us, the forgone rags of tattered time. There's tragedy in a chipped coffee cup and in six brand new alarm clocks and at sixteen minutes after midnight on one more New Year's Eve. Hey, that's a haiku, an American haiku, forget seventeen syllables, three-lined American Pops will do: Chipped coffee cup / Six brand new alarm clocks / Sixteen minutes past one more New Year's Eve. Meaning: if you're not an appreciator of modern verse — entirely under-standable given the ingrown-toenail and pin-the-tail-on-the-literary-influence essence of mid-twentieth-century Western prosody (remember, though, love of poetry is simply simple love of joy) — it's best to stay at home like I do in sweet, sweet Lowell along the Merrimack under tragic New England skies and dripping autumn trees and have homemade Sunday roasts and gentle moderate tippling and build a fenced-in yard for quiet outdoor reading and take care of your mother and of your cats and patiently and piously wait for what's going to happen next, la fin du monde, la fin du monde. But today I guess it's wrong for a son to take care of his widowed mother just because a bunch of bearded libertine Freuded-up pansies say it's psychologically abnormal for a grown man to live with his aging mother who only gave birth to him and supported him his entire life long and now only expects a little of that selfsame compassion. I guess that makes me abnormal, then. I guess Milarepa and I better get ourselves analyzed and get good and normal so we can hate our parents and hate our gov-ernment and get good book reviews in the Washington Post Book World *like all those amazing artists of prose like Edwin O'Connor and John O'Hara and Herbert Gold. Well, you know what old Milarepa would say about that? Let me finish that, you're not going to finish that, let me finish that and I'll tell you what old Milarepa would say. Okay, here's what Milarepa would say, has said, what I'm saying right now he said I say: "Though you youngsters of the new generation dwell in towns infested with deceitful fate, the link of truth still remains. When you remain in solitude, do not think of the amusements in the town. You should turn your mind inwardly, and then you'll find your way. The wealth I found is inexhaustible holy property. The companion I found is the bliss of perpetual voidness. Oh you innumerable beings, by the force of imaginary destiny you see a myriad of visions and experience endless emotions. I smile. To a Yogi, everything is fine and splendid. In the goodly quiet of this sky enclosure, I, Milarepa, happily remain, meditating upon the void-illuminating mind. The more ups and downs the more Joy I feel. The greater the fear, the greater the happiness I feel."* Ninth century AD, Mac. Ninth fucking century AD.

Jack said.

Who he was talking to, which roadside bar he and Joe were sitting in, what town along the retreat from Rivière-du-Loup they were nearest to, it doesn't matter.

Jack said.

Jack said Jack said Jack said Jack said. He was as sick of hearing the sound of his own voice as everyone else. Sicker, actually. Everyone else could just stop listening. Meditation, boilermakers, medication—nothing, however, can kill the ego's stubborn echo, echo. Yes, Jesus tells us so, yeah, Milarepa says you can, but anything you've got to memorize and repeat to yourself ten times a day, you know you don't really believe.

Have you ever been to Montreal, Joe? The bar stools separating them were empty, the man who'd been sitting beside Jack and the woman whose cigarette Joe had lit were gone.

A couple of times, yeah.

Well, I have. And it's Canada's birthday, Canada is one hundred years old this year.

I wasn't aware of that.

We have to go to Montreal, Joe, we have to go to this thing, this Expo 67 thing they're having there.

Maybe we should start thinking about going home, Jack.

To Stink Town on the Merrimack? To where the only two bookstores in town don't even carry my two most recent books, books principally set in, and about, said Stink Town? To the-sow-that-eats-her-young Lowell? Tell me, Joe, how foolish would you feel when we got back there and you remembered how close we were to Montreal and we didn't go?

We're actually not that close.

That's what I'm saying, that's exactly what I'm saying. We've already come this far. We're already so close.

I'd never even known anyone who'd been to Toronto. Stacey had—had visited with her family when her father had accepted some award for some building he'd designed there—but she didn't count because she'd said she hated it.

What's wrong with it? I'd said.

What's right with it? It's flat, it's ugly, and the people there are incredibly boring.

How someone who'd only been somewhere once—when she was fifteen, with her parents, for a weekend—knew enough about it to dismiss its entire geography, architecture, and citizenship outright didn't make much sense, but I didn't say anything. What was I going to say? Not counting Niagara Falls and the Walt Tkaczuk Summer Hockey School in St. Catharines, I'd never been anywhere.

Montreal—that's a real city. After my year as a House of Commons page is over—if I get accepted, I mean—I'm going to transfer from Ottawa U to McGill. Montreal, it's so . . . it's hard to explain to someone who's never been there. You've never been to Montreal, have you, Ray?

No, I said. *I haven't.*

I had seen what Toronto looked like, though, and not just in books or as moving background in bad made-for-CBC movies about people full of big, big dreams who move there from Canada's east coast but who soon discover that everything that is good and pure and real in life is back home, back in good old Newfoundland, or good old Cape Breton, or good old P.E.I. Sometimes on Saturday nights I'd end up home and hungry from a party or from Stacey's house, and I'd make a sandwich out of whatever was left over from dinner and sit with it and a glass of milk in front of the television in the basement, my parents hours ago asleep upstairs. By the time I'd finished eating and being fed up with what was on TV, the channel would get clicked to channel 41 and I'd sink into the couch and hitch an eye ride around Toronto with the Night Rider.

Whether the actual taxi with a camera mounted to its dashboard that allowed you to follow it fare to fare, here to there, was called Night Rider or whether that was just the name of the program, I didn't know. There wasn't any dialogue, none — you never saw or heard the cab driver or anyone getting in or out of the cab, never heard any narrating voice telling you what you were looking at or why — only late night light jazz that started when the trip began and faded out when it was over. All there was was the ride.

The taxi would trawl tree-shadowed empty avenues, stop and start in headlight-to-bumper traffic, follow the labyrinth of nameless Toronto street after nameless Toronto street, just like I imagined Sal and Dean doing, eating up the highway and swallowing down the miles and storing up the stories that made up *On the Road*. The camera always stayed steady on the road ahead, but you could see sideways glimpses of what else was out there. Viny brick buildings and shiny new business towers and neon-alive storefronts; expensive homes and low-income apartments and nothing like my parents' ranch-style split-level; and men and women white and black and colours I wasn't sure what coming and going but most of all just being there.

It was hard to tell whom the show was intended for. Midnight stoners, maybe, happy just to have a glowing TV flow to follow along with and slowly fade to test pattern to. Even though the station was in Toronto, it was hard to believe that anyone who wasn't from somewhere else would bother watching it. Who lives somewhere all day and then sits down in front of their television set at night to look at it? And it was dark, probably too dark to be worth waiting around to see something you wouldn't mind seeing again.

But the darkness was all right with me. Places, people, the future: everything looks better in the dark. What isn't there you don't know isn't there. Not yet. Who can not fall in love with a city in the dark?

He hated the sun. He hated the heat. Heat when it was supposed to be hot was bad enough — nothing like Florida summer heat, like sleepwalking through endless rooms of steamy fog — but the entire dumb-dumb citrus state of Fla. that was still a swamp in September was an affront, a personal insult, just one more way the contaminating world was always conspiring to keep him from being leave-me-alone Ti Jean happy.

Who cared if to most of his wrinkled neighbours in Orlando and later St. Petersburg it was normal never to have known spirit-waking September fresh mornings, October stirring breezes, solemn November winds? Seasons were to places what souls were to people. If sunshine all the time, then spring's (finally) sweet relief neutered to nothing, is just another season of purgatory blue skies. And how could it possibly be Christmas when it was seventy-two degrees outside and an orange tree in the leather-skinned guy next door's backyard was topped with a silver star that was somehow supposed to be . . . what? Apposite? Ironic? Funny? Nothing funny about New England winters. First lesson every New England schoolchild learns: something bigger than you exists. Give winter its due or die.

But Mémère wanted to live down here. No matter where the two of them called home—Long Island, Northport, Hyannis, back in Lowell—Mémère always wanted to move, always wanted to live down here. At first, she said, because she was so lonely, especially when Jack went away, she wanted to be near her daughter and her only grandchild. Later, because the New York and New England winters were, she complained, so hard on her arthritis, knotty-knuckled souvenirs of all those years working in the shoe factory. In the end—a stroke-stricken semi-invalid—because she demanded it, because Jack, *tabarnac*, he owed it to her.

Writing to friends, Jack, drunk—drunk by himself, alone and drunk at his desk—would lament having to leave behind long afternoon northern shadows and melancholic Atlantic skies and to dread the impending fluorescent Florida broil. Did have to admit, though, it would be nice to get a fresh start and be free of all the sycophants and troublemakers who forced him to drink too much and make a fool of himself and not let him be the kind of man he wanted to be.

Trouble was, though—and it really was the oddest thing— these pests seemed to breed everywhere he went. Everywhere. Without exception. How odd.

Stacey's brother and sister were both at university, Jamie's older sister too — was supposed to graduate from Queen's the same year, next year, that we went into grade thirteen, our final year of high school. Even Jamie's deaf brother Gordon was going away. Gordon even already knew where he'd be attending, some deaf college in Washington, D.C., that was the same as a regular university except that everyone who went there was hearing-impaired, even the teachers. If I'd had an older brother or sister or been born deaf I might have known what I was going to do with my life too.

CCI's guidance counsellor, Mr. Harnett, tried to help me find my way. Stacey was the only person I knew who voluntarily visited the guidance office — it was where all the different school calendars from all the different universities were kept, all in a row in alphabetical order along one of the office walls, shiny glossy with pictures of happy young people grinning up at you from their covers — but most everyone else went and saw Mr. Harnett only twice: once at the beginning of grade twelve for a career evaluation, and once just before Christmas of the following year to go over the paperwork involved in applying to wherever you were applying to. Before you showed up the first time you had to fill out a questionnaire listing your life goals and personal interests. When you sat down across from Mr. Harnett in his small office, though, he had the most important piece of information about you — a yellow file folder containing all of your grades since grade nine — opened up on his desk in front of him.

Mr. Harnett glanced up from my transcript and overtop of the black reading glasses resting on the tip of his nose long enough to open-palm me a seat in front of his desk; looked back down and held up a plump, hairy finger to let me know he wasn't quite finished studying my file.

Mr. Harnett was short and square and with a Brylcreem comb-over and raspberry red razor burn covering his entire neck. It was uncomfortable just to look at his neck. It looked like he'd tried to shave himself that morning with a butter knife and a bar of old soap. He finally dropped his finger from the air; pushed his reading glasses halfway up his nose in an attempt at putting a face to the rows of mostly Bs and Cs he'd just finished going over.

Ray Robertson, he said, as if he thought if he spoke my name aloud he might be able to remember it.

That's my name, I felt like saying, don't wear it out. I smiled, nodded — twice, contemplatively, I hoped — instead.

Mr. Harnett nodded slowly twice himself. He smiled like he wanted to sell me something I didn't need.

Philosophy, he said.

It was what I'd written down under Career Interest(s).

Ever since *Why I Am Not a Christian*, I'd wanted to be Bertrand Russell. Sitting around thinking about things all day seemed like a pretty decent job description to me.

My daughter, who's attending Trinity College, University of Toronto, as a freshman, is taking a philosophy course herself this semester.

Oh really.

She'll be majoring in International Relations, but a course or two in philosophy is a fine thing, just as language courses are an excellent way of fulfilling one's breadth requirements.

Now it was my turn to nod again, even if I wasn't entirely sure why.

As a career objective, however, I'm not sure that's what you want to pursue.

I could get a Ph.D., I said. I'd read enough About the Author notes by now to know that people who wrote philosophy books tended to have initials after their names.

You could, Mr. Harnett said. *Did you hear the one about the philosophy graduate? He had a B.A., an M.A., a Ph.D., but no J.O.B.*

This time he smiled for real. I knew it was for real because two long, thin bones on either side of his Adam's apple poked at his flesh, threatened to slice right through his neck. That and the razor burn were too much, I had to look away. I looked at one of the metal legs of his desk instead.

When I looked back up, Mr. Harnett wasn't smiling anymore. His glasses were back at the end of his nose and he traced his finger all the way down and then all the way back up my transcript like he was double-checking a dubious restaurant bill.

There's been a slight spike in your grades of late.

I've been working harder, I said.

To gain admission to a good graduate school—which you'd need to do to ultimately pursue a Ph.D.—it's important to have attended an equally impressive undergraduate program. I'm not sure that your grades—Mr. Harnett scanned my transcript one more time—*are strong enough to make that happen.*

But like you said, they've been going up. It turned out that smart people weren't really smart people, were just people like everybody else who happened to work harder at being smart. Who knew?

And let's hope they keep travelling in that direction, Mr. Harnett said, this time with the kind of smile that doctors on television used on grieving families when informing them that medical science has done all it can do and that everyone should just hope and pray now for the best. *Just keep in mind, however, that elite Canadian universities demand strong, strong academic records from their applicants. Trinity College, University of Toronto, for example, where my daughter is attending as a freshman, sets the bar at a minimum of 85 percent just to be considered for acceptance.*

But I heard that . . . I mean, someone told me that universities really only look at your grade thirteen marks, that if they're good enough you can go wherever you want.

Well, yes, that's essentially true, Mr. Harnett said, rubbing his chin. Jesus Christ, keep your hands above your neck, I thought, if you start touching your neck I don't think I'll be able to handle it. *But I think you owe it to yourself and your future to ask yourself this: do you really see yourself as an elite student by this time next year?*

I'm going to try, I said.

Certainly you're going to try . . .

My mother had always told me that if I did my best, if I tried as hard as I could, that that would always be good enough. My mother also said that I was handsome. What the hell else had she been lying about?

So keep doing the best you can, keep reaching for the stars. But in the meantime — by the clickity-clack of his boot heels Mr. Harnett propelled himself and his rolling desk chair across his office floor to his filing cabinet; opened a middle file drawer, stuck his hand in without looking at what he was grabbing, and clickity-clacked back behind his desk — *have at look at these.* He handed me three slim pamphlets.

They were glossy gleamy like the university calendars along the wall in the other room, but looked more like the leaflets stacked on the receptionist's desk at the dentist's office that outlined the importance of daily flossing and the different kinds of gum diseases to be aware of. Each brochure was from a different college — Mohawk, Fanshawe, St. Clair — but each outlined each respective school's program in Hotel and Restaurant Management.

Mr. Harnett was leaning back in his swivel chair now, feet up on his desk, one foot crossed over the other. His boots were black leather and ankle high and had silver zippers on the sides. They looked as if he'd slipped them on for a sock hop twenty-five years before and forgotten to take them off. He held his reading glasses in his right hand, sucked on the end of one of the arms.

You're a people person, he said. *I can tell just by the little talk we've had here today. And I'll tell you something else.* He removed the arm of his glasses from his mouth and pointed at me with it. *I have no difficulty whatsoever imagining you occupying a very important position in one aspect or another of the service industry. I'm talking suit and tie here, hiring and firing, the top of the pyramid. And here's the part I like best about getting a college diploma: you're in and out in a year, two years tops, and then you're right there in the workplace, ready to really start raking in the big bucks.*

If I got to wear a name tag, it wouldn't be all that different from working at Sears. A tie, a name tag, and people who hadn't gone to Mohawk College who'd have to call me Mr. Robertson. My mother would be so proud.

Jack never went in for any of that revolution shit. Even back in the dawn of days, kneeling and praying before sitting down to write (stealing the idea from a French movie he saw in Times Square about Handel), working by candlelight and blowing it out when done for the night, sacrificing a drop of fingertip-pricked blood to where he left off on the last page (until Burroughs dropped by one night and saw what he'd done and said, *My God, Jack, stop this nonsense and let's go get a drink*), it was all only part of his very own self-devised self-ultimacy program, oak-grown artiness entirely forgivable because born of teenage-notebook art-for-art's-sake daydream acorns. Salvationist at its core, though. Like Dostoevsky's holy sinners and saved sufferers. Like a mismouthed prayer.

Even the universities were in the social revolution business now. When Brandeis University invited him to participate in a forum entitled "Is There a Beat Generation?" Jack agreed because it was a chance to respond to some of his less evolved critics, to set the record straight, to make plain his point of view. It was only a little over a year since *On the*

Road had been published, and Jack was still news. Besides, fresh fame was sort of fun—a microphone; a full auditorium; a $200 honorarium. Jack carefully typed up an essay in his Long Island bedroom called "The Origins of the Beat Generation" and took it with him on the subway into the city. A few tables full of drinks later at the Kettle of Fish with Ginsberg and various New York friendlies and he was seated onstage beside the three other panellists. The usual red checkered shirt, black jeans, and ankle boots he wore weren't the only reason he didn't fit in.

Jack leapt to the podium and sang the essay he thought the organizers wanted and knew for sure that the world needed, a twelve-and-a-half-minute sermon on the essential beatitude of Beatness that was, in fact, founding-fathered by old-time America's (his own father's generation's straw-hatted, house-party-throwing, new-immigrant-thankful America's) half-buried wild glee and beautiful naivety and self-believing individuality. And if holy men were what you were aching to bow before, genuflect if you must before such saints of high holy goofiness as Harpo Marx and Krazy Kat and Lester Young and the Three Stooges. But most of all, remember yes yes yes, holy holy holy, all all all. The crucifix AND the Star of Israel. Mohammed AND the Buddha. The soul's gloriously soaring futility AND the body's sweetly rotting flesh. And gentle pity for all those who would spit on the children of the Beat Generation—the wind, as we all know, always blows it back.

Boos and cheers, but at least everyone was awake.

Uh, thank you, Mr. Kerouac. I think. More boos and cheers.

The sociology professor, the newspaper editor, the visiting British novelist—each yea'd or nay'd his respective respectable verdict in grammatically correct sentences before just as efficiently reclaiming his seat onstage. Polite applause, of course, after each, and forty-seven wristwatches covertly consulted when this thing would be finally over. And the moderator addressed carefully considered questions to the assembled guests who stroked their chins and crossed their legs and answered appropriately moderately.

Oh, no, though, Jack thought, this wouldn't do at all. We need needle and thread. We need form and content. We need declaration and deed. Otherwise, it's all just words. And words, words, words, as the great Dane once said, ain't worth a hill of beans. Less, actually: at least you can write a hymn about a hill of beans.

So, while the sociologist drearied and the newspaper journalist germalized and the visiting British novelist erudited, Jack tipsied around the stage making funny faces at the audience and tickling the out-of-tune piano at the back of the stage. And when the sociologist simply wouldn't stop talking, Jack grabbed his hat off his head and stuck it on his own head, perched in his seat and crossed his arms across his chest and frowned just like the sociologist, and everyone— even the other panellists and the moderator, even the people who'd booed him before—laughed, all except for the sociologist who squawked, *Give me back my hat!*

And Jack did. And the sociologist put it back on. And that was the end of tonight's lecture. And everyone will be tested. It may not be tomorrow, it may not be next week, it may not even be this year or the next, but everyone will be tested.

Afterward, back at the Kettle of Fish, happy boozing and backslapping joy and Ginsberg leaned across the beery table and pushed his glasses up his nose and shouted over the noise, *Look, Jack, we've done all this, we've made great literature. Why don't we do something really great now and take over the world?*

Grabbing Jack's sleeve, leaning in closer, *Yeah! And I'll be your henchman!* Corso yelled.

Jack laughed, drank, snorted, smiled, sighed, shrugged, slouched in the booth.

Ah, I just want to be Cervantes alone by moonlight, he said.

But, Jack, listen to me, we—

I just want to be Cervantes alone by moonlight.

Class dismissed.

Something something Susanna Moodie something something Margaret Atwood something something who we are as a country something something.

Everyone else was on page 578 of the *Oxford Book of Canadian Literature*, but I was two hundred pages behind the times, had my copy opened up to a selection of poems by Leonard Cohen. I liked the one about New Year's Eve and the hat-check girl who had syphilis and how the band was a sham, were all Nazis, and how the narrator had lip cancer but was going to put his paper hat on top of his concussion anyway. I had no idea what it meant, but it made sense.

Any comments or observations, Ray?

I looked up to Mrs. Ross and the rest of the class looking at me, waiting for my input into today's topic. I didn't flip forward to the proper page in the textbook, that would have only made things worse. I didn't have time to lie.

It seems kind of boring, I said.

A couple of laughs from the back of the room, but only because it was obvious I was too dim to realize that that was what literature was supposed to be, hadn't I been paying attention all year, didn't I know anything about art?

I don't think Margaret Atwood would agree with you, Mrs. Ross said.

Of course she wouldn't, I thought. She was the one who wrote it, how would she know if she was boring or not?

Stacey raised her hand and asked a question about pioneer life in Canada and I was off the hook, went back to what I wanted to read. Her question sounded more intelligent than any answer I could have come up with, but I didn't care, I knew I wasn't crazy even if everyone acted like I was.

It was like in my biography of Jack, the part where he was speaking at some university colloquium thing about the Beat Generation and everybody else onstage was full of shit and everybody in the audience knew it but no one would admit it and no one said anything that made any sense about anything except for Jack. That was what it was like. That was just what it was like.

And now the sonofabitch was asleep.

Joe flipped on the radio for company, said hello to three consecutive screams of static, clicked it back off. Jack didn't move, a rumpled raincoat tossed into the corner of the front seat. He should be awake, Joe thought, it's his fault we're going the wrong way. They should have been travelling in the other direction, home.

Even if they were there, though, even if they had been home, Billy still wouldn't be there, Joe knew. He'd called Mrs. Johnson from the last gas station. *I'm sorry, Joe, I haven't seen him. If he's in Lowell, he hasn't come home yet. I'm sure I would have at least seen a light on. Try not to worry, I'm sure he's fine.*

If he should have been travelling with anyone to Montreal, it should have been with Billy. Taking a road trip together to Expo 67 was exactly the sort of thing fathers and sons did. If Billy came back before fall was over, Joe thought, if he agreed to re-enroll in high school and if he promised to keep his curfew, then Joe would make a deal with him, would promise to take him to Montreal and see Expo and . . .

If he came home. If he even just called, or dropped a line, or even just told someone to tell his dad that he was all right. If.

Jack had said the same thing that Mrs. Johnson had said—*Don't worry, Joe, kids today are street-smart, a lot smarter than we were. Billy's a good kid, he's a Chaput, he's got a good head on his shoulders, don't worry*—but Mémère was the only one who'd made him feel any better.

Oh, pauvre Joe, she'd said, hugging him to her heavy flesh, not letting him go, *pauvre Joe, pauvre Joe.*

Jack didn't understand, didn't have any children of his own—only a daughter by his first marriage who looked remarkably like him and had his last name. He'd gotten Ginsberg's lawyer brother Eugene to pro bono him an inconclusive paternity test and a bargain basement child support settlement, but still denied Jan was his daughter, claimed that her father was actually a Puerto Rican dishwasher from Brooklyn by the name of Rosario. With close friends like Joe he'd occasionally take out the snapshot of Jan he kept in his wallet and seem pleased when they'd comment how much the two of them looked alike. Carefully putting it away, *Not my kid, though,* he'd say.

The only time Joe had ever visibly lost his temper with Jack was when, sitting at the bar at the Pawtucketville Social Club, sadness and Scotch had combined to compel him to show Jack a picture from his own wallet, of Billy as a new-born being cradled by his exhausted but obviously ecstatic wife in her hospital bed. It was around the time that Billy had first disappeared.

Jack took a quick look, a longer drink. *Why do people keep insisting on bringing something into the world just so that it can die?* he said.

Joe took back his picture.

Returning it to his wallet, *You can be a real insensitive ass-hole sometimes, you know that, Kerouac?*

Jack slowly straightened up on his stool like he was physically readying to defend himself; just as slowly deflated, ending up precisely like he was before, hunched over the bar. Into his empty glass, *I always appreciated the fact that you always called me Jack, Joe, that you never called me Kerouac like everybody else. That was the first time you didn't call me Jack.*

An apology. Unbelievable. This selfish fucking prick thinks he deserves an apology. Digging for and finding and tossing a handful of bills on the bar, *You really don't get it, do you?* Joe said.

Joe, Jack said, calling out after him, *don't go away like that, don't go away angry, you don't want to do that.*

But Joe was gone.

Jack told himself he should go after him, that they should work through whatever was wrong now instead of letting it build up and become something worse, but when he looked back down, a fresh drink had appeared in front of him on the bar.

He sipped his Scotch and water, considered.

If it's not one thing, it's always something else, isn't it, Len? he said to the bartender behind the bar.

You got that right, Jack.

Jack took another drink. *Hey, Len.*

Yeah?

Take a look at this. Who does this kid in the picture remind you of?

My dad had been on strike before so we weren't worried, even when negotiations that had begun in the spring edged into the fall. The first time had been when we lived on Park Street and my dad paid Mrs. Ruskowski's teenage son Henry fifty cents an hour to take his place picketing outside the plant. All I knew was that my dad was there in the morning when I woke up for school and was still there in the afternoon when I got home and that he was never too tired to take shots on me in net out in the garage or to play a game of tabletop hockey after supper after I'd had my bath. It was like he was on summer vacation, only in the wintertime, and when it was all over a couple of weeks later I was disappointed. If he was there when I got home from school now, he smelled like he used to smell, sweat and steel and dirt, and sat slumped in his chair in front of the television after dinner with his eyelids only half open and my mom telling me to come into the kitchen with her while she did the dishes, Dad was tired.

The only way the most recent strike affected me was when I asked my parents if I could chuck my glasses and graduate to contact lenses. I couldn't imagine Jim Morrison inciting a riot from the stage wearing tight brown leather pants and a pair of horn-rims, or Jack Kerouac hitching a ride outside Memphis in the pouring rain and having to lower his thumb so he could wipe his glasses clean. The first step to being what you wanted to be was looking like it.

We don't have your dad's health insurance while he's on strike, my mom said. *We'll have to wait and see.*

They're only a hundred and fifty dollars, I checked, can't we just pay for them?

We don't know how long the strike's going to go on, we have to be careful with our money. Besides, you've already got nearly brand new glasses that we bought you in the spring. And I don't like the idea of you wearing those contact lenses anyway. Those things are made of glass, you know, you can cut your eyes up pretty good with those things.

They make them out of plastic now, Mom, I checked it out, they're totally safe.

I don't care. Mrs. Jackovac had those things and one of her eyes got all infected and she couldn't see out of it for a week. It's lucky she can still see.

That was because she had glass lenses, they make them with plastic now, I told you. I might have said more, might have shown her the pamphlet I'd gotten from the optometrist's office at the mall, but it wouldn't have made any difference.

By the end of August, my dad and the rest of the workers had learned that the company wasn't afraid to call the union's bluff. Nearly four months after he and the rest of the factory had walked out on strike, instead of caving in to the union's demands, it seemed as if the company was quite comfortable letting them stay exactly where they were. Worse: the *Chatham Daily News* ran a story saying that the company was happy letting the union hang itself because they planned on moving their entire operation to Mexico the next year anyway. All the strike was doing, the article said, was saving the company money. Some people thought it was only a bunch of BS planted by the company to get the workers to panic and agree to whatever they wanted. Some people, like my dad, weren't so sure. Of course the factory wasn't going anywhere—it'd been in Chatham for nearly forty years; my grandfather and a lot of my dad's friends' fathers had worked there too—but no one had ever seen a strike go on this long before.

I guess we'll all have to move to Mexico, someone said, and everyone sitting around the swimming pool laughed. Because of the strike there'd been more parties at Mr. Roundy's house than in any other summer I could remember. Most of my mom and dad's friends worked at the factory, and the ones who had in-ground swimming pools were the ones who usually hosted the parties. The pool was mostly for the kids, who'd only come out of the water to go to the bathroom and when the hot dogs and hamburgers were done on the barbecue. The grown-ups sat in lawn chairs around the swimming pool drinking beer and smoking cigarettes and talking and, especially as the afternoon turned into evening, laughing. I didn't go to too many pool parties anymore—whoever heard of a beatnik at a pool party? — but it was hot and humid and August and, besides, there was a picture of Jack in *Jack's Book* goofing off on the beach in Tangiers. I made a point, however, of not doing any diving or actual swimming, just floated by myself in the shallow end with my elbows hanging over the edge.

We're gonna have to get you one of them big Mexican hats, Kenny, so you don't burn your head, Mr. Roundy said. All of the adults always kidded my dad about not having much hair.

A sombrero! someone else shouted.

Hey?

A sombrero, that's the name of those big Mexican hats — we gotta get Kenny a sombrero.

My dad upended his bottle of Blue and sucked down the remaining suds, pulled it out of its white Styrofoam cooler and set it down beside his lawn chair with a glass-to-cement clink. *Hey,* he said, *the Lord only made a few perfect heads, the rest he covered with hair.*

Everyone had heard him say that joke a million times before, but everyone roared with laughter anyway. Somebody handed my dad another bottle of beer. He pushed it inside his cooler and twisted off the cap.

Daddy, watch this! Mr. Roundy's daughter, Laura, yelled from the diving board. Laura was fat and dumb and bossy because she had an in-ground swimming pool and got every new toy as soon as it was advertised on TV. Mr. Roundy called her Princess. Sometimes Mrs. Roundy would smile and say, *You wouldn't believe the way Keith spoils her, she's a real daddy's girl.*

Daddy, watch this! she yelled again, this time sounding like if he didn't immediately watch her she was going to start bawling.

I'm watching, Princess, Mr. Roundy said. Everyone stopped what they were doing and looked at her.

Laura carefully stepped up to the edge of the diving board. Made sure all of her ten fat toes were aligned perfectly with the board's end. Slowly put her hands together like she was getting ready to pray. Inched up and down three or four times trying to find the right rocking rhythm. And, finally, dived into the pool, absolutely no differently than anyone else ever did.

Laura swam to the side of the pool where all of the grown-ups were sitting, smoothed back her long brown hair from her fat face, kept afloat by holding on to the side with both hands.

Did you watch me, Daddy? she said.

You bet I did, Princess, Mr. Roundy said.

How did I do?

You were awesome, Princess, Mr. Roundy said. *You were really, really awesome.*

But how does the keeper of the flame, no matter how fading flickering, keep alive the spark that twenty thousand winds daily and nightly conspire to extinguish? Where does Dracula go when the world—vampire enemies and vampire friends alike—has sucked him nearly pintless bloodless? To whom does God pray?

Forget booze drugs women, A to Z all of it. Good for a good time and even okay to blot out a bad one, but never enough of any of it in any sort of chemical/carnal combination to refill the well, to reset the compass, to replenish the source. Only by the source returning to its source is hope restored. Only when the river flows back into the sea have you got even an even chance. Give that compass a good swift kick in its magnetic ass and go wherever that motherfucker says. Back. Go back. Back to the source.

When you talk and talk and talk and still no one hears a single word you say, go back to where the talking stops, go back to Bach, listen to all those choraled voices, that single flawless voice. No sound to listen to at all, in fact, only towering clean green pines and a pure hawk wind moving among them, gently moving them.

And after only about the millionth time of being kindly instructed by critics, editors, and even occasionally your own agent to please write right, to please write like everyone else writes, please—maddening common sense a knife slash across the soul—go back to the ones who first taught the saxophone to talk, back to Parker, Prez, Hawkins, Jacquet, and get blissfully assaulted by a melody blown the way *it* wants to be blown and not the way it says to be played on some piece of pushy sheet music. Put the needle back to the beginning of the record and shout along. Scat, I mean, scat. Shout.

And when, after being at the typewriter so long, the sound of your own voice in your head an accusation—has started to sound like every exam you ever cheated on in high school and every three a.m. *I love you* you ever moaned but immediately knew you didn't mean—go back to Billie Holiday and get your face slapped and your gut punched and feel the hair on the back of your arms and your neck stand straight up at honest attention. Forget about singing the phone book. Who else but maybe Frank could take such absolute dross as *You love to see me crying, baby, and I sure don't know why* and turn it into something like "Lover Man" or "Mean to Me" or "Strange Fruit"? Lady Day, you sonofabitch, you make me want to die of love. Make me want to run straight out into the street right now and pledge undying everything to the very first skirt I see.

And sometimes, well, sometimes you just feel alone. Alone and impatient for eventually to be right now. Alone, and the only one, it seems, who gives a shit that the entire frothing world doesn't care that it's rotting out its already scant soul chewing bubblegum mood food twenty-four hours a day. Alone and feeling just like old Job down here, like, *Hey, c'mon, Big Guy, give me a sign, just one goddamn (sorry) sign that I'm still cheering for the right team.*

So take a voice down from the shelf and listen. Not a book—long gone the book-gobbling long days and longer loafing nights of eager youth; everything has been read, nothing's left to know—but a voice, a familiar voice, the sound, say, of Pascal's gentle sorrow, of Emerson's hard joy, of Goethe's bitter laughter. Ideas, irony, symbols, structure, themes, tropes—bah! Art is a friend when friendless. The voice of an old, old friend.

And as the river flows into the sea, so the sea empties back into the river. Fish, rocks, vegetation, even garbage: the weaker gets fed by the stronger and becomes itself again. All of us lonely little rivers dying of thirst and crying in our dusty riverbeds, thank God for the strong. Thank God for the sea. Thank God.

It probably ended up coming out even. New things you didn't want to do, sure — Clearasil-care for your acne, worry if you'd ever get a chance to get off anywhere besides in your girl-friend's hand, keep your mother from coming into your bedroom unless it was with clean clothes or to change the sheets — but because you were finally a teenager, things you didn't have to do anymore, too. Like go with my parents every time they visited Grandma and Grandpa Authier. I only went along this time because afterward we were going straight to the mall to buy me a pair of high-top Converse — to replace the dorky North Stars I couldn't believe I'd once thought were actually cool — and they promised we'd only stop in to say hello on the way there, they weren't even going to have coffee.

Let me put the pot on, Grandma said, pushing herself up from the kitchen table.

Sit down, Mem, we can't stay, we've got to get to the bank before four and then Ray needs new shoes and then we've got to get groceries.

Grandma slowly lowered her bulk back onto her chair, laughed, *Ah, Raymond, you're getting new shoes today, are you?*

Yep, I said, sliding past the kitchen table and into the living room. I'd given up a long time ago wondering why Grandma was always laughing. I turned on the TV although I knew there probably wouldn't be anything worth watching, Grandma and Grandpa Authier being the only people left in Chatham, it seemed, who didn't have cable yet. I sat down with the brown remote-control box on my lap and punched in the numbers anyway.

I got lucky, sort of, caught the last half of an episode of *Hogan's Heroes*, the one where Colonel Klink has to date General Burkhalter's dog of a sister or else get shipped off to the Russian Front. *Hogan's Heroes*, like all the shows I'd watched as a kid and seen every episode of at least twice, wasn't funny anymore. You knew what was supposed to be funny—the laugh track told you that—but it was like coming across old board games buried at the back of the hall closet that you hadn't played in years. It was hard to even remember the person who'd liked to play with them so much.

Let me tell you, we was drunk, boy—I mean drunk—*me and Giles and Loretta's brother Henri, us three, let me tell you.*

I leaned closer to the television, tried to block out Grandpa's voice. Hogan was making out with Hilda, Colonel Klink's secretary. Hilda was hot.

So we's drinking—and this is potato liquor, now, you

haven't been drunk until you've had that potato liquor that Loretta's brother used to make.

Grandma laughed with her hand over her mouth until she couldn't speak. *Oh, Henri, he . . . he . . .*

Grandpa laughed too, sucked deep on his cigarette. *So anyways, we ends up at the Paincourt Tavern that was there then, and in comes these fellas in their army uniforms and everybody's buying them drinks and slapping them on the back and I tell you, they was just about as drunk as we was, let me tell you.*

What year is this again, Mike? my dad said. My mom usually didn't say much when Grandma and Grandpa were telling stories, especially if they were stories where drinking was involved.

Oh, this was '40, '41 now.

Okay.

So these fellas and us, we ends up sitting there and drinking some together, and after a while they says to the three of us, "Why don't you fellas join up too?" they says. And then they starts telling us about how much they're getting paid and the pension a soldier gets and all about Europe and all the rest of it, and goddamnit, you know, the more we drank, the more it made sense.

I surprised myself, laughed along with everyone else.

So anyways, it can't be more than a week later, and I'm working in the field, bringing in the potatoes, you know, when these two other fellas from the army, they shows up and says I got to go with them, it's time to go.

No way, I thought. Nobody can just show up at your house and take you away, it's against the law. I turned down the volume on the television.

Jesus Christ, my dad said. *What did you do?*

There wasn't much I could do. They had guns. I went with them.

Everybody laughed, even my mom. I got up from the couch and stood in the doorway to the kitchen. Grandma had gotten up to get something down from one of the cupboards. Sugar, salt, flour, spices; old Mason jars full of beans and lentils and rice and oatmeal: everything was raw, something you used to make something else. Our cupboards at home were filled with things that you bought at the grocery store, things in shiny packages that were only what they were.

Taking one of Grandpa's hand-rolled cigarettes from its plastic case on the table, *What did you tell Loretta?* my dad said.

Well, I told her she was married to a soldier now and that I was going away for a while.

Laughing, having trouble getting it out, *And me pregnant with . . . me six months pregnant with . . . Paul,* Grandma said.

They knew you had a pregnant wife and they didn't even let you finish harvesting your potatoes? my dad said.

Let me tell you, boy, those army boys, they meant business. I was training up in Camp Borden there, up near Gravenhurst there, the very next day, let me tell you.

So what happened to your harvest?

Oh, Loretta brought it in.

But I thought you said you were pregnant with Paul, Mem, my mom said.

Yeah, yeah, I was, I was.

Turning to Grandma, tapping the ash of his cigarette into the same heavy glass Expo 67 ashtray Grandma and Grandpa had always had, *You're telling me you finished bringing in the potatoes all by yourself while you were six months pregnant?* my dad said.

Oh, câlice, no, Grandma said, *I didn't do it alone. We had a horse and a wagon, too.*

Everybody laughed, kept laughing.

I'd never realized how the kitchen table at our house was only for eating at, and how when we ate, we ate, we never talked. There wasn't any rule about it, we just didn't. At supper, at a quarter past six, my mom would say to my dad, *Your sports are coming on,* and we'd all listen to CFCO, already playing on the clock radio on top of the fridge, with silent purpose. After the sports there was a commercial break and then "In Memoriam," the funeral announcements. Unless it was someone my parents knew, we turned our attention back to our food.

Once things had quieted down, *Where's Bradley, Mem?* my mom said. I might have been a teenager, but Bradley was nearly twenty now, black-and-white horror films and bags of shared barbecue potato chips while the grown-ups talked at the kitchen table a long, long time ago.

Youse just missed him, he must of just pulled out of the driveway just before youse got here.

He wasn't driving, though.

Yeah, yeah.

I thought his licence was suspended.

What? I knew that Bradley spent most of his time since he'd quit high school working on stock cars out at the raceway in Buxton and that he'd gotten into some kind of trouble with the police over some stolen tires, but—

His car licence was suspended, Grandpa said, rolling a cigarette, licking the gluey edge of his rolling paper, *but you don't need no licence to drive a tractor.*

Oh, Dad, my mom said, smiling in spite of herself, *don't tell me he's . . .* and everyone started laughing again.

This ain't no regular tractor now, let me tell you, no sir. He put a '76 Toyota Celica four-cylinder in there with a six-speed transmission. He's got so much power in that damn thing, when he hits the accelerator the front wheels of that old tractor go right up in the air a good three feet, let me tell you.

It looks . . . Grandma said, trying to talk past her laughter and the hand at her mouth . . . *it looks like he's going to take off for the moon.*

My mom noticed me standing in the doorway. *Okay, son,* she said, *I know, we're going now.* She stood up.

No, I wanted to say, let's stay and hear more. But it was too late. My dad stood up too, jangled the car keys in his pocket.

Yeah, we better get going, he said. *It's Saturday, that mall is gonna be a real zoo today.*

There wasn't any room at the inn. Inns. At the last Montreal-bound motel they tried before giving up and turning around — Jack insisting he accompany Joe to the front desk to prove he wasn't the mess he obviously was and not the reason they'd been turned away from two other places already — the man sitting behind the counter, looking at Joe but referring to Jack, said, *Monsieur, you do not need a motel room, you need a hospital.*

It wasn't the first time an etymological road trip had turned ugly. Two summers before, here's a thought, here's a plan: jet away from spirit-sapping Florida for Paris and maybe Brittany and certainly the Bibliotheque Nationale, what a wonderfully invigorating idea (sensible solitary cognacs in the St-Germain district, writer's-block-breaking fresh French places and faces, and, of course, plenty of familial identity digging).

Jack spent most of the spring before his trip to France in the backyard in St. Petersburg, push-ups and sit-ups and headstands for his body, cold beer from a cooler he kept beside his lawn chair and volume after volume of Voltaire,

Rabelais, and Chateaubriand for his mind, nerve-steadying healthy humanism. Nothing cures *New York Times* envy and exterminates bad book review nit bites quite like two-century-old black squiggles on a white page advising amused indifference to everything but that which can't be ignored: truth, beauty, goodness. And fuck 'em if they can't take a joke. Especially fuck 'em if they don't even know what a joke is.

But the best-laid genealogical plans of mice and self-mythologizing *Homo sapiens* . . .

The Paris librarians smelled booze on his breath and saw stubble on his chin and couldn't place his French accent so were sorry, no, that particular volume was unavailable at this time.

But the card said—

Yes, of course, but I'm sorry, no, it is impossible.

You see, I'm the first Kerouac who's been here in 210 years, and—

Yes, as you have said, yes, but again, no, it is simply impossible.

Worse was the night he stepped out of the evening mist into the namesake of the church he'd been baptized in back in Lowell, the chapel of St. Louis de France. Fussy librarians and their fusty manuscripts go to hell, here was where his real roots were. Jack sank into a pew, hat in hand, and awed at it all all around him: the countless gleaming candles, the kaleidoscopic stained glass, the ancient organ music, the simple mystery of never having been here before yet here was where it all—his life—had begun. He bowed his head and prayed.

And then a middle-aged woman who reminded Jack of Mémère dropped twenty centimes into his upturned hat. Jack placed his tattered hat on his head and walked back into the mist. It wasn't until later, until his fourth cognac, that he realized he should have put the money in the poor box.

Calculus died first. It was an easy death, no one mourned it. Why I'd signed up for it in the first place was a mystery. I'd known that grade thirteen was the grade that mattered, the year that the universities paid attention to your marks, and yet I'd still selected not just calculus but physics too. Science: you miss one class, or spend it staring at your girlfriend's ass, and the next thing you know the following class everybody's chattering a foreign language. Three weeks and one dreadful mini-mid-term later and I could happily forget everything I knew about functions, derivatives, and quotients. It didn't amount to much, but it did mean more room for all of the things that really did matter. Stacey said the human brain didn't work that way — that in fact the more one used it, the more it was capable of remembering and doing — but even if she was right it didn't mean what she said was true. Not about my brain, anyway. I could *feel* it breathe better.

Mr. Koch, the physics teacher, spent most of the class speaking in scientific tongues too, but it was okay because I sat beside Don McClelland. Don worked after school and on weekends at APW Electronics fixing car stereos and rebuilding guitar amplifiers and was so science smart he was bored. He'd occasionally answer one of Mr. Koch's homework questions just to prove he was listening, but mostly he sketched pictures of his bass guitar on his notebook. When he did say something in class, you could tell he could actually somehow see what Mr. Koch only knew about from the textbook.

Class took place in the biology lab, which meant there was only a single-faucet sink separating your test paper from the person's next to you. Every Monday and Wednesday Mr. Koch recited all of the recipes he knew that used work, energy, and power as their main ingredients, and every Friday we had a test. Don would fill his page with numbers and letters in ten minutes, tops, and then gently push it a few inches to the right my way so that I could copy it all down. It seemed too easy at first, but Mr. Koch was also the defensive coordinator for the football team so I just figured he looked the other way to give one of his starting linebackers a break. And I always made sure to get a couple of things wrong so that my paper didn't look too much like Don's. Besides, it's never a good idea to get greedy when you get lucky. Going into the Christmas examination I had an 87 percent average and knew exactly where I'd be sitting when they handed out the exams.

Letting Don worry about what vectors were and how light travelled from Point A to Point B meant I had more time to consider the really big questions. Cranking the dial on the downstairs television one night, I saw an ad on the public education channel for something called *The Philosophical*

Question, a ten-session TV course that every week would feature real live philosophers discussing a different philosophical dilemma. You could just tune in and watch the intellectual fireworks fly, but if you officially registered they mailed you a booklet called *The Viewer's Guide to The Philosophical Question*. I wanted that booklet. I'd already decided that whatever university I ended up at I was going to major in philosophy, and this course was going to give me the head start I needed at getting caught up with all of the students in my future Philosophy 101 class who would have known all along that George Santayana was an American philosopher best known for his work in aesthetics and not the guitar player with the droopy moustache who'd had a big hit with "Black Magic Woman." I told my mom the course was for school and she wrote the station a cheque for fifteen dollars.

The big day finally arrived, a Wednesday night at nine p.m. (to be repeated Sunday night at eleven), and I was ready, had two pens, a fresh notebook, and, of course, *The Philosophical Question* booklet opened up to page one, topic one: "Moral Philosophy—What Is It?" I'd warned my parents about ten times that week not to come downstairs when my show for school was on—I had to concentrate, I couldn't be disturbed—so the basement was all mine. I hadn't told Stacey or Alvin or even Jamie anything about the course because I wanted philosophy all for me. The name of the show appeared on the television screen. Let the profundities begin.

The two guys who did most of the talking looked like lawyers and sounded almost as bad. You'd pick out the odd word or line that you knew was real-deal philosophy yack-ety-yack like *ethical truism* or *non-consequentialist theories of action*, but mostly the two of them took turns trying to out-polite each other while rubbing their chins and crossing their legs and readjusting their glasses on their noses. Who knew the search for the meaning of life could be so merci-lessly boring? I'd read that Socrates drank poison and died rather than renege on his quest for the Truth, and I won-dered if these guys had read the same thing. But they had to have—they were both professors of philosophy.

Every Wednesday night at nine I was loyally bored back in front of the TV with my booklet. I told myself it was probably all my fault, like somebody who judges somebody else stupid when they can't even understand the language the other per-son is speaking. I was eighteen, I was from Chatham, I was an idiot. Keep your mouth shut and just keep on keeping on, I thought, because, remember, Morrison did it, Kerouac did it, even Jamie was doing it, was learning Latin in his spare time by way of a correspondence course so that by the time he got to divinity school he'd be ready for his ancient language tests. Compared to that, I had it easy, all I had to do was learn how to look intelligent when I didn't have a clue what was going on.

When I showed up at school the morning of the Christ-mas exam, there was a sign on the classroom door saying that the examination had been moved to the gymnasium. When I got to the gym there were several single-file rows of desks set up up and down the gym floor with canyons of floor space separating one row from the next. We weren't allowed to go inside until five minutes before the exam was scheduled to begin, and everyone but Don was either crouching in the hallway with their faces pressed inside their textbooks or walking around clutching loose pages of handwritten notes and moving their lips, silently reciting formula after formula explaining how the invisible universe really worked. Don just shrugged when he saw me.

How much of our grade is the exam worth? I said.

Sixty percent.

Jesus Christ.

Don just shrugged again.

The exam was three hours long but you were allowed to leave after an hour and a half. I needed less than half of that to eeny-meeny-miny-moe the multiple-choice questions and bluff as best I could through the actual physics problems, with plenty of time left over to contemplate my higher-educationless future. The calculus course had been my backup course, the one I could afford to get a low mark in, but because I'd dropped it, physics was one of the six necessary credits I needed to graduate. I could always live at home for the rest of my life and take more courses off the television, I thought. Maybe I could become philosopher-in-residence at Sears.

When I got home, my mom said Stacey had called. I was supposed to have dropped by her house after I was finished at school. Now that all of her exams were over she'd decided it was okay for us to fool around again. I went to my room and shut the door and lay down on the bed.

And tonight was Wednesday, this evening's TV topic "Fear and Trembling: Can We Know God?" I may not have known anything about God, but after today I could teach the two suits on *The Philosophical Question* a thing or two about fear and trembling. Neither one of them was looking at forty years of wearing a plastic name tag and eight hours a day of ending every conversation with *Thank you for shopping at Sears*. Now I was just pissed off. What the hell could a professor of philosophy possibly know about fear and trembling?

Somewhere, Massachusetts, population approximately it really doesn't matter. They needed gasoline, caffeine, and someplace other than the side of the highway to urinate, and this was the off-ramp they got so this was the off-ramp they took. Joe figured that Lowell was less than three hours away, but it could have been another three days the way he was feeling. They'd only been on the road for a little over seventy-two hours, but clock time didn't have anything to do with it. It rarely did. Actor or audience, tragedy is exhausting.

Main street—not surprisingly called Main Street—and two out of three, anyway: a Mobil gas station and a key from the guy inside for the men's room. Joe considered offering to let Jack use the restroom first while he filled up the Chrysler and checked the oil, but ten minutes after announcing he'd have no other choice but to piss himself if Joe didn't find someplace for him to go in the next two minutes, Jack was snoring asleep. Joe would have liked to have let him stay asleep the rest of the trip home but knew that as soon as they got back on the highway Jack would wake up and insist upon pulling over, wherever they were. He'd take care of the car, then himself, and then shake Jack awake. Ten more minutes of peace for each of them.

Joe fed the car and paid for the gas and emptied his bladder and panicked when he came out of the restroom and saw the empty passenger seat. Almost immediately he spotted Jack wandering around a small graveyard in back of a very old, two-doors-down church, but didn't feel his heart begin to slow down or his face cool off until he'd parked the car and was standing beside Jack looking at a headstone.

People are here and then people are gone and it wasn't right. He remembered the last thing he'd said to Billy the day he disappeared. *Jiggle the handle on the toilet after you flush it, I'll fix it tonight when I get home from work.* How could those be the last words a man says to his own son? It wasn't right.

IN MEMORY OF MRS. ABIGAL ELIOTT
WIFE OF CAPT BENJAMIN ELIOTT
WHO DEPARTED THIS LIFE NOV. 12th 1790
AGED 69 YEARS

The town was a port town — you could smell the sea on the warm August wind — and the cemetery was dotted with the crooked and the cracked and the chipped headstones of several ship captains and their families. There were plaques on the wall of the church and on the two-storey insurance

building across the street testifying to their historical signifi-
cance as authentic pre-Revolutionary buildings. This was it,
America's pedigree. History in the rotting flesh.

Where's her husband? Jack said.

Whose?

Jack staggered down the row of graves. *Where's the captain?* he said.

Jack went from headstone to headstone like a tottering
two-year-old not quite sure how this whole walking upright
thing is supposed to work. He hadn't had a drink for a couple
of hours, but by now it didn't matter, his brain had finally
surrendered, gave him what he wanted.

Where is he, Joe?

Joe followed behind as Jack stooped and squinted at every
moss-blackened headstone. *Maybe he died at sea,* Joe said.

*He could be over here. He should be by his wife's side. The
captain should be buried beside his wife.*

They looked over here, they looked over there—it wasn't a
large cemetery, maybe a quarter of the size of a football field,
a knee-high white wooden fence all that separated the dead
from the living—but wherever Captain Eliott was spending
eternity, it wasn't here. They ended up near where Joe had
parked the car. Jack shut his eyes and stood in place, rocking
slightly, as if nudged by the breeze.

HERE LYES THE BODY OF JOHN BLAVERS
WHO DIED JULY 13th 1748
IN THE 16th YEAR OF HIS AGE

Just a kid, Joe thought. Even for back then just a kid. Sixteen years old. Billy's age next year.

Eyes still closed, *I don't know where he is,* Jack said. He said it like he was confessing a sin.

It's all right, Joe said.

He should be here. If he is, though, I can't find him.

That's all right, Jack, we tried. Let's go home now.

Jack didn't move or even open his eyes. Joe let him sway where he was. Suddenly there wasn't any hurry.

Jack made a pinched face like he was either furious or about to cry. *Sonofabitch,* he said.

What is it?

Jack didn't speak.

What is it, Jack?

I don't want to, Joe. I don't want to, but I have to.

You have to what?

Jack didn't speak.

You have to what, Jack?

I have to pee. I have to. I know I should have gone at the garage like you did, but I didn't. I'm sorry I didn't. I'm sorry.

Just pee, Jack. Just go ahead and pee.

It's a cemetery, Joe, it's . . .

It's all right. If you go behind that tree, it'll be fine. I'll watch out for you.

You'll watch out for me?

Sure, go ahead, I'll watch out for you.

Jack opened his eyes and unzipped his chinos and peed behind the old oak tree. Joe did a slow three-sixty. It had to be slow; not just because he didn't want anyone to think he was on the lookout for cops, but because it seemed like Jack would never stop urinating.

I feel better, Joe, Jack said.

Good.

I'm almost done now.

Good. The horn blast of a tug in the harbour replaced the sound of urine splashing against the tree.

It's time to go home now, Jack said.

Yeah, it is.

Let's go home, Joe.

Okay, let's go home.

It's time to go home now.

I had six, now I had five, I needed six, so now I had to have one more. This was math even I could understand.

Christmas exams were graded and returned the first class of the new year; in the case of my physics exam: Best Wishes, Happy New Year, Better Luck Next Time. Mr. Koch must have known all along that I'd been cheating off Don's tests, just like he must have known it would all equal out come exam time. I even thought I saw him smother a smile when he handed over my paper. It was covered in so much wrong-answer red ink it looked as if he'd sliced an artery while grading it.

Oh, come on, I thought. Eighteen percent? Even guessing gives you better odds than 18 percent. Everyone but Don and I was busy turning over pages, double-checking their marks, finding out where they went right and wrong. Don was sketching a fat stack of Marshall amplifiers on the back of his exam, thoughtfully not rubbing my nose in his more than likely astronomical grade. I did my best to imitate his consideration by pushing my paper away to the far edge of the desk with a single forefinger. I didn't want to risk whatever was wrong with it spreading.

Two days later, *I'll only have five credits then, so I need to have one more if I want to graduate,* I said. *That's why I want to take the correspondence course. Why* I need *to take the correspondence course.*

Only if you drop physics, Mr. Harnett said. *Which, as I've maintained from the outset, I strongly suggest you reconsider.*

Physics is a lost cause, I said.

It felt wrong to tell Mr. Harnett the truth about anything, but I needed his co-operation to get what I wanted. And what I wanted was to drop physics and to pick up an American History correspondence course so I'd have enough credits to graduate in June and go to university in September. I'd gotten the idea from Jamie, who'd been studying Latin through the mail for the past two years. The only difference would be that my course wasn't about self-improvement. My course was about survival.

Oh, I don't know, Mr. Harnett said, picking up the file folder on his desk, settling back in his chair, plopping his boots up on the edge. *It looks to me as if you just had a big fat case of exam jitters, is all. Your grade going into the exam wasn't so bad, I'm sure* — he studied the file, then studied it again, like he thought he must have misread it the first time — *was quite impressive, actually.*

I felt like levelling with him, like saying, *Look, cheating has taken me as far as it can, I have no other choice now but to be honest and to work hard.* Very hard. The correspondence course was intended to be completed over nine months, just like any other course, but I had only a little less than five, tops. Stacey had already warned me against it.

If it was me, I wouldn't do it, she'd said. *You're cutting it way too close. What if you don't finish in time? Then what?*

I'll have to finish in time, I said. *I don't have any choice.*

Stacey shrugged. I *wouldn't do it.*

I'm going to do it, I said to Mr. Harnett. *And I need to do it now. I talked to someone at the Ministry of Education and they said that as soon as they got all the forms they needed from you, I could begin as early as next week.*

You called the Ministry? He said it like I was a renegade butler who'd addressed his employer by their first name.

Yeah. I'd gotten the number from Jamie.

You shouldn't have contacted anyone at the Ministry of Education until you'd first talked to me.

Well, we're talking now.

And until you'd made a final decision.

I have made a final decision. And now I need you to fill out the forms. I want to get started right away. I've got a lot of work ahead of me.

For the record, there was one more stop. On the way home Jack insisted they hit Boston for just one game of pool and a beer, just one game of pool and a beer, justonegameofpool-andabeer.

No way, Joe said, Not a chance, he thought; not unless Jack grabbed the wheel and hijacked the car. Whatever amount of haranguing Jack could manage to hurl his way over the last leg home would be worth it if it meant the possibility of seeing Billy back at home and safe and sound sooner rather than later. Less than a mile before the Lowell turnoff, though: What if Billy wasn't there? Billy probably wasn't there. Billy wasn't there.

But if they spent the evening in Boston, Joe wouldn't know he wasn't there. Not yet, anyway. Joe clicked off the turn signal, missed the cut-off home, just in time. Next best to having is hoping.

"The Combat Zone" was Boston's red-light district: green beer, five-dollar blow jobs, medicinal-quality cocaine if you knew who to talk to. Joe didn't know who to talk to and Jack could barely talk. They doubled up against a couple of sailors at eight-ball and lost the table after a single game. Jack cracked his stick in half over the pool table and called the sailors a pair of no-good lying niggers. Neither one of the men was black. Joe stuck himself between Jack and a man at the bar who was, however, and said *Don't worry, we're leaving,* and the man said *Does it look like I'm worried, asshole?* and *And I'll tell you when you can leave, motherfucker,* and Joe pushed a crumpled twenty-dollar bill at the man and said *Please, my friend's not well,* and the man took the money and said *You got that right, douchebag,* and stared the pair of them all the way out the door.

Every story needs a denouement. This is this one's.

I convinced my parents to let me haul the old white Formica kitchen table up from the basement and set it up in a corner of the spare bedroom. I'd always done my homework at the kitchen table, but the correspondence course was different — was a clock that needed nightly punching — and my parents' police band radio keeping watch on the living room floor and randomly blasting out *Car eight, car eight, do you read me, over? This is car eight, go ahead, over. Car eight, we've got a domestic disturbance at 114 Wellington Street East, over. I'm on my way, over* while I was trying to puzzle through the intricacies of the Louisiana Purchase of 1803 wasn't helping me hit my target. I'd wanted to put the table in my bedroom, just like Jamie and Stacey and Alvin who had desks in their bedrooms where they did their homework, but between the dresser and my stereo and my records and my dumbbells, there wasn't enough room. But that was all right. The spare bedroom was for visitors, and no one ever visited us.

I did what my biography of Jack said Jack did, lit a candle before I sat down to work each night, blowing it out only when I'd eaten all the American Pie I could. Later, I found a hand-painted porcelain Buddha in the damp back room of Clem's, a second-hand knick-knack shop a few doors down from the Salvation Army, and I burned my scented candles at both ends right underneath the Buddha's indifferent gaze. I didn't know much about Buddhism, but I liked the way the fat man smiled, a smile that said, *Sure I know all there is to know, and you know what? Who really gives a shit?*

After a couple of weeks of lugging my boom box back and forth between my bedroom and where I was spending the majority of my evenings now, I eventually moved it and all of my cassette tapes into the spare bedroom permanently. There was only one rule, no Doors—I couldn't afford to pay attention to Jim's poetry when I was supposed to be studying the story of America—but music made the pages turn quicker, the words get written easier. In the course of another pointless expedition to the mall on the nowhere road to no *On the Road*, I came across a $1.49 bin at Woolco dumped full of deleted cassette tapes of bands I'd never heard of. Some of them, after I'd gotten their albums home, I never wanted to hear again—synthesizers, funny haircuts, mushy, robotic drumbeats—but others, if not always great, were never bad, twitchy new-wave guitar bands that you couldn't hear on the radio and no one that I knew knew the names of. They might not have been much, but they were mine.

And because orange pekoe tea and fear were all I had to help me stay awake and turning over tape after tape and pushing through question after question at the end of every lesson, I put together a handmade hall of fame on the wall over my work table to keep me going when the clock and common sense both said stop. Most prominent, of course, were photocopied pictures of Jim and Jack, as well as a red plastic sign swiped from the school library declaring PHILOSOPHY 1843.75.

Stealing from a library was wrong, I knew, but there were maybe ten books, tops, in the entire philosophy section, and besides, Mr. Brunt, the librarian, could help anyone who was really interested find them. But no one was really interested. And I needed that sign more than anyone else did.

Jack Jekylled himself as best he could: a gas station restroom makeover, an extra-large cup of very hot black coffee to go, a still half-full bottle of cognac sacrificed to homecoming semi-sobriety atop an overflowing garbage pail pyre at an Esso Station just outside of Boston. With an ETA of sixty minutes to their final destination of Lowell, Massachusetts, Jack decided to try out some sentences to see how human he could sound if he put his lips to it.

Foggy, he said.

It is, Joe said.

The windshield wipers squeaked left then right, left then right, left then right.

It doesn't . . . it doesn't look like it's going to turn to rain, though.

No, Joe said, *I think we're going to be all right.*

Left then right, left then right, left then right.

I think we're going to be all right too.

Satisfied he'd passed the test, Jack didn't say anything else the rest of the ride home. He watched the headlights of the oncoming traffic slowly appear then quickly disappear, listened to the rhythm the wipers made until he couldn't hear them anymore.

The house was bright with the lights from the living room when they pulled into Jack's driveway. Stella came to the screen door and waved but stayed inside. They both heard her shout, *No, no, it's just Jack, Gabrielle, it's just Jack.*

Jacky?

Yes, it's just Jack and Joe, they're back from their trip.

Jacky? Where's my Jacky?

Joe unlocked the trunk and Jack grabbed his bag. Joe slammed the trunk shut and a dog answered back with a bark. Barked again and again until, getting no reply, it stopped. Crickets and a warm treetop-rustling breeze fought a losing battle with the noise of the television set coming from the living room. The theme music of *Dragnet* leaked through the screen door. Mémère never missed an episode.

Jack kept his eyes on the pebbled driveway while he shook Joe's hand.

Thanks for everything, Joe.

Any time, Jack.

No. Really. Thanks for all your help. For everything.

Sure.

Jack looked up. *I think I got some good material. I think I got some things I can really use.*

That's great, Jack. I'm glad it worked out.

Yeah. Jack picked up his bag but didn't move. *I think overall it was a very successful trip.*

Joe nodded. Jack nodded too. Jack clasped Joe's shoulder then turned around and walked up the row of cement tile steps to the house.

Good night, Joe, Stella called out, waving again. She was holding the screen door open for Jack. *I'm glad you both made it home safe and sound!*

Joe waved back. *Good night, Stella. Good night, Jack.*

Jacky? Where is my Jacky?

I'm right here, Ma, Jack said. *I'm right here.*

Stella waved goodbye one more time and shut the screen door and then the wooden front door and turned off the porch light.

Joe backed out of the driveway, honked twice.

He drove for fifteen minutes before he realized he wasn't travelling in the direction of home. His clothes were dirty enough that they itched, and the last time he'd called Mrs. Johnson for any news of Billy he'd told her he would stop by for his mail as soon as he got back into town. He took a cigarette from the pack in his pocket and stuck it in his mouth and tried to remember where the nearest gas station was. If he was going to go anywhere but home, he was going to need more fuel.

It's like I can't believe it. It's like I'm actually having a hard time actually believing it, you know?

Yeah, I said. I kept the phone pressed to my ear and lay back on my waterbed as far as the telephone cord would stretch, rolled with the waves I'd made while Stacey kept talking.

I mean, think about it. My whole life—I mean, practically my whole life, since I can remember, anyway—I've worked toward being a page in the House of Commons, and now, with one letter I get in the mail, I'm actually going to be one. It's so weird. I mean, it's like the other me—the one that's always wanted to be a page—is more real somehow than the me who actually is. Or will be this fall. It's just weird, you know?

Yeah, that is weird.

I unbuttoned my jeans and pulled down my underwear and started playing with myself. We'd dueted a few sticky times before over the phone, so what was wrong with a secret solo performance, especially since I could tell that Stacey was too hot and bothered with her lifelong fantasy made right-now real to have any interest left over in helping either one of us get off? I still hadn't heard back from any of the universities that I'd applied to. Only the people who'd been offered scholarships had heard anything. Jamie, Alvin, and Stacey had all been offered scholarships.

You know what else is weird? she said.

What's that?

I tried to picture Stacey's mouth wrapped around my dick, but it wasn't easy. For one thing, the handful of times she'd gone down on me had happened either with the lights turned off or with her head buried underneath a blanket, so it was up to me to conjure and combine the image of her lips together with the reality of my cock at the end of my hand, and every time I did, words kept coming out her mouth, her lips wouldn't stop moving long enough for me to stick my dick in between. And even though it was only late March and my bedroom window was closed tight, my dad was celebrating the occasion of the thermostat nearly breaking sixty degrees by rolling the lawn mower out of hibernation and putting it to work for the season's first of many happy trips up and down and across our backyard. If I ever have my own house, I thought, I will never cut the lawn. Ever. Or water it or weed it or anything else to even remotely encourage it.

It's like I'm afraid to go outside in case I get hit by a car or something. Like, now that this great thing has happened to me, I've got to be super careful not to screw it up by stepping off the curb without looking both ways. Do you know what I mean?

Yeah, I said, *yeah, I do,* stroking, caressing, coaxing — everything short of snapping a vertebra and finishing off the job myself. But it was no use, it was like pulling taffy, my mind was empty, all I could see was what there was: a telephone in one hand and a lifeless penis in the other.

What's that noise? Stacey said.

The lawn mower was making its turn around the edge of the yard nearest to my bedroom window. It sounded like I was trapped inside the cargo hull of a single-propeller airplane.

Nothing, I said. *Just my dad cutting the lawn.*

Cutting the lawn? Is he insane? It's freezing out.

It's not freezing out.

Practically. And isn't it supposed to be bad for grass if you cut it before it starts growing again?

Who told you that?

I finally dismissed my dick back to my underwear, tugged up my blue jeans, leaned up against the backboard. I waited for the bed to stop rolling.

I don't know, she said. *My father, I suppose.*

Yeah, well, I think my dad knows a little bit more about lawn care than your dad.

I'm sure he does.

What is that supposed to mean?

Just what I said. I'm sure he does.

You know, just because my dad doesn't wear a fucking suit and tie to work doesn't mean he doesn't know a few things, you know.

Don't swear at me, Ray.

I wasn't swearing at you, I was just saying that—

If you're going to be abusive, I'm going to hang up.
Jesus Christ, I was just—
Goodbye, Ray.
Hold on—
Goodbye, Ray.
She hung up. I'd only seen people hang up on other people in movies. I put the phone back on the side table and leaned back again, started slowly rocking again, waited for it to stop again.

Almost immediately, the phone rang. *I've got it!* I yelled.

Of course she'd call right back. She was the one who'd insulted my dad and me, she couldn't be the one to hang up. It didn't work that way.

Hello? I chirped, like I didn't know who it was.

Man, who have you been talking to? Your phone's been busy for like forty-five minutes. It was Jamie.

No one, I said. *I wasn't talking to anyone. My mom was on the phone.*

Well, anyway, you're not going to believe this.
What?
Guess who wrote "End of the Night"?
Duh. Morrison.
No.
I was silent for a moment.

Okay, I said, *I know where you went wrong, you're going by the back of the album where it says "Words and Music by the Doors." But Morrison actually wrote all the lyrics on the first album, all except for the first stanza and the chorus to "Light*

My Fire" and all of "Twentieth Century Fox," *Krieger wrote those.* Jamie might have gotten scholarship offers from both Queen's and U of T and still be waiting on what McGill was going to come up with, but between the two of us, I was the undisputed Doors scholar. *Krieger wrote all of the simple pop songs,* I added.

You ever heard of a guy named Céline?

I had, maybe, but I didn't know where. *Maybe,* I said. *Why?*

I was looking for a quote from Churchill for my history essay in one of my old man's books of quotations, and I came across him. All his quotes were from the same book, a novel called Journey to the End of the Night.

Now I remembered where I'd heard of Céline. From *No One Here Gets Out Alive*, Morrison's biography. Céline was one of Jim's favourite writers, it said.

Actually, Céline was one of Morrison's favourite writers, so I guess it must have been some sort of tribute.

Yeah, and get this. Jamie wasn't listening. *That song "You're Lost Little Girl"? From the second album?*

Yeah, I know it, I taped you your copy.

Well, remember William Blake, from class last year?

Yeah.

Well, he's got a poem, and its first line is "You're Lost Little Girl."

The waterbed had stopped moving. I shifted my ass around so it would start again. *So, so maybe Morrison—*

What's the first line of "The Spy"?

What?

What's the first line of "The Spy"? From Morrison Hotel.

I know what fucking album it's on.

So what is it?

Why?

Do you know it or not?

Yeah, I know it.

What is it, then?

"I'm a spy in the house of love."

From a book called A Spy in the House of Love, *by some-body named Anaïs Nin.*

It took me a moment to think of something to say. *Just because they're the same doesn't necessarily mean that's where he got them.*

C'mon.

My dad was making a final pass underneath my window. The backyard was almost done. Soon, on to exciting new challenges in the front yard.

So what's your point? I said.

There is no point. I just thought you'd want to know.

What are you saying?

Don't drop a kidney, I'm not saying anything.

If you're not saying anything, I've got to go. My mom needs to use the phone again.

All right, Jamie said. *Talk to you later.*

Yeah, I said, *I'll talk to you later.*

He was on the can when he heard the chainsaws.

They'd only been able to finally turn the air conditioning off the day before, and for what? For the almost-breathable-at-last October air to be poisoned piercing with this roaring idiocy polluting through every opened window. He pulled up his pants and stomped to the living room and shouted at what he couldn't believe he saw.

Hey!

Stella thought he was yelling for her and came running from the kitchen. Mémère, asleep, woke up, called out, *Qu'est-ce qu'il y a?*

Hey!

Jack, Stella said, *what—*

Jack pointed out the living room window at the next-door neighbour's front lawn, at the two men with competing shrieking chainsaws tearing into the neighbour's soaring Georgia pine. *They're cutting down my tree, Stella. Those butchers, they're cutting down my tree.*

Stella rested her hand on Jack's trembling arm. The vein

in his forehead looked like a plugged garden hose ready to burst blue. *Jack, calm down, I'm sure—*

Stella? Mémère hollered. *Stella?*

Jack didn't bother shutting the front door behind him; marched across his own front lawn toward the workmen next door.

Jack, your shoes, Stella yelled, but Jack couldn't hear her over the screams of the chainsaws. Not that it would have mattered if he could. Even loneliness has its limits. Even the good kind. And his wasn't the good kind.

Wasn't the loneliness of an old man holding up the line at the bank because he can't help flirting with the pretty young teller because his wife's been dead for fourteen years this July, and depositing his social security cheque is worth putting in his false teeth and splashing on some cologne in order to remember what it was like to make a woman laugh. Wasn't the loneliness of an old woman having that nice Mr. So-and-So, the pharmacist, go over again just how much and when to take her medication even though she's been taking it for years and years now and it is, in fact, the only thing she really does know. Wasn't the loneliness of being young and in love and hating the mailman because he doesn't deliver the letter that should have arrived days ago.

A concrete-block, central-air-conditioned, two-bedroom-and-one-bath prison cell at 5169 Tenth Avenue North, St. Petersburg, Florida, loneliness. A $6.67 royalty statement loneliness. A 4:37 a.m. Pacific-time phone call loneliness,

Great, Jack, listen, I'll write you a long letter first thing tomorrow—first thing—but I've got to go now, I've really got to go, I'm hanging up now, Jack, I'm hanging up.

And now they were cutting down his favourite tree. The tree through whose branches he listened to the wind talking to him at night. *Used* to listen to the wind talking to him at night.

Why are you doing this? he shouted at the workmen. Even loneliness has its limits.

The men were wearing matching yellow hard hats and clear plastic goggles. One of them noticed Jack standing there. Without turning off his chainsaw, *What?* he shouted.

Why are you doing this? Who told you to do this?

The man pointed to his ear and shook his head.

Why are you killing my brother?

The man shook his head again and jabbed his finger in the direction of the white pickup truck parked on the street in front of the house, *Franklin Landscaping* and a phone number written across the passenger-side door.

So they're the murderers, Jack said, motioning with his chin at the neighbour's house. *But you're their paid assassins, there's blood on your hands too.*

The man pointed to his ear again and shook his head and wrapped both hands back around the chainsaw, eased the screaming machine into the guts of the tree. A blizzard of sawdust exploded in the air, a shower of wooden confetti falling over Jack's stocking feet.

Jack could feel Stella at his side.

They're murderers, he said.

I know, Jack, but let's go home.

They're murderers and they don't even know it.

Stella gave his arm a gentle tug. It was still shaking. *It's what the owners want, Jack. There's nothing anyone can do about it now.*

Jack turned, faced her. The vein in his forehead throbbed a fat blue worm in the happy Florida sun. *Why would anyone want to do that?* he said. *Why would anyone want to kill my favourite tree?*

If I couldn't be there to have the mailman hand me the letter, I wanted to take it out of the mailbox myself. It's what would have happened in the movie version, with maybe some stirring string music delicately overdubbed as I dipped my hand into the black metal box, recognized the university's crest in the upper left-hand corner of the envelope, and tore it open and raced through the words and realized that life was never going to be the same. There might even be tears bulbing in the corners of my eyes or at least a look of well-earned contentment etched across my face. Fade to credits. The end.

It was Tuesday, I had double spares, periods one and two, I didn't have to be up until ten. I yawned into the kitchen. My mother had leaned a letter against my cereal bowl before she'd left for the hairdresser. If she knew she wasn't going to be there to make me breakfast when I woke up, she'd put out the box of cereal, a bowl and a spoon, and a glass for my orange juice. Normally I just took it for granted, but this morning it made me mad. It's hard to feel like a hero when your mother makes sure you don't forget the most important meal of the day.

I ripped open the letter and flew through the first para-graph—. . . *pleased to inform you that . . .*—and didn't need to read any further. I wandered around the house a couple of times punching the air with my fist, the letter hanging from my other hand, but something was missing. Music, I thought, and went into my bedroom and lifted the plastic cover off the turntable. Except that I hadn't been able to listen to the Doors since Jamie had tipped me off about Jim's poetic plagiarizing. I knew the music was still good, but I also knew I wouldn't be able to hear it, would only be reminded of how the singer was, after all, just a singer. I turned off the stereo and went back into the kitchen, clicked on the radio. It was only CFCO, the same as it always was, but the house wasn't silent anymore. It had never occurred to me before that that was probably why my mother always had it on.

Maybe if I called someone. I picked up the receiver and listened to the dial tone while deciding who to phone. I couldn't call my dad, he was at work. After a year and a half of whatever he could get at half or less of what he used to make at Ontario Steel—which finally did move to Mexico, taking all four hundred of its jobs with it—a new factory owned by a German company had opened up in Tilbury and my dad was back on the line. My mom and him had stopped arguing. They were talking about redecorating the living room and putting in a bathroom in the basement. I couldn't call Jamie either, he'd be at school, in French class. But Stacey would be at home, she had the same spares as me.

That's great, she said, although she warned me she couldn't talk for long. Her mother and she were having lunch with our local MP, the one whose campaign she'd worked on and who'd written her a letter of reference for her page application. *He's actually a really nice guy,* she'd said. *I almost feel guilty I didn't vote for him.*

I can't believe that this time next year I'll actually be living in Toronto, I said. I needed to hear it for it to be real.

You know that York University's not actually in Toronto, though, right?

No, I know, but—

Of course you can always transfer. As soon as my year as a page in Ottawa is over, I'm out of there, I'm off to McGill.

I know.

I've already looked into it. You're allowed to transfer as many as five credits to the school you end up getting your degree from.

I know, you said.

When?

Before.

Did I?

Yeah.

Oh.

I heard Stacey's mother singsong her name, tell her it was time to go.

I've got to get going, she said.

Me too. I really did, but would have said it even if I hadn't.

Okay, bye.

Bye.

We wouldn't be saying goodbye for good until the end of August, but Stacey had already said, and I'd agreed, that we weren't going to ruin our summer vacation with messy emotional farewells and unrealistic talk about continuing to date when we'd be hundreds of miles apart. *It's not just unrealistic*, she'd said, *it's not even healthy.* She wasn't wrong. She rarely was.

If I wanted to make Canadian Literature class I needed to be out front and waiting for the bus in twenty-five minutes, just enough time to take a shower and eat. I dropped my underwear and T-shirt where I stood, but picked up my copy of *Jack's Book* lying on the dresser on the way to the bathroom. I sat down on the edge of the waterbed.

It didn't look like the same book I'd brought home from the mall three years before. The spine was as cracked and wrinkled as an old man's forehead, three of the four corners on the cover torn and frayed. I'd done this. It was hard to believe you could do something like that just by reading.

I turned to chapter two, "The City," the section where Jack leaves Lowell for school. I steadied the sloshing waterbed with an open palm, read. Jack had had no idea what was going to happen to him, good, bad, tragic, none of it. I liked that. I liked that a lot.

Books are good liars. The lie that life is one existence-altering epiphany after another, one long, uninterrupted learning experience always resulting in a brand new, oh-so-wiser you every single super-satori-sized step of the way. As frauds go, it's not bad—better, anyway, than the prevalent disease of understanding the march of modern literature as the careful cultivation of one gigantic fucking headache finding its ultimate aesthetic expression in *Finnegans Wake*, the sound of literature crawling up its own snickering asshole. The birth of the reader as second-class schmuck. Cleverness as spirit killer.

Dreams might not come true, but—next best thing— sometimes clichés do. Sometimes, for instance, life imitates art. Spring 1951, for instance, Jack typed the last words of *On the Road* onto the Scotch-taped scroll of ten twelve-foot-long sheets of tracing paper he'd rigged together so he wouldn't have to stop writing in order to bother with changing sheets of typing paper, the same reason he didn't bother stopping to change any of the characters' names from their real names. It was a 120-foot-long, 120,000-word single paragraph poured directly onto the page in three coffee-quicked weeks because the pump was primed and the road is fast. His second wife had left him and was pregnant with a child he didn't want, he had a $12.38 overdraft in the bank, and none of it mattered because someone—him—had finally kicked American Literature's tired ass into the twentieth century.

He walked away from his typewriter and stood underneath the stars and lit a cigarette. It was spring and everything was trying to be alive. He inhaled, he exhaled, he blew a halo of smoke into the warm evening air. He watched the smoke rise, lose its perfect form, but continue to climb, up and up until it became part of the sky. A sky full of the same stars under which Shakespeare had once stood tremblingly content after completing *Lear, Hamlet, Macbeth*. He felt like a character in a novel who realizes something.

He was part of the chain.

Even if he'd written just a book and not *the* book—even if he'd only done what tens of thousands—millions—before him had done—made his little noise in the big silence to keep himself company—he was part of the chain.

He took a long drag on his cigarette. He let the stars swallow him.

The car was packed and ready to go, the gas tank filled up, the oil and windshield-wiper fluid topped off. My dad had even washed it although it wasn't Saturday and it didn't really need it. All that was left was to go to bed and get up and leave. This time tomorrow night I'd be calling somewhere else home.

What about your spare pair of glasses? my mom said.

I got them, I said.

And what about your extra contact lens cleaner, the one underneath the bathroom sink?

I got it, Mom. I told you, I got everything.

We were sitting in lawn chairs on the back deck, my dad standing by the rail, smoking. The light from inside the kitchen shining through the patio doors illuminated the deck but left the rest of the backyard in darkness. My dad was blowing smoke rings into the night.

Well, now's the time to double-check, not tomorrow morning. Once we get on that highway we're not coming back for anything you forgot. That traffic to Toronto is crazy.

My dad caught my eye, winked. My mother had never

been to Toronto either. I didn't know what was making her more upset: my leaving home for university or her having to pass through the gates of Gomorrah. All summer I'd been subjected to hearing about whatever articles she came across in the *Chatham Daily News* detailing Toronto violence, Toronto pollution, or the rising cost of living in Toronto. But every week she'd also bring home something else she thought I might need for when I went away: more Bic pens that had been on sale at BiWay than I could ever use in a single year; a red and black checked wool jacket *For walking around campus, for when it's cold*; new underwear, new socks, new undershirts. If she couldn't stop me from dressing like a beatnik, she could at least make sure I was warm and clean underneath.

We've double-checked everything three times, Mom, relax.

We watched my dad ground out his cigarette in one of the homemade ashtrays he'd made after he'd built the deck, a plastic margarine tub filled halfway to the top with sand. He snapped the lid back on. The lid kept out the dew and the rain.

Oh, I know what I forgot, my mom said, popping up from her chair. *There's your good jeans still in the dryer. I better get those ironed.*

Don't worry about it, Mom, I'm wearing them tomorrow, we're just going to be in the car.

You can't wear clothes that aren't ironed.

I will once I start doing my own laundry. My dad and I grinned at each other. He was sitting in one of the other lawn chairs now.

Well, you shouldn't, she said. She opened the screen door. *And until then, you're not going to.*

My dad and I laughed, stared out into the backyard. You couldn't see it, but it was there, you could smell it. He'd cut the lawn that afternoon. The freshly chopped blades of grass, the cool dew, the warm night. We sat and listened to the crickets, to someone else's screen door slamming shut, to the single bark of a dog, to the crickets.

She's just worried, that's all, my dad said.

I know. It's just funny.

It may be funny to you, but to her she's losing her baby.

It's not like I'm dying, I said. *I'm just going away to university.*

My dad took his pack of cigarettes out of his shirt pocket. *Oh, I understand, but mothers, they take these sorts of things hard.*

What about fathers? I said, laughing.

My dad put the cigarette he'd taken out of his pack back inside, shut and tucked in the top. *I think I better shave,* he said, standing up. *That way I won't have to do it in the morning.*

I nodded.

With his back to me, talking to the lawn, *And your mother's right, you can't be too careful, it wouldn't hurt to do one last check around the house just to be on the safe side.*

Okay, I said, and he left me on the deck by myself.

I went and stood by the rail, where my dad usually did when he smoked. I'd never felt sorry for my parents before.

I'd have to do like I'd said I would and call them every two weeks, more if it seemed like they needed me to. I'd have to make sure I didn't forget.

And after they dropped me off, and after I got settled into my room in residence, the first thing I was going to do was find out how to take the subway to Yonge Street. Because everybody knew that Yonge Street was where you went to get anything you wanted. I was going to find a bookstore where I could buy *On the Road*. And I was going to read it, I was finally going to read it.

And I did.